Christmas Wishes at Pudding Hall

Kate Forster

HEAD
ZEUS

An Aria Book

This edition first published in the United Kingdom in 2021 by Aria,
an imprint of Head of Zeus Ltd

9 7 5 3 1 2 4 6 8

A CIP catalogue record for this book is available
from the British Library.

ISBN (PB): 9781801108034
ISBN (E): 9781801108010

Cover design © CC Book design

Typeset by Siliconchips Services Ltd UK

Printed and bound in Great Britain by
CPI Group (UK) Ltd, Croydon CR0 4YY

MIX
Paper from
responsible sources
FSC® C013604

Aria
5–8 Hardwick Street
London EC1R 4RG

WWW.ARIAFICTION.COM

For Josie Cameron, who asked me to keep writing.
Thank you for reading.

ENTRÉE

I

Christa Playfoot shivered in the cold December air as she adjusted the heavy bag on her shoulder. Checking the pocket of her pink puffa coat once again for the keys, she noted that the silver spoon key ring that Simon had given to her when they opened the restaurant was cold to the touch. She had always said he was born with a silver spoon in his mouth, so he attached it to the keys to their restaurant as a joke. Only he had laughed.

Looking at the restaurant from a distance, she saw the navy gloss wooden features on the outside of the old building, with white window boxes she had filled each season with different flowers. Magenta pink geraniums in the summer. Pots of creamy butter-coloured daffodils in the spring. Warm amber violas for autumn, and vibrant red poinsettias for Christmas. Now the window boxes were empty and there was a *For Lease* sign above the blue and white striped awning. She had once dreamed of having a restaurant in London, and now letting go of the dream was proving to be more painful that she had ever imagined.

Her thumb ran over the bowl of the spoon in her pocket. She had always felt this gift was actually a little dig at her for coming from poverty and was Simon's reminder she would be nothing without his silver touch.

Perhaps that was true. Simon's family had bankrolled the restaurant and she had been so excited to build something with him, she had ignored the fact there were no specific ownership papers.

And now she was handing back the keys in exchange for almost nothing. Maybe enough to put down a deposit on a flat in London but she didn't have a job, only restaurant reviews that mentioned him first in every single one. No bank would loan her money because she made a wonderful soufflé, even if minor royals had taken a photo of it for Instagram when they came to Playfoot's.

Now Simon no longer wanted to work in the restaurant, because he had a fancy new role as a television judge on a cooking show called *Blind Baking*. Never mind that she was the pastry chef in the relationship, her desserts winning awards and acclaim, instead the production company had called Simon because he was posh, witty, and handsome. Not to mention he had been voted 'Spiciest Man in Cooking', wearing an apron and nothing else on the front cover of a magazine.

She should be a judge on a TV show called *Blind Dating* where she could advise the female contestants to never give over their financial choices to a man who spends more time in the bathroom than you before you go out and asks how he looks before he comments on your outfit.

When Christa had seen the magazine cover of Simon stripped bare, she knew their marriage was truly over. Simon was on a trajectory to fame and Christa was still trying to decide if being a chef was her true calling now she had lost the restaurant. She loved to feed people more than anything else but all the pomp and ceremony of restaurants made her anxious. She much preferred a meal around a kitchen table with wine and laughter, swapping stories with friends until late in the evening.

The streetlamps switched on above her and Christa noticed the Christmas decorations were up in the street. The red bows and green garlands usually cheered her but today her heart ached. There was a hollow feeling that sometimes took her by surprise when it returned unannounced like now. The sense of a piece missing inside her but she did not know what to put there. It had followed her around ever since she could remember, popping up uninvited.

She walked to the front of the restaurant where the lights were off. Pressing her face against the window she saw Simon sitting at the table with a bottle of wine open in the dim light and a woman sitting opposite him. They were laughing and the woman's hand was on his knee.

She opened the door and stood in the doorway inviting the cold air in. The weather report was threatening snow for Christmas but she would believe it when she saw it. Every year they said it would snow and it never came until after New Year when she would have to be back at work.

'Christa, come in, you must be freezing,' Simon said benevolently, giving her a look as though she was the little match girl down to her last strike.

'No thanks, I'm late for something,' she lied.

Simon gestured to the woman sitting opposite him. 'Christa, this is Avian. She's a producer on my new TV show.'

His new TV show? As though it was all about him. God she hated him.

The woman looked Christa up and down and she saw a little smirk on her face.

'Oh, hey babe. So, you're Christa. Simon speaks of you with such good vibes.' Her California hippy act wasn't fooling Christa. Oh yes, they were definitely together.

Christa couldn't help herself. 'Avian?' she asked. 'What an unusual name.'

'It's French for bird,' said the woman as though Christa was an idiot. 'My mother lived in Paris for a year.'

'No, it's English for birdlike,' corrected Christa. '*L'oiseau* is French for bird. I worked there for two years in fine dining before Simon and I opened this.' She gestured around her at the restaurant.

'Avian loves food, don't you, babe?' said Simon.

Looking at how thin this woman was, Christa doubted this morsel of information very much.

She was so thin it pained Christa to see the bones on her chest jutting out like a ladder. With her long hair and a face carefully made up in the artful way that looked like she wasn't wearing any makeup she was a beautiful woman and the exact opposite of Christa. Christa pushed away the comparisons because she liked how she looked, with her short dark hair, cropped in a pixie cut, and bright blue eyes with eyelashes usually only bestowed on undeserving boys. And she was healthy and didn't really drink very much and had never smoked, so all things considered she was in pretty good shape, she told herself.

Simon used to tell her she was chubby. He had called her Chubs at Le Cordon Bleu, which he said was cute. It wasn't cute.

Christa wasn't angry with this woman, she reminded herself, she was angry with Simon and she was angry with herself for staying so long when she knew the marriage was over a long time ago. What she couldn't work out was why she had stayed so long in a loveless marriage that was purely a business relationship – except she didn't have equal shares – until it was too late.

'So you're a TV producer? That's amazing,' said Christa, trying to be nice but wanting to run as far away as she could.

'Is it?' asked Avian who then picked up her phone, showing Christa their brief tête-à-tête was over.

Simon glanced from Christa to Avian and back again. He was terrible with uncomfortable moments. She paused to make him do the work for once. She was forever filling in the gaps in their marriage, their business and their communication. Let him carry the weight of this moment with his little bird-inspired friend. He shifted in his chair. 'So, you all set then?'

The question sounded like he was enquiring as to whether she had all her things for a school trip, not the end of the last ten years of their life together.

Christa threw the keys at him from the doorway. He panicked and dropped them. He never was good at ball games – only mental games.

'As set as a jelly,' she said and she paused. 'Okay, well, bye then. Good luck with the show.'

Avian glanced up at Christa and gave her a sliver of a smile while Simon seemed to see something interesting on the floor.

'Ta,' he said, and she turned and walked away from the place and person she had poured her heart and soul into, feeling the tears stinging her eyes. She wasn't enough for Simon. He had used her all those years and traded off her skills and talent and then claimed them as his own.

Outside on the street, she leaned against a wall and took several deep breaths. Ta. He ended their marriage and business with the word *ta*.

Her stomach churned as she put the heavy bag at her feet, as she tried to focus on her surroundings to keep her present in the moment. For the past twenty years and more, she had thought this feeling would never return. All the work she had done to make sure that her life was shored up so these feelings of anxiety and uncertainty couldn't find their way aboard. And yet here she was with no job, no direction, and nothing to anchor to now that Simon had pushed her out of the life they'd built together.

She felt the hot flush of shame of not having enough, of not being enough. Just like when she was twelve and she had stood in line at the food bank. Her dad had been sick, coughing all the time and hadn't worked for a week. She had a list of things they needed but with no money and little in the house, that had been their only option. With a letter from her dad and a shopping bag, she tried to stand tall to give them impression she was older than she looked.

She tried to push the memory away but it insisted on being acknowledged.

It had been cold, just like today...

'Next,' said the man at the food bank.

Christa walked towards the door but the man stopped her.

'Where's your parent?'

'He's sick; he's at home,' she said and shoved her hand into her shopping bag. 'I have a letter from him with his number.'

'We don't allow kids to come down on their own. Tell him to come down and you can get what you need.'

Christa started to argue but the man was gesturing to the person behind her.

She turned and walked to the back of the line, feeling tears welling, wondering how she was going to get the food until her dad recovered.

Crying, she hated herself for not being older and being able to get what she needed for them.

She had vowed then to never let this happen to her ever again.

And here she was, thirty-five years old, without a plan or a direction. Simon had been her safety net for so long, she had put up with more than she should have to be secure but at what cost?

She realised that she had put her security into the hands of someone else, and instead she should have woven her own net. Whatever she needed to learn before was back to remind her that she still didn't get it. That hiding behind Simon was avoidance. And now she had to do the work. She had no one to blame but herself for not standing up to him more, for not insisting on looking at the paperwork, for not owning her talent and asking to be recognised for her contribution to Playfoot's.

The rush of awareness made her head hurt but it was the clearest thought she'd had in six months. Whatever she was going to do next wasn't in London and it wasn't with white tablecloths and a wine list.

She heaved the bag back onto her shoulder and started to walk down the busy street, seeing some of the usual faces who often came to the back door of the restaurant.

'Hiya, Sam,' she said to the man in the overcoat and she reached into the heavy bag on her shoulder, pulling out a container of her best chicken stew with rice and vegetables, pressing it into his hands. She had cooked it low and slow and always stirred with a little hope that the people she gave her cooking to would find some care and support.

'And a little sweet treat for after, because I know you love the lemon slice with coconut.'

Sam smiled a toothless grin at her.

'You're a good egg, Chrissy. We'll miss you.'

Christa felt her eyes prick with tears. 'I'll miss you also, Sam.'

'Here comes Darryl and Allen,' said Sam and soon Christa had walked up the street and handed out her containers of food, with little care packages of wet wipes, and plastic cutlery, Chapstick and some deodorant, and sanitary items for the women.

It wasn't much but it was her goodbye present. For ten years she had been feeding the homeless six nights a week from her kitchen door. She would worry about them, and though Simon told her they had choices and were like human seagulls, Christa viewed them as her community and it eased the burden of the waste that she saw in the kitchen.

'Where you off to then?' asked Mary, scooping stew into

her mouth with the wooden spoon that had been taped to the side of the container. Mary had been on the streets since Christa had been at the restaurant and she was as wise as she was erratic, but if you got Mary on a good day she could have given Brené Brown and Oprah a run for their money in life advice.

'No idea yet – I'll see what comes up,' she said.

'Whatever you do, cook with love. I can taste the sadness in this stew. He's not worth it, love. Used to tell us to piss off when you weren't around.'

Christa wasn't surprised at this titbit of information about Simon. She had heard it before from others on the street. 'Not enough salt in the stew?' she asked, avoiding Simon as a topic.

Mary smiled at her, her long grey hair matted to her scalp. 'Cooking is like love. You should fall into it with complete abandon or not at all.'

'That's very poetic, Mary,' she said.

Mary shrugged. 'I didn't write it, I read it somewhere, but you can tell when someone doesn't like cooking, you can taste it in their food, I reckon. My gran's golden syrup dumplings were always sweeter than my mum's. She hated us kids; that feeling flavoured everything she did.'

Christa looked at the homeless woman who was spooning the food into her mouth, and wondered if you ever stopped thinking about the painful times you endured as a child. How those times changed the course of your life and how you could run from them and then the reminder would come disguised in a simple dish, or the scent of something simmering on the stove, in a song or a saying from a stranger. And she knew deep inside her that she had avoided confronting her past because Simon made it easy for her to ignore it by taking control of her life. She had no idea who she was anymore, let alone what she wanted, but she knew she needed to do something that made a difference to the twelve-year-old Christa, and to the Sams and Marys of the world, and if it was with food then that would be what she did, because food had given her a lifeline once upon a time and she suspected it might just do it again if she trusted whatever was to come next.

2

Christa walked back to the flat she'd once shared with Simon and entered the perfectly beautiful and minimal space – carefully curated by him, of course. Christa preferred a more eclectic environment, but Simon had said it suited their aesthetic for the restaurant and would get them more magazine coverage.

And he was correct. Their home and restaurant were covered in every important interiors magazine with them looking smug, leaning against their expensive joinery and sitting on the arm of their Italian sofa.

They looked so perfect and yet they slept on opposite edges of their shared bed and were polite but cold to each other. They were such different people. Christa wondered how they had ever thought to get married.

But people change and she doubted she would even speak to Simon if she met him now at a party. Once she had been impressed by his money and confidence. Now she wanted to see what people cared about and how they helped others.

Christa turned on the kettle and looked out the window. A sparrow was bouncing around the bird feeder in next door's tree and she thought about the woman called Avian with Simon. What a terrible name to give a child, she thought. There was no doubt Simon was a flirt but now she wondered if he had seen other women during their marriage. The waitresses who smiled a little too long at him, or the patrons who seemed to always want to play with their hair or adjust their breasts in his vicinity.

Avian was the polar opposite of Christa to look at, she thought. While Avian was wearing black leather trousers and a tight turtleneck, Christa must have looked like a giant Christmas ham in her pink puffa jacket. She was surprised Simon hadn't stuck cloves in her and carved her up.

The pink puffa had seemed cute on the website but when it came Simon had screamed laughing and called her blancmange for the day until she had cried and then he said sorry and told her she looked cute, which she hated. Being told she was cute was so patronising. She shivered at the word as she put a teabag into a mug and poured the water in.

The doorbell rang, and she went and pressed the buzzer.

'It's Selene,' came the throaty French voice.

Selene always seemed to know when Christa needed her, even when Christa didn't know herself.

Selene had studied at Le Cordon Bleu with Christa and Simon, and while she and Simon went into hospitality, Selene had become a restaurant critic and was now one of the most highly regarded in Europe with her own page in a luxury magazine and a column in a paper, along with her own website.

Christa buzzed her in and poured her a cup of hot water with a slice of lemon. Keeping the calories down wasn't easy when you were eating out most days.

She knocked and Christa let her in. '*Salut*, did you return the keys?'

Christa rolled her eyes. 'Yes and I met his new bit of thin rib: Avian.'

Selene laughed. 'She is a little bird lady. She's the producer on the show. All the way from the USA.'

'She seems to have migrated for the winter,' said Christa. 'I hope she and Slimon fly to the warmer climes asap.'

Selene sat on the sofa and crossed her legs, her elegant frame belying that she reviewed restaurant food for a living. 'Slimon. Very funny. I like it. He shall be known as that from here on in. So how did it go? All done?' she asked.

Christa nodded and sighed. 'And I have signed the papers, so I'm no longer married. I am also jobless and once I put this place on the market I will be homeless.'

Selene sipped her hot water.

'What do you want to do next?'

'Feed the poor? Clothe the naked? I don't know, something to help people,' she admitted.

Selene didn't roll her eyes but she was nothing if not a pragmatist. 'That takes money and connections. You will have to get a job first.'

'I'm aware,' sighed Christa. She had worked on enough charity events to know the huge pressure on the organisations to keep everything afloat while trying to get donations and support from wealthy individuals.

'Someone I know asked if you wanted to cook for a rich family over the Christmas period. The lawyer for the client messaged me, all very cloak and daggers. He said he had eaten at Playfoot's. It's obviously someone famous or important. But the money they mentioned was ridiculously high. Out in the country somewhere, at their house.'

Christa's ears pricked up. She needed more money to

support her while she worked out what she wanted to do next in order to realise the dream that had been planted in her mind.

'Me? They asked for me? Who are they?' People rarely asked for her. 'Surely they meant Simon?'

'No, he said you by name,' Selene said. 'I could ask the lawyer who it is, but I doubt they would tell me unless I signed a non-disclosure agreement.'

Christa was tempted. They knew her cooking, they knew her food and they asked for her personally. It was kind of nice to be recognised for once. Especially when Simon was being featured as the best thing to happen to British cooking since Gordon Ramsay.

'Over Christmas? I could do it. I mean it's not like I'm going wassailing with my family.'

Selene reached over and gave her arm a rub. 'You could come to Paris with my family but we will just drink and fight and you will not be paid for it.'

Christa thought of the holidays with Simon's family at their country house, perfectly chic and very Sloane Ranger with the silver cutlery all lined up on the white damask cloth and Fortnum and Mason Christmas crackers on the table. The first year she had Christmas with Simon's family she had nervously drunk too much champagne and asked when the photographer was arriving for the catalogue shoot. She knew it was rude but it was true. The perfection of the table had made her wonder about the silliness of Christmas. Simon had been furious with her little dig, which she apologised for but he had said that not everyone could enjoy the bonhomie of the shelter Christmas she had told him about. She remembered the shame then and even now it smarted to think of it.

Of course the food was also perfect. Every year it was the same. Always catered with smoked salmon to start, followed by roast Norfolk bronze turkey with all of the trimmings. Then there was a Christmas pudding with brandy custard and mince pies and a platter of cheese and biscuits to finish. It was all perfectly fine but that's all it was: fine. There was nothing spontaneous about the day, no bustling about the kitchen or fighting over whether the turkey was done or not. So rehearsed, she felt she could have recited the conversation word for word from Simon's parents about the cooking of turkey and how nice it was to avoid the line at Waitrose for the smoked salmon.

Christa thought back to the Christmas lunches of her younger years when it was just her and her dad. Simon might have thought it was sad but she remembered there was life, unlike in his family home. It wasn't what everyone would want to experience for Christmas but there was a sense of being in it together. Everyone would wear the paper hats and share the small gifts as though they were priceless. It wasn't what some children would think was a wonderful Christmas but for Christa it was generous and filled with hope.

Her dad had died the year she started at Le Cordon Bleu and she started to date Simon in second year. God he was handsome in a sort of posh foppish Hugh Grant way. And he could speak French and he drove a green MG and he said he went to school with one of the members of Coldplay. He was, to Christa, the most wonderful, exciting and different man she had ever known. All the girls wanted to date him but after first year, when she topped the class in everything, he chose her.

'I've always been into talent over looks,' he had told her the first time they made love and she'd thought it was romantic. Now she wanted to shake herself awake from the spell he had her under back then.

In second year she came first in everything again and Simon became even more serious about her. He was planning a restaurant, he had told her; he had investors, he confided; and he wanted her to be his sous chef.

Instead she went to Paris after she graduated, and lived with Selene's family and worked at a Michelin-hatted restaurant, returning with a perfect soufflé recipe and a fluency in French.

It was the only time she defied Simon in their relationship but the head of her course told her she had something special. She could cook in a Michelin-starred restaurant if she worked hard enough, because he thought she had the talent. She was the only one to be offered the apprenticeship in France and, looking back, she realised Simon knew he couldn't outshine her, so instead he would use her talent for his own gain.

Simon had then gone into full wooing mode. He came and saw her as often as he could, and he complimented her constantly on her talent and how clever she was. When she had mentioned the hotel where she worked were thinking of promoting her, he told her he supported it and he couldn't wait for her to eat at his restaurant he was opening.

And then, just before his restaurant opened, he called her crying, saying his sous chef had pulled out. He would be open in a week. He would lose the money from the investors. What could he do? He was desperate for an idea; he needed Christa's brilliance. And so she said she would come back to London for a while. Just until he found the right person. And fifteen years later she was still there.

She had been played by the Playfoot, she thought, stuck in the restaurant and spending every Christmas with his family, even though Christmas Eve was her birthday.

Once she had suggested that she and Simon start their own tradition and he responded as though she had suggested he smother his parents in the night with an oven bag.

Instead, Christa always received a birthday present on Christmas Eve from Simon, "but something small, because it's Christmas tomorrow". And she had accepted it because she didn't think she deserved anything more. Christmases and birthdays were small when she was a child because of her dad's issues and lack of money. So to want something more as an adult made her feel like she was a materialistic, pathetic fool.

And she always received a little present from his parents, given in hushed tones away from the nativity set on the mantelpiece, as though they were worried that Jesus would be cross with them for celebrating someone else's birthday.

Christa shuddered at the memories.

'It's funny how you settle in life,' she said aloud.

'Some do – not me,' said Selene.

Christa smiled at her friend. She would never settle the way Christa had but perhaps it was because Selene hadn't been through what she had.

'I'll do it; tell whoever it is, I will do the gig. I need to get out of London. It's making me sad. And I want to be busy. I need space to think, you know?'

Selene put down her mug. 'Really? Staying with strangers, cooking for them?'

'Why not? I'm not achieving anything here, am I? I need the money. I need the distraction. It'll be good for me,' she said. Was she trying to convince Selene or herself? She wasn't sure.

Selene pulled out her phone and typed onto the screen.

'Okay, I have told them you're interested. Let me see if I can get the price up though. You deserve birthday tax also.'

Christa laughed. 'You're the best non-agent I could have.'

Within a minute Selene's phone rang and she picked it up and spoke.

'Yes, that's correct… Another ten. It is Christmas and she will be away from her family.'

Christa thought about her friends, all spending the time with their families. She would have been alone, not wanting to intrude on anyone's lunch or dinner even though she knew she would have been more than welcome.

'Correct, that should be fine. Yes. Email it through and we can review and return the paperwork and the signed NDA.'

Selene put down the phone.

'It is done. You head to York on the third of December and stay until the third of January.'

'God that's longer than I thought,' said Christa.

'It's also a fifteen-thousand-pound fee,' Selene added.

'What? Are you joking? That's ridiculous money.'

'I can ask them for twenty if you like.'

'I mean that's very overpaid.'

'It's what you could be earning in the restaurant though. Don't undervalue yourself.' Selene scolded her. Christa was silent as she knew her friend was right. She always undervalued herself in her work and in her relationships.

'In York? You say?' Christa sat back and tapped her chin. 'York. Who is famous and rich who lives in York?'

'The cast of *Emmerdale*?' Selene asked and Christa burst out laughing. 'They are sending through the paperwork now. I will forward it to you to print out. And they want your bank account details so they can pay you half upfront.'

Christa felt her eyes prick with tears.

'How do you always know when I need help and then just show up like some sexy French fairy godmother?'

Selene shrugged. 'We are soul sisters, Christa. I will always support you. I chose you not Slimon in this divorce so whatever you do, I'll cheer you on.'

Christa closed her eyes and felt her body relax for the first time since she and Simon split. She had a plan, even if it was only until January the third; but it was something to do and she was needed, and that was enough for now.

3

The city disappeared behind her as Christa sipped her coffee while she drove her Jeep along the A1. She had Christmas songs playing in the car to try and get into the Christmas spirit but she had the feeling that she might have bitten off more than she could chew.

Once she had signed the NDA and the money entered her account, a list of food to be avoided for some meals came through, including anything with gluten, onion, garlic, certain berries and fruits, and even spices.

She still didn't know who she was cooking for but judging from the list of prohibited food she imagined they were very used to having things just the way they liked them and nothing else would suffice.

She stopped in Leicester for some lunch. The wind was biting when she got out of the car so she headed to the nearest café for a toasted cheese sandwich and a cup of tea to warm her up. Sometimes simple food was the best kind. Not every chef would admit they ordered takeaway food or made toasted sandwiches as often as they do. The last thing Christa felt like doing was cooking for herself when she was at home.

Now she had a month of cooking in a place far away from Simon and the memories of London. She loved cooking for people, although the list of banned food was a red flag. Probably Americans, she thought, maybe a movie star who was on a strict diet for a new role. She tried to guess who it might be as her stomach rumbled, reminding her she needed to eat.

The café she stopped at was very old-fashioned and the old tables looked like there had been forty years of news passed across them, but the tea was hot and strong. The best food often came from old places like this, which focused on what they were good at and ignored the trends. She could have done without the television suspended from the wall but at least the sound was turned down.

Christa bit into her sandwich when she saw a television advertisement playing for the new cooking show and Simon's face came on screen. He was smiling at her as she ate her lunch, as though he was a benevolent food angel above her, sending blessings to the small café. She stared out the window of the café, thinking about all the times she let Simon have the spotlight because she didn't think she was worthy of being proud of her work. God, she wanted to slap herself.

There was food critic also judging, a pompous git who was Selene's rival in the world of restaurant reviews. Christa hated his braces and the cravats that he now wore and the way he licked his fingers as he looked at the camera. Ewww. The final judge was a YouTube cook who became famous for cooking in the woods behind his mud-brick house, handmade by him of course.

None of the judges were women, which Christa found

surprising when there were many women who were making their mark in the culinary world. But she also knew from her female friends in the industry that it was hard to work in a restaurant and have children. She had wanted children but Simon didn't, which is why she didn't have any.

She paid the bill and picked up some homemade lemon curd for sale on the counter.

'I'll take one of these,' she said to the woman serving her.

'I made it myself,' said the woman. 'I had too many lemons this year. I couldn't give them away – all my friends said they hadn't used the ones I'd already given them.'

'You know the saying though,' said Christa. 'If you have to buy lemons then you don't have any good friends. Your friends should know how lucky they are to have you.'

The woman handed the change back to Christa. 'Oh I like that. I might remind them for the next batch. Have a good day, love.'

Christa hopped into her car and, filled with tea and a fine sandwich, she drove towards York feeling better and her thoughts clearer.

Leaving London was obviously good for her. Perhaps this was what she had needed all along. Some space to think and be open to possibilities. Anything could happen, she told herself as she drove through the countryside.

Simon had moved on, and she needed to as well. She didn't want what he wanted, perhaps she never had, but he made her path smooth so she didn't have to worry about food shelters and the heating bill and lining up for supplies on cold winter days.

What she couldn't understand, she thought as she drove, was why she forgot she could do those things and survive.

She was resilient but Simon had made her dependent on him and she hated that she had allowed it to happen. She was once a brave child, a courageous teenager, the best in her class at cooking school, and somehow she had forgotten who she was when around Simon.

The nerves she had felt about driving to the job dissipated because she remembered the one thing her dad always said about her: 'Christa, you can do hard things. Not everyone can but you can.' And he was right. He would have hated Simon. She laughed to herself.

She was thankful Simon never met him. He wasn't Simon's sort of person, with his rough smoker's voice and lack of decorum about people whom he called piss-elegant. No more piss-elegant, she told herself. No more hiding behind a man. No more not being herself and saying what she wanted in life. This was the new Christa Playfoot, ready to do hard things.

Feeling empowered, she checked the sat nav directions and realised she hadn't paid attention and missed the turn-off.

Maybe she could do hard things but reading a map or listening to directions wasn't one of them, she thought, giggling as she took the next turn-off to get back onto the right path. The journey back to self might take a few wrong turns, she reminded herself but at least she had a sense of where she was going now.

The map was sending Christa off the road and onto a gravel driveway. She drove slowly, the large oak trees creating a tunnel of branches, while a light rain began to fall. The address she put into the GPS had told her she was heading into a forest, and as though proving the fact, she saw a large stag standing by the side of the drive. She slowed down so as to not startle the magnificent animal but perhaps she was the one startled, she considered as she caught its eye as she passed. She could have sworn it dipped its head in greeting.

Even with the heater on in the car, she could feel the temperature dropping outside as the sky became darker and the rain heavier as she came to the end of the driveway. In the not so far distance was a house that was beyond anything she had imagined she would be staying in. An enormous palatial building that looked like a wealthy child's doll's house had been blown up one hundred per cent and then some more.

'Are you serious?' she said to herself as she stopped the car at the top of the driveway to fully take in the view. She expected Mr Darcy to run down the stairs to see if Lizzy had returned home but sadly it was just her and no Mr Darcy was to be seen. The rain turned up its setting to pouring now and a clap of thunder announced her arrival, followed by a bolt of lightning that made the house glow for a brief moment.

She dialled Selene.

'I'm working at Downton Abbey but on steroids,' she said as soon as her friend answered. 'There is a storm and a deer on the side of the road and I'm not sure if I am in some gothic horror film or walking into my own death.'

'Are you serious? That's amazing, babe. Take photos, lots of them. I want to see but I have to go right now. I'm heading out to an early event. Text me, yeah?'

Christa drove up to the house and parked next to a large

four-wheel drive Bentley. Simon wanted one of those, she remembered, thinking how much he would love the house and it's grandiosity. *Stop thinking about Simon*, she told herself. He was gone. He didn't think about her every minute so why did she think about him? She was so used to conferring with him about everything to make sure he was happy that she forgot to think about herself. No more, she told herself. She closed her eyes for a moment to rebalance her mind. Simon was gone. She was here and never the twain shall meet again.

Opening her eyes, she took in the whole house – well as much as she could with the enormous wings and stairs and columns. There were so many windows.

It was magnificent but Christa wondered who would clean it. So much to Hoover, she thought as she reached for her umbrella in the back seat. She opened the car door as a gust of wind blew so fiercely that the umbrella flew out of her hand and was out of sight in a moment.

Taking her chances, she ran from the car up the many front steps to the front door just as the thunder crashed again. Banging on the door with both hands and then ringing the bell next to it, she shivered as the rain hit her back like a cat o' nine tails.

Just as she was about to give up and run back to her car, the door opened to reveal a young boy on rollerblades with a hockey stick in his hand.

'Hey,' he greeted her in an American accent.

Christa was about to speak when another child appeared, who was identical in every way – including the accoutrements on his feet and in his hand – except he held a small, space-age-looking video camera.

'Are you the chef?' he asked, pointing the camera at her.

More lightning and thunder so close Christa screamed. Was she in *The Shining*? What was happening?

'Seth, Ethan, let her in for God's sake,' said a booming voice with a Californian drawl.

Christa stepped inside the foyer of the home and looked up to see a man standing at the top of the staircase. He was tall or maybe that was because he was looming large above them all, like an omnipotent god in a hoodie, jeans and sneakers. He leaned over the railing to peer down at her.

'You're Christa the cook? Yes?'

'Chef,' she corrected.

'Chef, okay, sure,' he said. 'If that's what you want to be called.'

For some reason his dismissive comment felt like he had scolded her. She was sick of being overlooked, invalidated, and patronised by men, and this person was giving her the same energy as Simon.

'Actually, I earned that title,' she said, crossing her arms and tilting her head back further so he could see she was serious.

'Pardon?' He frowned at her, dark blonde hair falling into his face, and he pushed it away.

'I'm not a cook, I'm a chef. I worked in a Michelin-hatted restaurant in Paris and owned a restaurant in London for over ten years. And the *Sunday Times* said my hot cross bun ice cream served with spiced wine-soaked quince tart was a miracle and resurrected the once maligned fruit.'

As Christa was speaking, she heard herself and tried to stop but the words just kept coming out of her mouth.

'So yes, I am a chef. Not a cook,' she finished, feeling

weak at the knees from looking upwards for so long and feeling her blood pressure rising.

The man laughed. 'This is Christmas, not Easter, so you can leave your hot cross bun ice cream for next year. But thanks for the CV. I am sure you will chef for us very well,' he said, putting emphasis on the word chef, which annoyed Christa, but she had already said too much.

This whole taking charge of her life thing wasn't going quite to plan.

'I didn't catch your name,' she said, holding her ground.

'I didn't throw it,' he said and she stared at him, her eyes narrowing, as she tried to take in this level of arrogance and entitlement.

He paused and she saw his shoulders drop. 'Marc, Marc Ferrier,' he said in a softer tone.

She nodded her acknowledgement, trying to recall if she had ever heard his name before but it drew a blank.

Two men in raincoats ran up towards the door, one holding a fancy green umbrella with a gold handle.

'God, it's hideous outside. We're drowning,' called one of the men in a booming voice, also with an American accent. A crack of thunder was heard closer than Christa would have liked.

The children were skating on the marble floors, which she was pretty certain couldn't be good for the floors, or the children if they fell.

'Stop skating on the marble,' yelled the man above, as though reading her mind. 'And shut the door – it's freezing.'

'Shut the door,' one of the children yelled.

'Shut the front door,' yelled the other and Christa couldn't stop herself.

'Stop yelling. You don't get anything done faster or better by yelling, okay? There will be no yelling at me or around me or I will leave. Shut the door, stop skating and stop dripping water everywhere,' she said to the men in raincoats.

Everyone stared at her and Christa wondered if she should turn and head back to her car and drive back to London.

The man at the top of the stairs looked over the ornate bannister at her.

'I thought chefs liked to yell.'

'Not in my kitchen,' she answered, tipping her head to look up at him again and feeling the blood rushing to her face.

He caught her eye. 'And not in my house – you're right. I hate yelling,' he said and he gave her a slight nod and then walked away as though he had her approval despite the unorthodox entrance.

The children were already skating away now the small disturbance in the atmosphere had settled.

'You're Christa, yes?' one of the men said while taking off his rain jacket and hanging it on the array of hooks near the front door.

She nodded. 'Yes. Sorry about that but it was all very chaotic. I don't like chaos.'

The man looked her up and down and then laughed a little but not meanly. 'Then you better get prepared for when his ex visits. She is the original Goddess Discordia.'

Christa stared at him. 'When does she arrive?'

'Whenever she pleases,' he said. 'She's the one with the list of intolerances.' He gave Christa a knowing look and she smiled respectfully in response.

It wasn't for her to say what was an allergy, intolerance or disordered eating, but God knows, every year there were more and more requests at the restaurant for accommodations and substitutions. Perhaps the world was becoming more intolerant in general, she often reflected.

'I'm Adam, Marc's lawyer, and this is my husband Paul. We're here for Christmas also. I have to make some calls. Paul, can you show Christa to her room?'

Adam was gone in an instant but she could hear his voice barking down the phone as he left.

Paul smiled at her kindly and she felt herself relax.

'Hey, Christa, grab your things and I'll take you to your room. We usually have a housekeeper but she's gone in to York to get some supplies. FYI, she's terrifying.'

Christa laughed. 'That's something to look forward to. Don't worry about my things – I can get them when the rain stops,' Christa said. She looked around the foyer and didn't see any Christmas decorations.

This foyer was crying out for a tree and some cascading pine branches and bows down the bannister.

'Did you just arrive?' she asked Paul.

'No, we've been here about a week but Marc and Adam work all the time. I'm the corporate wife, so I'll be hanging around the kitchen, if you don't mind.'

'I don't mind at all,' she said, meaning it. Paul had a pleasant demeanour and was more relaxed than the other two men.

The twins were rollerblading away, their war cries and slapping of the hockey sticks competing with the storm outside.

'Come to the kitchen then,' said Paul. He had a New

York accent and wore a beautiful cashmere jumper, and she followed him through the house that was impeccably decorated but without a whisper of the time of the year. There was a mix of modern and period furniture, muted tones of grey and indigo and black, with art to match. It was certainly elegant but very masculine and impersonal.

'Will Christmas be celebrated?' she asked looking around.

'Of course,' Paul said as he pushed open the door to the kitchen. 'Why do you ask?'

'It's just that there aren't any Christmas decorations,' said Christa, wishing she had kept her mouth closed.

'Marc isn't the festive type,' said Paul with raised eyebrows that silently spoke volumes. He gestured to a beautiful professional kitchen, big enough for six chefs to make a banquet for fifty people. 'They usually do Christmas at their house in San Francisco. I think that was more the ex-wife than him. I do remember them having holiday décor when I went for a cocktail party, but it was all very silver and blue, not my style. I'm more of a traditional, Martha Stewart style.'

'Oh my gosh, me too – I love traditional decorations. The more old-fashioned the better,' Christa agreed. 'I did a big tree covered in tartan ribbons last year. My ex hated it.'

Paul grabbed her arm. 'Oh that's perfect.' He sighed. 'It's hard for me. I'm an interior stylist. I keep turning around corners in the house and see where a gorgeous Yuletide moment could be.' He shook his head. 'Anyway, have a look around and let me know if you need anything else and I can let Adam know.'

Christa looked around the space. Stainless steel was mixed with wood panelling and marble countertops for baking. It was better than the kitchen at Playfoot's. Simon would be green with envy at this space.

Christa opened a drawer and saw Alessi cutlery lined up in perfect order.

'How many will I be cooking for each night?' she asked.

'For now, it's myself, my husband Adam – the lawyer with the loud voice – the twins and Marc.'

'No dinner parties or cocktail events? Christmas drinks?'

'No, we don't know anyone here and Marc isn't the event type. Hates dinner parties.'

What a shame, Christa thought looking at the kitchen set-up. 'What time is dinner?' she asked.

'Seven is fine. Usually, the twins eat in the kitchen and the adults sit in the dining room. It's very formal.'

'Wow, okay.' Christa couldn't understand when people didn't want to eat with their children. How would they learn manners or appropriate behaviour if they didn't have good role models? That's why she always admired the French and them taking children out so early in life to cafés and letting them sit at the table like young adults.

'What do you want me to make for dinner?' she asked as she heard Adam's voice calling Paul.

'I should go,' he said but he turned as he was leaving the kitchen. 'Selene said you're amazing, so surprise us.'

'Love her,' said Christa.

'Same!' said Paul.

'Sorry about yelling about the dripping from the rain – I shouldn't have spoken to you like that,' she said. 'I worried about the boys on their skates with the marble and the water.'

Paul shrugged. 'No offence taken. I didn't think about

them actually, so it was good you did. They don't always get thought of first in this house,' he said he with a wry look at her.

He walked to the door. 'Sing out if you need anything. I'll be around.'

And then Christa was alone again, wishing everything about the arrival had gone differently and wondering how she would make it through the next few weeks.

4

Walking through the hall to go downstairs, Christa wondered about the house and its belongings. Everything was artfully placed and expensive, from the carpets that sunk under her feet, to the art in the elegant frames that were probably by famous artists she didn't know and the furniture that all seemed to be covered in silk and beautiful prints.

She had seen people who were well off like Simon's parents but this was next-level. Every room was decorated sympathetically to the style of the house but no one was in them. So many rooms unlived in, when so many people were living without a home. It felt jarring as she walked down the quiet hallway and turned at the sound of a fire crackling. She looked inside and gasped at the sight of the most beautiful wallpaper she had ever seen – gold and black with deer, squirrels and rabbits amongst ferns and flowers. The room's furniture was all dark wood and leather, and there was a large desk and a fire in the grate.

'Can I help you?' she heard Marc say behind her.

'Sorry, I was just admiring the wallpaper,' she said and turned to him. 'It's so beautiful.'

He looked at her and then the wallpaper and back to her and nodded. She felt silly for commenting. He probably looked at it every day and was tired of it, or he thought she was a snoop. Everything about this man told her he had money. His expensive hoodie with the luxury label sewn onto the left breast. Well-fitted dark jeans and the trainers she had only ever seen in magazines with the unmistakable branding. Christa wasn't impressed by labels, but she did notice how Marc ran his hands through his dark blonde hair and that his tan seemed real. There were flecks of grey in his hair, just a few, and she respected he kept them there. He was tall and slim, and she noticed he had some bracelets on one arm. One of them spelled out Dad in beads and she felt herself soften a little at his gesture to his children.

'Excuse me,' she said and she walked towards the stairs to go to the car to get her luggage and special chef knives that she took everywhere.

'Is your room okay?' she heard him ask.

Adam the officious lawyer had shown her to the floor and had pointed at the room that would be hers for the next month.

'Sure, I mean there's no gold wallpaper of forest animals frolicking but it will suffice,' she joked.

Marc looked at her and frowned.

'That was a joke,' she said. God, this guy was a barrel of laughs.

'Okay,' he said and he walked into what she now presumed was his study and closed the door.

She immediately regretted her pithy comment. What she wanted to say was her room was lovely. It was nicer than she had expected or assumed she might be afforded for her time here.

She thought perhaps it would be a single room with a bed and bathroom. What she got was a true suite, similar to one she had stayed in on her wedding night at a fancy hotel. A large bedroom with a king-sized bed and a sitting room with a television and sofa set and new glossy magazines on the table. The bathroom was stocked with all the appropriate Penhaligon's toiletries and a soft robe was hanging on a hook against the tiles.

She stood at the top of the stairs and wondered, and then went back to the room Marc had disappeared into and knocked. 'Come in,' she heard and she opened the door.

'Yeah?' he asked, looking up from his laptop from behind the desk.

'I wanted to say the room I've been given is lovely. It's much nicer than what I thought it would be and really generous. So thank you,' she said, feeling awkward.

Marc leaned back in his chair, his expression unreadable.

'So you have everything you need?'

'I do.'

'And it's warm enough? The housekeeper can get you more blankets if you need them.'

'I think I'll be okay. I'm used to the cold winters.' She smiled at him.

He laughed and pushed his hand through his hair again – his little habit, it seemed.

'Those from California aren't so lucky. I'm still acclimating. Those winds are brutal.'

'Gloves, hats and thermals are the thing for the wind,' she offered.

'Yes, I have it all from our ski lodge in Aspen but it's different when you're trying to exist in it and not flying down runs, hot from the exercise.'

Christa didn't know what to say to that. Skiing in Aspen was so far away from her reality.

'All right then, I'll go get my things,' she said and she turned and closed the door behind her.

When she returned from the car with her things, she had peered out the window of her room to see fog covering extensive lawns and the beautiful silhouettes of trees in the dusk. Hopefully, she would have time to walk the property, she thought as she pulled on her work pants and chef whites then slipped on her clogs and headed downstairs to the kitchen.

It was nearly four in the afternoon, and Christa wondered what she should make for dinner since Paul had given her carte blanche in the kitchen.

The fridges were filled with fresh vegetables and more cheese than she thought was possible for the small number of inhabitants of the house.

Another fridge held meat and then another wine. It was ridiculous, she thought, thinking of all the meals she could make with this food to give to those who needed it most.

She pulled out packages marked salmon, duck, quail and goat.

'Bloody Nora,' she said.

'Who's Nora?' she heard a voice say and turned to see the twins behind her.

'Whoever bought all this food. It's enough for a formal dinner every night until the middle of next year.'

'It wasn't Nora, it was Peggy – she's the housekeeper. Dad gave her a list of everything he thought we might need.'

'What happens if we don't eat it all?' she asked. This was as much as they would order for a weekday lunch at the restaurant. How on earth would they get through it all?

'They throw it out I guess,' said one of the boys with a shrug.

Christa closed the fridge with a sigh.

'I'm Christa,' she said.

'I'm Seth,' said one of the boys. They were blonde, thin, with dark eyes, and utterly identical except one had a small freckle on his cheekbone.

'And I'm Ethan,' said the other.

'Really?' Christa crossed her arms. 'I went to school with twin girls who were always messing about and pretending to be the other. It's part of your DNA to play tricks on people.'

They laughed. 'Nah it's the other way around but you won't remember anyway. Dad has never got us right.'

Christa saw a flicker in their faces and she studied them closely.

'I will try my best to remember who is who,' she said. 'You,' she pointed at the one with the freckle on his cheekbone. 'Are Seth.'

He looked at her suspiciously. 'How can you tell?'

She touched his cheek. 'Your little hallmark,' she said. 'Gives you away.'

The boys seemed impressed with her deduction and they sat on the kitchen stools at the bench, their rollerblades making loud noises as they crashed against the woodwork.

'We're not really that similar,' Seth said, as he touched the knife roll.

37

She quickly moved it out of the way.

'Ethan likes gaming and metal music, and I like K-pop. He likes to film things and I like to make things, like with Lego.'

Christa nodded. 'Good to know. And what do you like to eat for dinner?'

'We like burgers.' Seth said. 'And pasta. And sushi. And Mexican food.'

Christa thought for a moment.

'What does your dad like to eat?'

'Stuff we don't like,' was all Ethan said and then he made a vomit noise.

'He likes pasta,' said Seth. 'He had the little round things, like little squashed eggs. Knocko?' he asked.

'Gnocchi?' she asked and he nodded.

'Yeah, that's the one.'

Pasta was a good start she thought, as she dug through the fridge and found some wagyu beef she could mince and make burgers with and found some potatoes to make pommes frites.

Ethan was up again and went sailing past her on his skates.

'Sit down. No skating in the kitchen,' she said firmly, and surprisingly he obliged and sat next to his brother.

'Can you teach us how to cook?' asked Seth.

She looked around the fridge door to see if they were being silly but saw they were serious.

'How old are you both?'

'Ten,' they answered in unison.

Christa thought about it. A little company during prep could be fun and she could learn why her boss was always so angry. Besides, teaching people to cook was something she was passionate about. She never understood when people said they were terrible cooks and couldn't cook. Anyone could cook if they followed the recipe. If they could learn to drive they could learn to cook.

If she had her way, cooking healthy food, and learning what to buy at the supermarket and budgeting, would be taught at school.

Those were real life skills.

'Okay then,' she said. 'You can both be my commis cooks. You're just old enough otherwise I would breaking the labour laws.'

'What's a commis cook?' The boys seemed thrilled with the title.

'It's the name for the newest cooks in the kitchen. The ones who will become chefs one day if they work super hard,' she answered.

The back door opened and an older, stout-looking woman holding shopping bags walked into the kitchen. She wore a green woollen coat and a scowl. Her grey hair was pulled into a bun and she had a face that could have made you admit to murder, even if you were innocent.

'Oh, Cook, you're here finally,' said the woman as though Christa was late.

'Christa Playfoot – I'm the chef,' she corrected.

'Peggy Smith, housekeeper of Pudding Hall.'

'Pudding Hall?'

'That's the name of the house,' said Peggy putting the bags on the bench.

Christa looked at the boys. 'What a wonderful name for a house. But it's called Pudding Hall and you don't have a single Christmas decoration? That's very sad.'

The boys shrugged as though they didn't know the answer to her question.

'Why are they in here?' asked Peggy, looking at the boys suspiciously.

'They're my apprentices,' Christa answered, trying to get a reading on Peggy, who seemed put out to have the children in the kitchen.

'We're commi cooks,' said Ethan.

'Commis,' said Christa laughing. The boys were delightful and funny.

But Peggy didn't seem to find them amusing. 'Well don't be messing about in here – Cook has a busy job.'

'Chef,' said Christa but Peggy ignored her and kept talking.

'Mr Ferrier sent me out for more food, just in case you didn't have what you needed.'

'More?' asked Christa thinking of the filled refrigerator.

She sighed. 'I don't know what else you would need. There will be nothing left in Waitrose if I head back there again.'

'We have more than enough; don't buy any more,' said Christa. She watched Peggy unpack the bags of shopping.

More cheese, she noticed.

'What do you do with the food that isn't cooked?' she asked Peggy.

Peggy shook her head. 'It is thrown in the rubbish. I had to dispose of a lot of fruit and vegetables as they said they would be here earlier than they were and it went off.' Her look spoke volumes to Christa. At least they agreed on something.

'What sort of things does Mr Ferrier like for dinner?' she asked Peggy who shrugged.

'No idea – they've eaten in York for the past few nights.'

Christa looked to the twins who were fast becoming the fountain of knowledge for her induction at Pudding Hall.

'What did your dad order for dinner?'

'I don't know. We weren't invited,' said the boys.

'I made them shepherd's pie and they didn't eat it,' said Peggy glaring at them. 'In my day you ate what you were given and liked it.'

'It was gluggy,' said Ethan.

'And smelled weird,' added Seth.

Peggy gave a snort. 'Rude little beggars,' she said and left the kitchen.

Christa set about mincing the meat and then checked the cupboard for bread rolls for the burgers.

There weren't any so she started on a dough to make her own rolls.

'Shepherd's pie isn't for everyone,' she said. 'Feel like burgers then? Let's make some rolls.'

'We get rolls from the supermarket,' said Seth.

'These will be better than supermarket rolls,' said Christa with a smile. 'Want to see how I make them?'

'Yes,' the boys shouted.

'Wash your hands and then let's get baking,' she instructed.

Every step of the way the boys asked her what she was doing. She let them knead the dough and then punch the air from them, which they took great pleasure in.

And then she set them aside to rise.

'Is that how bread is made?' one of the boys asked. 'I never knew that. Mum doesn't like carbs. She says they're bad.'

Christa shook her head. She had no idea what carbs were

at ten, let alone calling them bad. She knew it as bread or potato and that was that.

'How did you learn to make bread?' asked Seth.

'I was taught by a lovely Italian man who owned a bakery that I worked at when I was at school,' she said.

'Did you just make bread?' asked Ethan, as she worked.

'Nope, I made all sorts of yummy things like Italian donuts and biscotti, which is lovely with coffee.'

'Why did you have a job when you were at school?' asked Ethan. 'Is that even allowed?'

Christa smiled at him. 'Yes it allowed and it's good to work and earn your own money. The people who owned the bakery gave me a job right through school. I was very lucky. There is nothing like the smell of freshly baked bread,' she said to the twins.

She remembered that was the scent that stopped her on her way home from school. The smell of bread was hypnotic, causing her to stop and look at the window.

Il Forno, the fancy gold lettering on the sign had read. A handwritten note with Help Wanted on a brown paper bag was taped to the window below the gold writing.

'Have we been to a bakery?' Seth asked Ethan.

'I don't think so,' said Ethan with a frown.

'What do they look like?' asked Seth.

Christa thought about Il Forno. 'This was an Italian-style bakery, not an American-style, so instead of shelves, there were baskets of bread and rolls and loaves of all shapes and sizes. Some had olives in them. Some had herbs on top. And they were all delicious.'

'I like olives, but Ethan hates them,' said Seth.

The boys played with the measuring spoons as Christa told

them about the Italian croissants, different types of biscotti and panettone in the prettiest boxes she had ever seen.

The boys listened and watched her intently as she peeled the potatoes.

With the potatoes dried, ready to be turned into pommes frites, she looked inside the refrigerator and thought about Adam and his husband and boss's dinner.

She picked up a container of eggs complete with feathers attached. Real eggs, she thought.

'Do you have chickens here?' she asked the boys who were now warring with their hockey sticks.

'No idea,' they said in unison.

Seth added, 'We've only been here a few days and it's rained every day. And Dad won't come out walking because he's busy with work.' They were back to skating around the kitchen now, which was slightly dizzying for Christa as she tried to spot who was who again.

'Can you stop skating please? If you're in the kitchen you have to learn that there are hot liquids, sharp knives and people carrying things. You can't carry on like this or I will have to let you go and find other twins who can work respectfully.'

The boys stopped skating and came back to the bench.

'Do you know any other twins?' they asked, looking at her suspiciously.

'Not yet but I can ask in town,' she stated firmly.

The boys looked disappointed at her lack of twin connections and she felt a little sad for them.

'Let's make pasta,' she said brightly.

The boys dropped their sticks with a clatter and turned their attention to her.

'More carbs? Mom would die,' Seth said. 'She says carbs make her crazy.'

'Lucky she's not here then,' said Christa, slightly annoyed that the children already had such a dim view of certain foods.

'Do you have children?' asked Ethan.

'Nope. Go and wash your hands again at the sink behind me.'

The boys did so.

'Why not?' they asked, wiping their hands with the tea towel she handed them.

'Because I work long hours and I would want to be with them instead of being at work.'

The boys looked at each other, as Christa tipped pasta flour in front of them in small mounds.

'Make a volcano shape,' she instructed and the boys followed her lead. 'Now crack an egg into it.'

'Can I film it?' asked Ethan.

'You can't film and cook, so make your choice,' she answered. 'You don't want flour all over your camera.'

Her egg yolk was orange it was so fresh and perfect, and she sighed with pleasure.

There was nothing she liked more than fresh, home-produced food.

The twins carefully broke their eggs into the well and she instructed them to drizzle over some olive oil and salt and then showed them how to whisk the eggs with a fork, eventually adding more of the flour as they went.

'Don't worry if the eggs spills out – move it back in with your hands. It's all part of the work. And now let's knead the dough, like we did with the bread. This will take a while so don't give up. The more stretchy it is, the better,' she encouraged.

She watched their faces as they worked, their young hands kneading the dough while she occasionally sprinkled more flour over the top.

She enjoyed showing people what she knew, and when children were engaged, she enjoyed teaching them.

She and Simon had decided against children during the last few years of their marriage because he had said they didn't have time. She wasn't sure she ever said an outright no but it became part of their narrative as a couple when asked and soon she repeated it until it became something she had believed. When she looked back on it now, she realised that Simon didn't want her to have children because she would have taken time out from the restaurant.

A sadness gripped her and she wondered if she had missed out on something.

'I'm pulling mine like we saw in that horror movie where they pulled the man's skin,' said Seth, interrupting her thoughts.

Ethan laughed and followed his lead. 'This is his stomach as we pull the fat away.'

Christa made a face and turned away from them. Maybe she wasn't missing anything if that's what boys were like.

'When you have finished cooking your horror show, we're going to use the pasta maker to roll it really thin,' she said pulling the pasta maker from the cupboard. Honestly, this house had everything she would ever need.

The boys looked at the contraption and nodded their approval.

'I saw something like that in a video game. They put people's hands in them to torture them and make them tell the truth.'

'My God, does your dad know you watch that sort of stuff?' she asked as she set up the pasta maker.

'I don't know,' said Ethan shrugging and Christa wondered what sort of parent the man was. And then she remembered her own father, passed our drunk on the floor outside their flat, Christa trying to drag him inside even though she was only eleven. And the landlady coming upstairs to tell her that he had urinated on the landing and Christa had to clean it up. She had, telling him in the morning, and he'd promised to never do it again, which was a lie. She brought herself back to the room and away from young Christa. She didn't often go back and look at her past because it was painful and complicated but lately the memories had been coming up more often that she liked.

'Okay, no more horror movie references – now we make fettucine. Do you know what fettucine means in Italian?'

The boys shook their heads. 'Nope.'

'Little ribbons,' she said. 'Isn't that lovely?'

'Like sinew and veins,' said Seth. 'I saw that on a medical show.'

Christa rolled her eyes. This wasn't going to be easy after all.

5

Marc Ferrier was in a revolting mood. The figures he and Adam had worked on didn't add up and the research he was waiting for was late. And there was a stranger in the house. The new cook, whom he'd caught standing outside his study, staring in like a lunatic. He hated being around new people; he found himself often tongue tied and then saying the wrong thing. This is why he had Adam to do the legwork on these matters. It was just a shame he had yelled when she arrived. He had set the tone for their professional relationship, he was afraid.

There was a knock at the door of his study.

'Come in,' he said, and then it opened.

Peggy stood in the doorway, reminding him of a menacing hedgehog.

'Yes?' he asked carefully. Why did she make him feel like he hadn't done his homework?

'I have concerns about the cook,' she stated grandly.

'Why? Did she ask for wallpaper in her room?' He was only half joking. But he didn't want to have to deal with this when he had work pressures to iron out.

'She is encouraging the boys to lark about the kitchen and they're making a mess, which I will have to clean up in the morning. They are making food and skating and generally being nuisances.'

'For God's sake,' he spat out and stormed past Peggy and down to the kitchen. He couldn't leave those boys alone for a moment. He knew they needed to be in school but he wasn't sure they were staying for longer than the Christmas period and a nanny or babysitter was out of the question. If he did hire one they would have terrorised them away. They knew exactly what to do to cause chaos and confusion.

He pushed open the kitchen door and spoke firmly to the boys.

'What are you two doing? Peggy said you're in the way.'

Christa, who was cooking, looked up at him. 'The boys aren't in the way. Not in the slightest bit. I invited them to learn how to make pasta.' She smiled at him, which disarmed him. 'We're making fettucine, which means, boys?'

'Little ribbons,' answered the children in unison.

Marc found himself lost for a response. The boys were sitting calmly at the bench, with the cook on the other side, and ingredients between them.

'You're here to cook, not to childmind,' he snapped at her, unsure why this woman unnerved him. 'Leave Christa alone. You have a room filled with video games; go and use them.'

The boys jumped off the kitchen stools and skated away in silence, hockey sticks and camera in hand.

Christa looked at him and at the pasta dough on the bench.

'Are you going to stay help me knead this then? It is for your dinner after all.' She pointed at the dough.

Marc caught her eye and held it for what felt like the longest time.

She straightened her shoulders, stared him down and smiled. A slow, disarming smile that threw him completely.

'Let me guess? You're joking again?' he said.

'Maybe,' she answered with a small laugh.

He finally spoke. 'If my children get in the way, please let me know.'

'They weren't in the way. They're lovely company, truly,' she answered as she worked the dough.

He frowned at her, trying to think the last time anyone had said the twins were lovely company. He wasn't sure it had ever been said since his divorce. God knows the children took it badly. Even though they weren't great parents, the children wanted them to be together.

He had wanted to tell them that sometimes parents staying together is actually worse in the long run for everyone but he couldn't explain that to his children because then he would have to tell his kids about his own childhood and he never wanted expose them to that level of drama.

A gambler for a father and a faded nightclub singer for a mother whose toxic marriage made Elizabeth Taylor and Richard Burton's seem like a fairy tale. And as the eldest of the four children, he did the parenting in lieu. He'd been parenting since he was nine and he should be good at it but he realised it was different with your own kids. He was so used to barking orders at his siblings he assumed this would work on the twins but it didn't. It just made them fight for his attention by behaving badly. He walked upstairs to his study, thinking.

He shouldn't have spoken to the chef like that but he

was truly surprised to see the boys so happy at the kitchen bench and he wasn't often surprised.

And Christa wasn't fazed by him at all. She stood there and stared at him in such a way that he felt both bothered, offended and extremely intrigued.

Marc wasn't one of those people who called themselves foodies. To him, food was simply a necessity to survive. He would eat the same thing every day if he could as long as he didn't have to prepare it.

He had a chef back in San Francisco but he made a lot of sushi and ramen for the boys and he preferred protein shakes and the occasional salad.

This chef was making pasta with his sons? It was as though he'd walked into an alternate universe where carbs were back and his children were well behaved.

Adam walked into the study and put the laptop in front of him. 'Those figures have been fixed,' he said. 'And I've backdated your address on the financial compliance forms to Pudding Hall from June, when you decided to buy Cirrus. That way you will have been in the UK for the right amount of time to own a media service.'

Marc nodded and checked the figures again.

'Then you will be the biggest media owner under fifty,' Adam crowed. 'I'm already lining up the interviews in my head. *Fast Company*, *Wall Street Journal*, NBC, CNN, BBC Stock Report – it's going to be huge.'

Adam worked harder than Marc some days, and when he told him he had to come to the UK to live for enough time to be eligible to buy the streaming service Adam hadn't paused for a moment. He came to Pudding Hall because he loved to work and Paul came with Adam, which was fine with Marc. As long as Adam could get the deal through, he didn't care where he spent the holidays.

'You can't tell anyone yet though,' he reminded Adam, even though he knew he didn't have to. He thought for a moment. 'Did you get Christa to sign the NDA?' he asked.

'Yep, all done,' Adam said.

'And Peggy?' he asked. 'She seems nosy.'

The last thing he needed was her spreading information about what he was working on.

'Peggy? She's signed,' said Adam. 'Thought I doubt she would be the one to call *The New York Times* about the big media deal that will put Lachlan Murdoch on notice.'

Marc wondered about Peggy but she had been a part of Pudding Hall for thirty years, and had overseen it from the last owners to Marc buying the home, managing the contractors and decorators while he was in the States.

But when he arrived, it felt empty. There was no doubt it was beautiful. It had been on the cover of *Architectural Digest* and was the most pinned country house on Pinterest yet it felt like a movie set. Christmas should be joyful and fun and instead the house felt like an Airbnb. He thought about getting Christmas decorations or getting someone to decorate it for the boys, but it felt hollow.

He would apologise to Christa at dinner, he thought.

'Tell me about Christa.'

'Christa Playfoot. She and her ex-husband had a restaurant in Mayfair. Very well reviewed. Paul and I ate there a number of times. It's everything a brasserie should be.'

'Why is she cooking for me then?'

'Because she's getting a divorce, the restaurant is closed

and you're overpaying her to make protein shakes and hotdogs for the boys.'

Marc rubbed his temples and sat back in his chair. 'The boys were making pasta with her and I ruined it.'

'Pasta?' Adam seemed surprised. 'Is that a healthy option? Considering their mother loathes them having carbs.'

'I guess so,' Marc said. 'I'm not great at this parenting full-time thing. But I don't have the time to micromanage their macro intake at the moment.'

'You don't have to micromanage them, just love them,' Adam reminded him.

'Thanks, Dr Phil,' said Marc but he knew Adam was right. Since he and his wife had separated he had the boys full-time while she decided to take her share of the settlement and invest in all sorts of schemes from movie producing, collagen juice bars, to investing in new mobile phone technology from Latvia. Marc had no idea if anything she was spending her money on was a good investment but what he did know was she didn't want to parent at the moment and he was left holding the babies.

Back in San Francisco they had nannies but the boys claimed they were too old for nannies now and made their feelings known by terrorising them until no nanny agency would take the job, no matter the price.

Adam stood up and stretched his back.

'Dinner is at seven thirty for us. She is feeding the boys at six,' said Adam. 'If you wanted to say hello to her and pretend the other version of you was a twin, then I would suggest a change of top and parting your hair on the other side to make it believable.'

Marc rolled his eyes at Adam. 'Thanks for the tip but this isn't an adult version of *The Parent Trap*.'

Adam shrugged. 'I help where I can.'

Marc sighed and thought about how he came across to Christa. 'I don't think I made a great first impression.'

Adam peered at him. 'Why does it matter what she thinks of you? You don't care what anyone else does.'

Marc couldn't answer for a moment. 'That doesn't say much about me if I'm a rude prick to everyone though. I mean, I just don't really want to spend time with many people.'

Adam scoffed. 'You just don't get impressed by anyone anymore because most people want something from you.'

Marc couldn't argue with that. It was true and he wondered if that was why Christa challenged him so much. She was doing her job her way, which he could respect and understand. Perhaps they were more alike than she realised.

'I'll talk to her,' he said to Adam. 'And show her I am not a complete arsehole.'

'I still think the twin ruse is the way to go but you do you,' quipped Adam as he left Marc to his work.

Just after six in the evening Marc walked downstairs where a delicious smell guided him to the kitchen. He could hear the boys laughing and talking loudly as he stood by the door, unseen by them.

'Can we have ketchup?' asked one of them.

'Of course – what is a burger without ketchup?' he heard Christa reply.

He took a deep breath and stepped into the kitchen.

'Burgers? Who is having burgers? Why wasn't I invited?'

Christa and the boys turned to him, surprise plastered on their faces.

'You're welcome to have one but the boys made you pasta for dinner.' She seemed slightly on guard, which made sense since he had acted like a total idiot every time they had met before.

He looked at the plates of food on the bench. The burgers and fries looked incredible and his mouth watered at the sight of them.

Peggy came into the kitchen.

'I have set the dining room for the adults,' she said, which sounded like an order.

'Oh, it's okay, we'll eat in here, I know Adam said seven thirty but it might be nice to eat together.' Marc looked at Christa. 'Or are you making something that requires extra time? Otherwise we can wait – I don't want to be difficult.'

He thought he saw a little smile cross her lips. 'Of course that's fine. I have prepared homemade fettucine with a simple but delicious carbonara sauce.'

'Sounds perfect,' he said.

Peggy was wringing her hands. 'I set the table in the dining room. With the good china.'

'I know you did, Peggy, but I want to eat in here with my boys,' he said and paused, waiting for her to understand his tone as he texted Adam and Paul to come down earlier.

Peggy, to her credit, nodded.

Adam and Paul came into the kitchen soon after.

'Are we eating in the dining room?' Paul asked.

Peggy almost snarled, 'No, Mr Ferrier wants to in eat in

the kitchen.' She spoke as though he'd said he wanted to eat in a pigsty. 'I will move the place settings in here though the fine china will look out of place.'

'Don't worry about it. We can put it away,' said Marc. 'You head home – it's dark. Please.'

Peggy went to the hook by the back door and took down her coat.

'I can stay if you need me,' she suggested.

'It's fine, head home.' Marc hoped his words were firm but not mean.

She nodded at his instruction. 'Goodnight, Mr Ferrier, Mr Abraham, Mr Salter, Master Seth and Master Ethan. And to you, Cook.'

She closed the kitchen door and Marc let out a sigh of relief.

'She is truly something else,' he said as he went to the wine fridge and opened it, searching for the one he wanted and then grabbing it. 'Like a scary housekeeper in a horror film.'

He uncorked a bottle of wine and started to open and close cupboards randomly.

'Speaking of horror films, stop with the cupboards,' said Adam. 'What are you looking for?

'Wine glasses,' he said.

'Butler's pantry, right-hand side, long cupboards,' said Christa as she tossed a salad.

'How do you know this after an afternoon here and I'm still searching after owning this place for several years?'

Christa smiled at him. 'It's my job,' she said. He felt a tug of interest in her and it was foreign but also pleasant. He was glad he had decided to eat with the boys.

'Boys, set the table for us. We're eating in here tonight.'

He saw Adam and Paul glance at each other. 'Don't share looks. It's lovely in here and smells incredible,' he said.

Seth and Ethan rushed to get cutlery and plates, while Paul found placemats and napkins.

Adam was putting out wine glasses and Christa was whisking egg yolks.

It was a hive of industry and Marc felt something he hadn't felt before.

Contentment.

'It's funny how a kitchen can create an instant atmosphere,' he said to Christa as he opened the wine.

'The kitchen is the heart of everything, in every culture, at any time. Food brings people together,' she said to him as she pan-fried some bacon pieces in a pan, the spitting of the fat not fazing her for a moment.

'Do you mind us eating in here?' he asked, aware that he might be encroaching on her space.

'Not at all – it's nice to have some company,' she said and he noticed the blue of her eyes.

He opened the wine and poured a glass for himself, Adam and Paul.

'Would you like to join us for one?' he said, wondering if that was okay. In San Francisco he never ate or drank with the staff but this felt more intimate and right, since they were in her space.

Christa looked at him. 'I don't drink when I'm working but thank you.'

She plated up the pasta onto three dishes and then carried them to the table.

'Where is your dinner?' he asked.

'Oh, I'll get something later.'

'There is more in the pan,' he said to her. 'I won't take no as an answer. Please.'

Christa sighed. 'Okay, I shouldn't do this really, but it's been a day, you know?'

Marc laughed. 'I don't think you saw the best of me any of the times we crossed paths today. I'm sorry about that.'

She shrugged. 'I try not to make snap judgements of people.'

'Really? I do but it's something I'm working on,' he admitted, wondering if the wine was actually truth serum.

He held out his hand. 'Can we start again? Marc Ferrier.'

She took his hand in hers. 'Christa Playfoot.'

'Pleased to meet you. Now have some wine and let's eat this incredible-looking meal.'

Marc sat at the head of the table as Christa placed down a leafy green salad and bread, while the boys carried their burgers to the table and sat down opposite Adam and Paul.

Christa sat at the end of the table, with her plate of pasta in front of her, looking awkward.

'Dad, we made the pasta. Try it, try it,' Seth said excitedly.

Marc took a mouthful. The yolky sauce tasted like a dream and the salt of the bacon cut through the richness, creating a symphony of flavour in his mouth. The pasta was the perfect texture and al dente. He looked up at the twins.

'This is unbelievably good.'

The boys smiled with pride and he felt a stab of guilt for yelling at them earlier.

He looked at Christa at the other end of the table. 'So it seems you are a chef and not a cook.'

Christa gave him a wry smile.

'My degree and work pedigree would agree with you but thanks for confirming.'

'Was I being condescending then?' he asked. 'Oh God I was. I was trying to be funny.'

Christa said nothing as she ate.

Marc laughed but it sounded false to his own ears. *Try harder*, he thought and he turned to Adam and Paul. 'I apologised to Christa for being an absolute idiot today. I'm surprised she's stayed here.' He looked at Christa. 'But after seeing what you have taught the boys, you can stay forever.' He laughed and everyone joined in, not because he was funny – he was self-aware enough to know that – but because he had apologised. That was something he was trying to improve in his life. When you were rich, not many people expected apologies. But when you were a billionaire, you were told never to say sorry for anything because you could buy forgiveness. Christa looked at him for longer than he felt comfortable with and he worried she could see through him. She returned her focus to the food on her plate and he wondered what she was thinking. Was she impressed by him? Did she dislike him? Did she think he was rude? Arrogant? Probably all of the above, he thought, wishing he could start everything again.

He watched the boys eat their burgers, which looked incredible, while Paul chatted with Christa about her restaurant and a mutual friend they had.

'Good idea on the chef,' he whispered to Adam.

'She's pretty great,' answered Adam. 'The boys love her, which is no easy feat. Although this pasta is so good I will be up a pants size if she keep this up.'

'Don't bring your California food anxiety here; it's a holiday and this food is incredible.'

Marc watched the boys listening to Christa talk and noted the way she included them in the chatter.

She was a natural with kids, he thought as she switched easily from talking to them and then Paul and back again. She offered bread and salad and cut the boys' burgers in half to make it easier for them to eat but she didn't look at him unless he asked her a question or spoke directly to her.

The discomfort of her dismissing him made him realise something. This is how he made her feel, he thought, and he hated himself. He needed to think before speaking, he reminded himself but he wanted her to know he recognised her work with the dinner and with the boys.

He raised his glass and held it up to the room.

'To Christa, our chef and pasta queen! And wrangler of recalcitrant people of all sizes. May you never leave Pudding Hall!'

Christa picked up and glass and raised it to him.

'Thank you,' she said and he caught her eye and he nodded at her and she nodded back. An agreement of sorts had been made, and he had never wanted to impress anyone more than this woman who had turned Pudding Hall upside down in an afternoon.

Homemade Fettucine

Ingredients

2 cups plain (all-purpose) flour

3 large eggs

½ teaspoon sea salt
½ tablespoon extra-virgin olive oil

Method

1. Pour the flour on a clean and clear work surface and make a volcano shape. Break eggs, olive oil, and salt into the centre. Use a fork to break up the eggs while keeping the flour walls together, Be gentle. Then use your hands to coax the flour into a dough until it is a messy ball

2. Knead the dough. To start with, the dough will feel dry, but continue until it finally comes together around the 8-10 minute mark. Then it should be malleable and smooth. If the dough feels too dry at any point, wet your fingers and sprinkle it with a little water to bind. If it's sticky, dust more flour onto the bench and then shape the dough into a ball. Wrap in plastic cling film and leave resting at room temperature for 30 minutes.

3. Dust two large baking sheets with flour while the dough is resting.

4. Once ready, cut the dough into four pieces and carefully flatten each into an oval disc. Run the first disc of dough through the pasta machine roller attachment three times on level 1 (the widest setting).

5. Place the dough piece flat and fold the two short ends in to meet in the centre, then fold the dough in half to form a rectangle.

6. Run the dough through the pasta roller in the following order:

7. Three times on level 2

8. Three times on level 3
9. One time each on levels 4, 5, and 6.
10. Lay the pasta sheet onto the floured baking sheet and sprinkle with flour before folding it in half. Sprinkle more flour on top of the second half. Every side should be floured so that your final pasta ribbons won't stick together.
11. Run the pasta sheets through the pasta machine again, using the pasta cutting attachment.
12. Repeat steps 4-8 with the remaining dough
13. Cook the cut pasta in a pot of salted boiling water for 1 to 2 minutes.
14. Enjoy your fresh pasta with your favourite sauce or oil.

6

When the dishes were cleared from the table, which Adam and Paul had helped with, and the two dishwashers were on, Christa went up to her room and showered.

Her room was beautiful, she thought as she closed the curtains on the dark windy night.

She opened a cupboard and saw a small fridge and kettle with a selection of tea and a French press for coffee. A tin of shortbread was unopened and in the fridge was milk and some fruit.

Did Peggy do this? At Marc's insistence? It seemed like a very personal touch in an impersonal house.

She took out the kettle and filled it in the bathroom, plugged it in and turned it on. A night-time cup of tea was exactly what she needed. Moving the heavy curtains back, she looked outside but it was so dark she was shocked. She had forgotten what the dark was after living in such a light-polluted city like London.

The weather report was still claiming snow was on its way, and according to news reports York would be looking at a very cold Christmas.

Marc had taken the boys upstairs to get ready for bed, since they had stayed up later than usual. There had been a lot of laughter and chatting over dinner, and Adam and Paul had great stories about when they met in New York and Paul's work as an interior stylist for celebrities in Los Angeles.

'Pick up any *Architectural Digest* and I can tell you the budget, who is selling and if it's a divorce about to be announced and why my work is the best on the West Coast,' Paul stated.

'He's right, it is the best,' said Adam. 'You know he said no to the family starting with K because they buy their artwork by the metre.'

Christa made a face. 'Horrendous.'

'I know, right?' said Paul. 'I mean one of them looked at a Rothko and asked if he could make it bigger? The man's been dead for more than fifty years.'

Christa laughed. 'I get it. My place in London was decorated by my ex and it's very impersonal. Not me at all.'

'Photos?' asked Paul and she looked up the listing on her phone and handed it to him. He swiped through the photos. 'It's very masculine, sort of Four Seasons, Hyatt inspired?'

'Yes, he wanted it to feel like a hotel.' She sighed.

'I went to a conference at a place like this once,' Paul said.

Christa started to laugh again. 'God, it's not me,' she said. Marc had returned and was holding the phone now, swiping through the images.

He looked up at her. 'What is you? What is your style?'

She paused and thought for a moment. 'Warmth. Colour. Fun. Something pink and flowers and gardens and teapots and things that I love around me. Probably too girly for most men but I am unashamedly in love with the colour pink and anything fun.'

Marc handed her back her phone. 'You shouldn't ever apologise for what you like,' he said and she appreciated him saying that.

There was one tense moment when Paul, after a few glasses of wine, asked why there weren't any Christmas decorations.

A cloud seemed to cover the dinner for a moment until the boys cheered and said they wanted a tall tree and stockings over the mantel and could they make a gingerbread house? 'Please, Christa?' they begged.

Marc hadn't said anything but the energy in the room changed and he ordered the children upstairs to shower and bed.

Christa didn't ask what it was about but the spell was broken and she was back to being chef and a staff member.

Not that it troubled her now as she stepped from the shower. Her room was snug with the gas fire on and the lamps dimmed. Christa had never had an open fire in her bedroom before and now she wondered how she would ever not have one again. There was a small mantel above the flames and she wished she had some Christmas trinkets to place on top. Even a little garland of holly would suffice. Perhaps she might buy a few things and place them in her bedroom. Marc Ferrier couldn't say anything about that if it was in her room, could he?

Christa dried herself and pulled on her favourite Christmas flannel pyjamas with cute little puddings on them and the complimentary robe from the bathroom.

There was a soft knock at her door and she opened it, surprised to see Marc Ferrier outside her door.

'Oh, hi, did you want something to eat?' she asked, wishing she wasn't wearing the namesake of the house on her body.

She saw Marc's eyes take in her nightwear and he gave her a small smile. 'You have puddings on your pants.'

'Um, yes, yes I do,' she said, wishing she could fall into a hole and never climb out.

'They're fun,' he said and then seemed to catch himself.

'Thank you,' she said wishing she was in a sensible pantsuit and not PJs. 'How can I help you?' she prompted him.

'Oh I just wanted to say thanks again for today and tonight. And to make sure we're okay.'

She nodded. 'Of course. I have no issues at all.'

Marc nodded and stepped away as though to head back down the hallway and she couldn't stop herself.

'Do you think we could buy some decorations? I know you're not keen but the boys would like it. Might add some spirit to the house, you know?'

Marc stared at her, his face stony again.

'I will do what needs to be done when I'm ready, thank you.'

Christa nodded. 'Of course, your house, your décor, your timeline.'

He went to speak and then closed his mouth again.

Christa couldn't help herself. 'My dad hated Christmas but he learned to love it because I loved it and he made sure I had nice memories, even if he struggled with the season.

He didn't let his own rubbish times affect mine. I was always grateful he put my emotional needs above his own.'

Marc nearly snarled at her, his lip curling. 'Thank you for your therapy lesson, Christa, but you're here to cook.'

Christa rolled her eyes. 'You can't help yourself can you?'

'What?' he said, his eyes narrowed.

'When people suggest things, or when things aren't in your control, you act like this. You apologised to me and now you do this again.'

'It is not your business whether I have a Christmas tree or not.'

She shrugged at him. 'I know it's not, but take it from me, your kids will remember not having a tree more than having a tree.'

Marc stalked away and Christa felt a flush through her body. She never spoke to anyone like that but Marc just really made her want to speak her truth. After so many years of not being herself, this new improved version was both thrilling and terrifying.

Men like Marc Ferrier never liked an idea that didn't come from themselves. He was rude, imperious and moody. Clearly his previous brightness was a rare emotional eclipse. Marc seemed to not like Christmas for whatever reason. Perhaps it had been a hard time for him at some point but it didn't mean he should deprive the boys of the enjoyment of this time of the year.

At least she could have some fun besides cooking and she could see if there were people in York to help.

She couldn't help thinking about all the food in the

fridges downstairs that would go to waste. There was no way they could eat it all before it went out of date and was ruined.

Christa took off the robe and climbed into bed, and googled Marc Ferrier on her phone.

Notoriously private.

Very few photos of him. None of his ex-wife and children.

He was worth nearly one billion dollars.

Christa put down her phone. It was so much money it was stupid, she thought. No one needed that amount of money and she wondered what he did to help people. That was too much money to spend in a lifetime, just as there was too much food downstairs to eat.

She looked up whether he did any charity work but there was nothing listed. For some reason it made her angry that he wasn't doing anything to help the world – to fight hunger and poverty.

She turned out the light and lay in bed thinking about all the things she could cook with the food that could go to the homeless or the vulnerable. He wouldn't even know that it was gone and besides, she reasoned, she wasn't stealing the food, she was redistributing it, like Robin Hood but of the kitchen.

The thought thrilled her as she pulled the covers up under her chin. Having so much to give away and help so many people? It was a dream come true. She just had to hide it from Marc and the rest of the house. Anyway, who would notice a few things missing from such an overstocked kitchen?

★

Only the twins came to breakfast and they requested pancakes and bacon and maple syrup, which Christa whipped up in no time. She had been up early checking the contents of the fridge, working out what to cook and when before the food went off.

She could make a hearty stew with the beef and Thai chicken patties. And she had a lovely recipe for a goat curry, which she could serve with some naan bread.

She had so many ideas but she also had to see where the need was in York.

There was always need in every city. Always children in shelters, like she had been, eating nervously, looking around and hoping there wasn't a fight over the gravy or apple pie. Men missing their children, mothers trying to find enough to buy their children something for under the broken tree, if there was a tree.

She hadn't seen Marc that morning but she had given Peggy a tray with coffee, muesli, fruit and yogurt as requested.

Peggy was now supervising the cleaners who had arrived, looking terrified of her and waiting by the front door.

Christa wasn't sure where dust would dare to settle under Peggy's watchful eye but she was grateful Peggy was occupied so she could do some planning for cooking for the house and for organising where she could distribute the excess food.

With the house busy she could drive to York, pick up some containers for food and then drop into a refuge or homeless centre to see if they needed food or whether there was anywhere else she could deliver meals. A sense of purpose for the morning made her feel excited as she looked inside the fridge. So many ideas and since Marc was a wasteful Grinch she felt no guilt about sharing his abundance with people less fortunate than herself.

She checked the time and mentally worked out how long she could be out and explore York and then come back in time to make lunch. It was doable, provided she was efficient.

Peggy came into the kitchen just as she was writing a list.

'It's going to snow,' she announced to Christa.

She looked up. 'Today?'

'Not today but soon,' she said ominously like a human version of a speaking weather predictor machine.

'They say that every year and it never does.' She laughed but Peggy stared her down.

'I am not they,' she stated. 'I am never wrong and I know York. Lived here all my life. If I say it's going to snow then it will snow.'

Christa realised she had offended the woman and changed the topic from weather to food, which might be more soothing to the housekeeper.

'I have to head into town and pick up a few things,' she said. 'I'm going to freeze some stock and make some soups.'

Peggy lifted her chin, clearly insulted by Christa's inference that she hadn't bought the right groceries. Obviously this was a touchy topic just like the weather, she thought.

'If you give me the list I can arrange the items to be delivered to the house. It's Saturday so you will have to wait till tomorrow for the delivery.'

Christa smiled. 'No thank you. I like to shop for things myself sometimes so that I get to see local produce and so on.'

Peggy grimaced. 'Then you'll want to head to Shambles Market, over on Parliament Street.'

'A market? I love a market,' exclaimed Christa. 'Should I see if the boys want to come?'

Peggy was taking some tea towels from under the sink.

'Mr Ferrier did say you weren't here to childmind, remember?'

She left Christa before she could say anything in reply. She knew she wasn't here to childmind but everyone loved a market and it might be nice to check if the boys wanted to see some of York, but again she reminded herself, this wasn't her circus and they weren't her monkeys.

The market was as delightful as she had hoped, set next to a cobblestone street with medieval buildings. Christa felt like she had gone back in time. People milled about – both locals and tourists – and there was a lovely Christmas feel that made up for the lack of it at Pudding Hall.

'Would you like to try some fudge, miss?' asked an older man as she passed a stall. 'It's tusky triangle. Very good this time of year.'

Christa stopped. She had already tried an orange truffle covered in white chocolate and a thick slice of York Cheddar and had drunk a coffee and eaten a blueberry Danish but she was intrigued by the name.

'A tusky triangle – what a fun name. What is it?'

The man handed her piece. 'You taste and tell me what you think it is. No one ever gets it right but they always head home with some in their shopping bags.'

Christa took the little napkin with the pinky marbled fudge sitting atop, waiting to be discovered.

She put her shopping down and looked at the fudge and then picked it up took a bite, then she took another bite and then finished the sweet off and wiped her mouth with the napkin.

'Any guesses?' asked the man who was old enough to be her father. He had twinkling eyes and a weather-beaten face. She liked his energy immediately.

'It tastes like champagne but it's not champagne. It's tart but it's not sour. The sweetness comes from the fudge not from the flavouring.'

He nodded enthusiastically. 'You're closer than most.'

Christa paused and closed her eyes as she tasted the last remnants in her mouth.

'Rhubarb!' she exclaimed.

The man cried out, 'She guessed it, Robert, she guessed the tusky triangle.'

A man from another stall selling gin laughed. 'You might as well retire now, Petey – she knows your secret.'

'Aye she does,' said the man called Petey. He smiled warmly at Christa. 'And for that, you get a box of assorted fudges, including the mystery one that you guessed.' He handed Christa a ribbon-wrapped box.

'That's so kind but I can pay,' she said.

'No, it's a pleasure to give to someone who knows their

rhubarb from their crab apple. And it's good to be generous at this time of the year, don't you think?'

Christa placed the box into her shopping bag. 'I do, thank you. I will come back and buy some more next week. I'm sure these won't last long with my sweet tooth.'

She was about to keep walking when she thought of a question for Petey.

'Are there many homeless or people in need around here? I would like to do some volunteering, mainly around food as I am a chef, but I'm not from here and I wasn't sure if maybe you knew any places or organisations?'

Petey leaned in over the display of fudge. 'I knew you were special,' he said and she saw his old blue eyes crinkle as he beamed at her. 'I help down at St William's food bus. It's usually from ten till midnight. I used to help a few times a month but since the weather has been cold and people are away for Christmas it's been hard to get people to help or even provide food.'

'Oh yes, I want to help; I need to help. I'm Christa Playfoot. I'm new in town,' she said to him. 'Who can I call?'

Petey was writing down a name and number on the back of a brown paper bag.

'Call Zane, he's the social worker who runs the bus and outreach programme. He's a good fellow and he will guide you. Tell him Petey told you to call.'

Christa carefully folded the paper and tucked it into her purse.

'You are a dream, Petey, thank you.'

'And you, Christa, are a gift to me and to the people of York. Welcome.'

Petey's Tusky Triangle Fudge

Ingredients

  1kg/2¼lbs of fresh rhubarb, chopped
  2 cups white sugar
  2 teaspoons grated orange zest
  1/3 cup orange juice
  ½ cup water
  340ml/11½fl oz evaporated milk (unsweetened condensed milk)
  600g/21oz caster sugar
  30g/1oz butter
  275g/9¾oz of the rhubarb mixture
  2 tablespoons lemon juice

Method

1. In a saucepan, combine the rhubarb, sugar, orange zest, orange juice and water. Bring to a boil, then cook over medium-low heat for 45 minutes, stirring occasionally, or until thick. It will thicken more as it cools.
2. Butter a 23x23 cm (9x9 in) dish.
3. Combine evaporated milk, sugar and butter in a large saucepan over medium heat; boil. Stir in rhubarb mixture and lemon juice. Heat, stirring constantly, to between 235 and 240°C (455 and 464°F), or until a small amount of the mixture dropped into cold water forms a soft ball

that flattens when removed from the water and placed on a flat surface.

4. Remove from heat and quickly spread in prepared dish. Allow to cool before cutting and serving.

7

'Dad, Dad, Dad, Dad, Dad,' said the boys in turn until Marc looked up from his laptop.

'You only have to say my name once,' he reminded them.

'Not true, that took five "Dads" for you to look up,' Seth answered.

'The record is twelve,' said Ethan.

'Twelve? That's not true,' Marc replied, insulted at the insinuation from the boys.

Marc tried to remember when that might have been but he knew he didn't always show up for his kids and he knew what that felt like. He closed his laptop and put it beside him.

'It is so true – I have video evidence,' Ethan said. 'I can get it down from the cloud and play it on the TV if you want?'

'No thanks,' said Marc feeling exposed. 'You have my attention, so what would you like to say.'

Seth lay on the floor of the large sitting room, staring into the fire that Peggy had laid and lit for them.

'We want to go and get a Christmas tree. A real one, not a plastic silver one, a real one, like in *Elf*.'

Marc didn't know what the one in *Elf* was like but he assumed it was the gold standard for trees.

Why hadn't he bought a tree yet? Why was he being such a Scrooge? When Christa had asked him if he wouldn't mind getting some decorations he had been so rude to her. God he needed to stop being such a moody bastard. He had come to Pudding Hal to give the boys a proper English Christmas and he was fighting it every step of the way. Christa was right in her assessment that he didn't like being told what to do but it was more than that: he didn't want a tree because of his memories of Christmas as a child. He didn't want to look at a plastic tree with a star perched drunkenly on top while his drunk parents created a war below.

What would happen if he gave the boys the Christmas he never had?

Their Christmases in California had been low-key and usually run by his wife who knew his aversion to the holiday. The boys received presents but sometimes they went to St Barth's or Maui and spent the day on the beach.

But what if he gave them the memory of the tree and the cooking, and the present buying? What would happen? His parents wouldn't come back and ruin it. He wouldn't have to carry the burden of caring for his siblings and trying to get enough food for them for the day, telling them Christmas was bullshit because no one really lived like you saw in the movies or the TV shows.

He was holding the power to heal himself in his hands and he was ruining everything for the boys.

He remembered the yelling and the police coming and his dad being dragged away to spend Christmas night in the cells. The turkey on the kitchen floor, next to the foil container, the grease mark against the wall from where his dad had thrown it mid screaming match with his mom. He thought Thanksgiving had been bad with his mom locking his dad outside for spending the rent at Caesar's Palace but Christmas really outdid itself for family toxicity. After that his mom told him that Christmas was a piece of shit holiday and there was nothing to be thankful for at Thanksgiving and they wouldn't have Christmas again as long as she lived. The memory of the disappointment took his breath away. Why was he putting his own pain onto his children?

'We can get a tree,' he said, feeling his eyes sting, and he blinked fiercely to stop the emotion. Why was Christmas so heavy with love and pain for so many? He knew he wasn't the only one. He saw it when Christa spoke of her father and her Christmases.

'Can we go into the city and get one?' Seth was sitting up now. 'Now?'

'If you want.' He had planned to do more work this afternoon but he could at least get a tree. That wouldn't hurt would it?

'Okay, get dressed. We'll head into York and get a tree.'

The boys yelled and cheered and ran upstairs.

He sighed and looked at his laptop, which he was tempted to reopen, but if he did then he would lose the momentum to go.

Be a better father, he heard himself say to his own father when he was younger. Maybe he should take his own advice for once.

The tree was only the start of the Christmas project at Pudding Hall. They needed a tree holder and then decorations – which the boys bought far too many of – but he liked their selection. Toy soldiers and little angels and sprigs of holly tied to red ribbons and more.

And the lights. So many lights. Marc looked at the ropes of lights on display and wondered which ones would be right and if there was a method of putting them onto the tree.

'Can we get an ornament each?' asked Seth. 'And then we can use it next year and the year after and forever and it will be our own ornament – just ours.'

Marc was deciding between cool white twinkle lights or multicoloured globes and wishing he knew which option was the best. He put both into the basket and figured Paul would be able to help him choose.

'Yes, get what you like,' he said.

'You have to choose one for you and Adam and Paul and Christa too,' said Ethan. 'So we all have one.'

Marc wanted to roll his eyes but looked at the huge array of ornaments.

He chose a navy and silver painted glass bauble for Adam and a red and gold one for Paul.

What would he get for Christa?

There were cooking ones, which were cute, but she was more than that and he wanted her to see that he knew. Choosing the right ornament mattered to him, and he looked through the options.

There were silly ones with Santa Claus and champagne bottles and traditional partridges and even glass squirrels.

Then he saw one that made him smile. A family of deer. A stag, a doe, and a little fawn standing in front of a pine tree. It was mercury glass and hand-painted in shades of gold and green. He didn't know why he liked it but he did and he thought it would make her smile. Holding it, he felt the cool glass, heavy in his hand. It reminded him of Christa, maybe because the doe had blue eyes and long lashes, like Christa's.

'Is that for you?' asked Seth, peering at the ornament.

'No, it's for Christa.'

'Does she like deers?'

'I don't know,' he replied. 'I hope so.'

'Don't forget to get one for you,' reminded Ethan.

He looked again and saw a Christmas pudding with a sprig of holly on top. It reminded him of her pyjamas and he smiled as he picked it up. Perfect, he thought.

After he had paid and corralled the boys he guided them from the store, telling them they didn't need a life-sized blow-up Santa for the living room.

Finally the tree was tied to the roof of his four wheel drive and the decorations in the boot of the car when he heard the boys yell.

'Christa, Christa.'

He saw Christa across the road in a pink coat and white woollen hat with a pom-pom on top. She looked like cupcake and he smiled at her, feeling shy but not sure why.

Christa was carrying many shopping bags filled with all sort of goodies poking out of them.

'Hello there,' she said and she looked at the tree on top of the car. 'A tree – how wonderful! You can have a fun time decorating that. We can make sugar cookies to hang on the branches if you have some ribbon.'

The boys jumped with excitement. 'Can we get some ribbon?' they asked.

He laughed. 'Sure thing. Do you want to put your things in the car? I can drive you back.'

Christa shook her head. 'I drove here but thank you.'

She really did have the prettiest smile and he liked that she ignored that he had been rude about the decorations the night before. His ex-wife would have gloated at him changing his mind.

'Why don't you put them in the car, come and help us choose some ribbon and then you can head back without breaking your shoulder with all of your shopping?'

'I have to cook lunch,' she said.

'We can eat here in town. Why not? Make a day of it?'

He wasn't sure why he wanted her to stay but the boys were now pulling the bags from her shoulders and handing them to him so he could put them in the car.

'Gosh, you Ferrier males are very persuasive.' She laughed. 'What about Adam and Paul?'

'They have gone sightseeing, much to Adam's horror,' said Marc as he locked the car. They started to walk down the street, while the boys ran ahead.

He cleared his throat. 'I was thinking about what you said about your own dad and Christmas. You were right, I was putting my own stuff onto my kids. Thanks for showing me that I was being a bit of an idiot. People don't often do that to me, well except Adam but that's usually about work stuff, not life and kids' stuff.'

Christa said nothing so he went on.

'Christmas wasn't a happy time for me as a kid and I guess I thought it didn't matter to my kids, even though I want them to have a great English Christmas. I thought if I had Christmas in another country like the UK, which is beautiful, I would be able to get over my own Christmas issues.'

People passed them on the footpath, carrying shopping bags and flowers and pushing prams and holding hands. The spirit was infectious even to a Scrooge like him. 'This...' He gestured around them. 'This is not like anything I know. I thought this was all just stuff you saw in the cheesy Christmas movies; I didn't know it was a real thing. I send my assistants out to buy presents. I don't wrap them. I don't even choose them. I mean what does that say about me?'

He looked at her and she threw her gloved hands up at him.

'I am only here to cook, not to give you therapy,' she said and he saw a glint in her eye and a smile at the corner of her lips.

Then she laughed and it was a real throaty, hilarious laugh that made him join in with her.

'I was also worried about it being tacky, like silver trees and pink flamingos.'

Christa was still laughing. 'While my pudding PJ bottoms might say the opposite, I do have excellent taste in Christmas decorations but I understand this time of year can be hard for people. Not everyone loves Christmas!'

'Do *you* like it?' he asked as the twins stopped outside a games shop, pointing out new video games to each other.

'We have that one, that one, and that one. And those there. And those at the back. Dad we have all of these,' yelled one of the boys.

'Christmas?' she asked. 'I love it, but it's also around my birthday so I'm biased.'

'And you're working for us over your own birthday and Christmas? That's crazy.'

He glanced at Christa who was looking at the boys but she had a tightness around her mouth.

'Money makes choices for you, and limits them sometimes,' she said and he heard the edge to her voice.

'Dad, can we get the video games in the window that we don't have?' Seth was pulling at his jacket sleeve.

Usually he would have bought them for the boys because he thought it would keep them occupied for a while and he could work but he saw Christa frown and turn away from them, walking to another shop window and leaving him with the boys.

'No, you don't need any more games – you have enough already,' he said firmly.

The boys stared at him as though he was making a joke and then they realised he was serious.

'Dad,' one of them started to complain.

But he put his hand up.

'Enough. You have enough games. And there are other things to do back at the house, okay?'

He was surprised when the boys were silent.

And then Ethan nodded. 'Okay, but we want to make a gingerbread house. Can we do that? Can you help us? We can do it together.' The look on their faces pained him and he felt sick at what sort of a father he had been lately.

'I can film it for my documentary I'm making,' said Ethan and he nodded encouragingly at his son.

'That would be cool,' he said to him and saw the happiness in his face.

'Christa,' he called to her and she turned, her face expressionless. 'The boys want to make a gingerbread house for Christmas. If you can help us, we would love to do it as a project. Ethan wants to film the process for his doco.'

She smiled at the three of them, her face relaxed, cheeks pink with the cold.

'Wow, what a cool idea. I'd love to help but why don't we make it more than a house? Why don't we make a gingerbread house of Pudding Hall?'

The boys started to yell ideas at each other. 'We can do all the windows and the stairs. What do we make stairs out of? Can we do the garden?'

They started to walk again, the boys running ahead to talk excitedly about the gingerbread house and the Christmas tree.

'It doesn't take much to make them happy. I need to remember that,' he said. 'Thanks for reminding me.'

'I hope I'm not some morality tale for you because I'm low on cash and have to work through my birthday and Christmas.' She laughed.

Marc felt embarrassed. He was always terrible at explaining anything other than a business deal.

They came to a café in an old Tudor-style building. The window was filled with delicious-looking pies and sandwiches and cakes and slices. Someone walked outside and a gust of warm air and the scent of coffee escaped.

'This looks good?' he said but it was more of a question to Christa who was peering in the window.

'It looks fantastic,' she said. 'I'm hungry.'

Soon they were seated and the boys were happily discussing Minecraft blocks, which Christa knew nothing about.

Marc was studying the menu when the waitress came to them.

'Hello, is this lovely family ready to order? Your boys are very well behaved,' she said to Christa, who seemed to be grasping for words. For a moment, Marc wondered if this was what it would be like as a family. His ex-wife didn't like going out with the boys because she said they weren't old enough to behave. They had always eaten separately at home in San Francisco, eating different food, prepared by a different chef. He had eaten out with the boys many times but not as a nuclear family, he realised.

He smiled at the waitress. 'Thank you, and yes, we're ready to order. Christa? What would you like, darling?' He tried not to laugh as she gasped.

And then he saw her blush from her neck to her hairline and he realised he liked teasing her. In fact, he liked it more than anything else he had done in a very long time.

8

On Monday morning, Christa called the number Petey had given her and asked for Zane. She had spent Sunday evening cooking two roast chickens with all the trimmings for the family and had eaten with them but quickly cleaned up after and headed upstairs.

'Sorry, Zane is out but he can return your call when he's back. What's your number?' said the person on the end of the line.

Christa gave her number and then put down the phone.

She felt slightly dithery, hoping Marc would come into the kitchen but also hoping he didn't because she needed to get on with her work.

She would make some stock for the soups using the quail, which would give her a beautiful broth.

Soon she had the birds in the roasting pan and in the oven. Then she started chopping the onions, carrots, celery and garlic. She used the fresh parsley from the market and the pig's foot she had bought at the butcher before she'd seen Marc and the boys. Then she dug into the shopping bag, hoping she hadn't lost the precious small ingredient.

'There you are,' she said and she opened the bag and held it to her nose and took a deep inhalation and then sighed.

'Wow. Seems like you have some good stuff there. Is it legal?' she heard Marc's voice say and she felt her stomach flip.

Damn, it was a crush. How embarrassing.

Pulling the bag away from her nose, she handed it to him. 'Take a sniff and tell me what you think it is.'

'Oh a sniff test – I'm good at this. I once smelled a baloney sandwich that had been in my sister's school backpack for a full semester.'

He held the bag to his nose and closed his eyes.

'I can smell...' he opened his eyes and looked at her '... spice. Wood. Something like incense but not cheap stuff like at Venice Beach but something like I smelled in the Atlas Mountains in Morocco.'

Christa wasn't sure if he was being pretentious or silly but he seemed serious.

'They're juniper berries,' she said.

Marc seemed thrilled with this news.

'Oh my God, I'm gifted. There were juniper bushes where I was. These super rare ones that I was asked to help fund a protection programme for.'

'Did you?' asked Christa, trying to get her head around what he was saying. 'Fund the bushes?'

'Of course. I love gin,' he said and then he laughed.

For a moment she thought about telling him her plans to cook for others with his food but how could she say it without sounding like a thief or as though she was judging him for having so much more than others. She would tell him, she thought, eventually, when she found the right time. She needed to think about it, she told herself. But deep inside, she knew she was avoiding it because he'd probably think she was some sad do-gooder who was trying to make him feel guilty about having so much. Who was she to think she could solve homelessness and world hunger, like a foodie Bob Geldof?

She opened the oven and turned the meat, making sure she was scraping up all the bits caught on the pan.

'That smells incredible,' he said. Peering into the pan. 'Is it for dinner?'

'No, it's stock for soup.' She shoved the pan back in and closed the door and her phone rang.

She picked it up and answered, 'Zane, how are you? Can you hold a minute?'

She put her hand over the receiver. 'Sorry, I have to take this.' She took the phone and walked outside, shocked at how cold the air was and wishing she had her coat but Marc was inside the kitchen now. He was looking inside the refrigerator, which was his right, but she wished he would go away at least until she had spoken to Zane.

'Hi, Zane, I'm Christa. Petey from the market gave me your details. He said you might be looking for volunteers?'

'Yes, we are actually. What sort of help are you hoping to give?' Zane asked.

'I'm a chef, so I can cook some of the food, like soups or stews and I can help in the van a few nights for the next few weeks. I'm not in York for long but I was helping homeless people in London and I want to support the people of York.'

'That sounds incredible, Christa. Do you want to come down tonight and see what we do? Say nine o'clock?'

'Yes! I would love to,' she said seeing Marc now eating the fudge from the refrigerator.

'I'll text you the address to this phone number and

remember to dress for warmth. Those night winds can be deadly.'

Christa knew this wasn't just a figure of speech. The cold air would actually give people hypothermia and she had heard of dead bodies being discovered in parks and on benches during very brutal winters.

She shoved her phone in her pocket and went back into the warm kitchen.

'Everything okay?' asked Marc.

'Fine, I will be heading out after dinner tonight, if that's okay with you. I don't think you need me once the boys are all sorted and in bed.'

Marc's eyes looked away from her and seemed to settle on something outside.

'That's fine. I hope you have a nice time.' His jaw was set now and Christa knew he wasn't happy with something. His mood had changed.

'It's professional not personal,' she said. Though she knew she didn't need to justify it, she wanted to.

'That's fine. You're an adult; you can do what you like.' His hands were in the pockets of his jeans now. 'I came down to ask you if you can please arrange a cake for Adam. It's his birthday tomorrow. He loves chocolate and drama, so if you can work with that brief, it would mean a lot to him.'

Christa laughed. 'Cakes, chocolate and drama are my specialty. Consider it done,' she said.

Marc walked to the door of the kitchen. 'I ate some of the fudge also – hope that's okay. Did you make it?'

Christa smiled at him. 'I bought it for everyone from the

market actually. I was going to share it after dinner tonight with coffee.'

Marc nodded. 'It was okay. I think I ate one that was sour. Tasted like my grandmother's rhubarb strudel, one of my most hated desserts as a kid.'

'That's exactly what the pink one is. It's very hard to pick, according to the man who sold me the fudge. You picked rhubarb and the juniper berries – you must have the nose for it after all.'

Marc laughed. 'Don't forget the baloney sandwich.'

'Never,' she answered as he walked away.

Christa had made a large pot of vegetable soup for the family and saved one for the St William's food bus. She had made several baguettes to have with the soup and once dinner was cleared up and put away and the boys were still decorating the tree and arguing about the placement of decorations, she had slipped out the kitchen door with the soup in a large pot she'd bought in town and put it in her car, along with some bread, making sure it was safe for the drive.

The house was quiet as she drove away, feeling uneasy at not being honest about telling Marc she was using his food to help others, but she tried to remind herself that he wanted to help. He liked helping. Tomorrow, she told herself, she would tell him tomorrow. Besides, tonight might be a dismal failure and they wouldn't need her or her food. She drove down the dark driveway, her car lights showing the way when she saw the stag again, majestic in the centre of the road. Behind him walked a doe, elegant and graceful. She stopped and waited for them to move. Eventually they did, watching her car as she passed.

She made a mental note to never eat venison again after witnessing such beautiful animals.

After finding her way to the headquarters of the charity that ran the food bus, she parked her car and carried the pot of soup and the bread to the door and rang the bell.

The street was well lit but she still felt nervous being out at night in an unfamiliar environment. The door opened and there was a man in his thirties with a broad smile. 'Christa?'

'Yes,' she said, feeling awkward shoving the soup pot at him. 'I brought soup.'

'Lovely,' he said. 'I'm Zane.'

She stepped into the reception area and then followed Zane down a hallway where she could hear voices in the distance.

'Come down and meet everyone,' he said. 'We park the van out the back so we can load it up and then we head out. Some people do the food and we have some nurses who help with basic first aid and health checks. On weekdays people can come here and shower and get their clothes swapped or washed and they can have a haircut on Tuesdays.'

He was handsome and had a lovely energy about him, she thought as they entered the large commercial kitchen.

Zane put her soup down on the bench. 'Everyone, this is Christa. She is a chef and she brought us some of her soup.'

Looking at the large pots on the stove and various items

cooking, she felt silly with her pot of vegetable soup but no one responded poorly.

'Christa.' She heard Petey's Yorkshire accent. 'You came.'

She saw her new friend buttering slices of bread.

'I did, thank you for this, Petey. I hope I can be of some help.'

Zane was talking to someone by the stove and there were two women who had stethoscopes around their necks and were pulling on large jackets.

'You can help me butter this bread if you want, and then we can load it up for the truck.'

Christa looked at the trays of bread. 'How many will come for food tonight?' she asked.

In London she had fed maybe ten people on a busy day out the Playfoot's kitchen back door. She knew the soup kitchens in London fed hundreds of people but she liked to help those around the restaurant who couldn't get to the kitchen or didn't want to line up. She had thought about helping there more and more as she and Simon grew apart, but there simply wasn't time with cooking six days a week. She felt the nerves surface she hadn't felt since she was young.

A memory shot into her mind with a force that felt like a slap. Her father taking her hand as they stood in line; Christa, cold in her red coat and wishing they were home in the flat in front of the radiator, but Dad hadn't paid the power bill and it wouldn't be on until tonight.

'Jimmy? Jimmy and daughter Christy?' She heard her dad's name called and she glanced up at him. He looked tired and his skin had a sheen to it that came after he had been asleep for a long time.

'Here,' he said and he walked to the front of the line, her hand still in his.

There were mumbles from the line, and someone said, 'Oi he's got a bairn,' and then the mumbles stopped.

'Dad, what's a bairn?' she asked but he didn't answer as a woman with a clipboard checked his name and then pushed open a door for them.

The smell of cauliflower hit her first but then there were other smells of chicken, some sort of red meat – maybe lamb. Yes, it was lamb.

There were round tables with plastic tablecloths in faded colours and unmatched chairs surrounding them. A small vase of holly and sat in the centre of the table and at each place setting was a single Christmas cracker.

'Get some food for the girl and then yourself and take a seat,' a man said, wearing a red paper crown, with a name tag that read 'Dennis'.

They walked to the bain-marie and Christa looked inside the glass windows, the heat welcome as she peered at the choices.

'What can I get you, love?' said a woman who was wearing a Santa hat and a slash of orange lipstick.

'Christa?' She heard her name and she returned back to the present.

'Yes, sorry,' she said to Zane who was in front of her, trying to get her attention.

'Petey is ready for you to jump in whenever you're ready,' he said.

'Of course,' she said and she rushed to Petey's side.

'It's a Monday, so we usually get around one-fifty or so. It's cold so they might be more likely to come tonight, especially if they hear about the soup you made,' said Petey kindly. 'It's not only rough sleepers. It's parents struggling to feed their kids for the week, or pensioners who can't make ends meet. We'll package them up with some food boxes also.' He pointed to the shopping bags already tied up, filled with pantry items that she could see through the plastic.

Christa felt silly not realising how many people they helped and she wished she had made more but they seemed to have enough food judging by the number of pots and containers heading out the door.

Soon the van was loaded up and Christa was offered the passenger seat next to Zane while the other volunteers sat inside the van.

Zane turned to Christa. 'You warm enough?'

'I hope so,' she said. She had on her pink puffa jacket, thermals, her beanie and gloves and boots with warm socks.

'Okay then.' Zane started the van. 'You ready to help some people?'

'Absolutely,' said Christa and she felt that for the first time, she was doing what she was meant to do in life.

Italian Vegetable Soup

Ingredients

2 each of onions and carrots, chopped
4 sticks celery, chopped
1 tbsp olive oil
2 tbsp sugar

4 garlic cloves, crushed
2 tbsp tomato purée
2 bay leaves
few sprigs thyme
3 courgettes, chopped
400g/14oz can butter beans, drained
400g/14oz can chopped tomatoes
1.2 litres/40½fl oz vegetable stock
100g/3½oz Parmesan or vegetarian equivalent, grated
140g/5oz small pasta shapes
small bunch basil, shredded

Method

1. Gently cook the onion, carrots and celery in the oil in a large saucepan for 20 minutes, until soft. Splash in water if they stick. Add the sugar, garlic, purée, herbs and courgettes and cook for 4–5 minutes on a medium heat until they brown a little.

2. Pour in the beans, tomatoes and stock, then simmer for 20 minutes. If you're freezing it, cool and do so now (freeze for up to three months). If not, add half the Parmesan and the pasta and simmer for 6–8 minutes until the pasta is cooked. Sprinkle with basil and remaining Parmesan to serve. If frozen, defrost then reheat before adding pasta and cheese and continuing as above.

9

Marc was still awake when Christa's car came up the driveway. He checked the time. One in the morning. Whatever professional event she had been at ran late, he thought and then checked himself. It was none of his business but still it made him curious. She said she didn't know anyone in York and now she was out at events until one in the morning.

Leaving his office, he entered the foyer of the house just as Christa walked inside.

'Oh hello, I hope I didn't wake you,' she said.

'Not at all, I was finishing some work and about to head to bed but was going to turn the tree lights off first.'

Christa looked at the tree. 'It's a magnificent tree. The boys did a beautiful job.'

Marc looked up at the tree that was twinkling in the semi darkness. The scent of the pine was soothing and the little angel on top was looking down at them.

'Even for a Scrooge like me, this is pretty nice,' he said with a small laugh.

'Do you want a cup of tea?' she asked him. 'I'm going to make a decaf one. Always helps me sleep.'

Marc was tired but he wanted to stay up with Christa.

'Love one, although I hate tea. Can I have coffee?'

Christa turned to him as she opened the kitchen door. 'Coffee? At this time? Will you sleep?'

Marc shrugged. 'I'll get a few hours' sleep – it's okay.'

He turned on the kitchen lights and Christa made them their drinks and sat down at the kitchen table.

'I can smell sausages,' Marc said, sniffing the air. 'Did you eat sausages tonight?' He paused. 'God sorry, that was rude. It's a nice smell, just in case you were worried.'

Christa laughed. 'That's good to know. Yes, there were sausages at the event I attended.'

'So it wasn't a black-tie affair I guess?' he teased.

'Are you saying sausages can't be fancy?' she said, pretending to be offended. 'Not everything is foie gras and caviar in the world.'

Marc laughed. 'I actually hate both of those things.'

Christa took the fudge out of the fridge and he watched her carefully cut the remaining pieces into little squares. 'Don't worry I won't give you the rhubarb one,' she said as she put down the plate.

Marc looked at the plate and took a small piece of chocolate fudge and popped it in his mouth.

'The tree was a good idea. Thanks for the push,' he said.

Christa pulled off her woolly hat and he watched her hair stick up with the static as she sipped her tea. 'It wasn't a push, it was a suggestion.'

'Thanks for the suggestion then,' he said supressing the desire to smooth her hair down.

'So, what's your Christmas battle scar?' she asked.

'What do you mean?' he asked but he knew what she really wanted to know.

'Why you hate Christmas so much? Was it terrible behaviour from family? Poverty? Addiction? Mine was poverty and addiction. Dad was an alcoholic. He eventually got sober but we had a rough few years there for a while.'

'Um…' he said, thinking. 'I try not to think about it too much. There's not much happy stuff in the memory board.'

Christa picked up a piece of the rhubarb fudge. 'You don't have to answer. I was just curious. I'm nosy. I shouldn't have asked.'

'No, it's fine. I know I've been giving mixed messages about Christmas.'

Christa laughed but not meanly. 'You don't want a tree, then you buy the biggest one ever cut down. You say no decorations and now the house is beginning to look like Santa's wonderland. It's hard to stay on what is what day to day.'

Marc put his head down on the table. 'I know, I know.' He raised his head and looked up at her. 'I've been pretty crazy.'

And she smiled at him so kindly he thought she might already know his life story but he knew that would be impossible.

'Not crazy, but I have learned the more you try and push the memories away, the more they come shooting back like a pinball in a machine, harder and faster every time you try and avoid them.'

He thought for a moment. 'You're right,' he said. 'So put me in the second category. Parents who spent their money at the bar instead of on food or even a small present under a shitty plastic tree is what I dealt with. Three younger siblings who didn't know anything about what was going on and me trying to keep them fed with my money as a delivery boy. I think I hoped it was all fake. Then I would be the one who knew better, you know?'

He looked down at his coffee, thinking about the debt collectors coming on Christmas Eve and taking the car. The one thing they had that made life easy for them to get to the shops or Dad to get some work as a handyman. Without the car they were stuck in the outskirts of Los Angeles and without a car, they were sitting ducks for homelessness.

'I'm sorry,' she said. 'You deserved better than that. So did your siblings.'

He nodded. 'What about you?' he asked. 'Was Christmas especially difficult? Besides it being your birthday, which is what date, by the way?'

Christa smiled at him. 'Christmas Eve. Which is why I am called Christa.'

'A Christmas Eve baby. Did you hate it growing up, having to share your birthday with a baby named Jesus?'

'Not at all. My dad was great about it. We always had a separate celebration and presents.'

'And your mom?' he asked.

'She died when I was four. I don't really have any memories of her but I know I was loved. I guess that matters doesn't it? Knowing you are loved and cared for?'

Marc thought back to the apocalyptical fights with his parents and the police coming and the arguments and the violence between his parents at Christmas. It was strange how it could be such a special date for someone and the worst date for another.

'Yes, you're right. I hope my boys know they're loved.

I'm not always great at telling them. I need to get better at it.'

She smiled at him. 'They're such great kids, Marc. Honestly, they're a delight.'

'That's not something I hear very often,' he said. 'It's nice to hear.'

A sadness washed over him. He looked at Christa. 'What is it about you that makes me want to tell you my whole life story? You're like some sort of emotional siren.'

The blush on Christa's neck rose again. 'Oh I don't know, people do seem to tell me things. I guess I'm just a good listener?'

'It's more than that,' he said. 'You get it, whatever "it" is.'

He hoped he wasn't coming across too strong. He wasn't even flirting; he was being his true self and it felt foreign and yet liberating. He didn't talk about his feelings to people, especially people who worked for him, but Christa wasn't here for long and she challenged him in a way that wasn't combative but instead thoughtful and putting the boys first.

Her finger was circling the rim of the tea mug, slowly as though she was performing telekinesis on the cup. He wouldn't have been surprised if there was a small whirlpool in the cup.

'My dad went through some tough times. As I said, Dad struggled with alcohol. I mean it can't have been easy raising me from so young and trying to keep up with bills and rent and trying to grieve for your wife.'

Marc nodded. He knew what it was like to have alcohol ruin a childhood.

'When I was nine, we didn't have any money or food, or heating, so Dad took me to the shelter for Christmas lunch.

I remember thinking it would be awful but it wasn't. I mean it wasn't the Pudding Hall experience but it was okay.'

'Tell me about it,' asked Marc.

Christa paused for a moment, as though gathering her thoughts.

'I remember the presents,' she said and smiled at the memory. 'There was one that set my course to sail to where I am now actually.'

'What was it?' He was genuinely interested in her story.

'First I got a pink diary with a lock and key. Oh that was exciting and it came with some glitter pens – even more thrilling.' She laughed. 'But the final present was something called The Beginner's Cooking Set. It came with an apron and a chef's hat. A cutting board. A set of measuring spoons in different colours. Wooden spoons of different sizes. A recipe book for children. Spatula, tongs, a serving spoon and some kitchen scales. And I was shocked. What a horrible thing, I thought at the time.

'And then a woman who had served me lunch looked over my shoulder and said, "You and your dad will never want for food again with you cooking up a storm", and I thought about it and realised she was right. If I could learn how to cook then I could care for Dad. And then he wouldn't drink because he didn't have to worry about it anymore.'

Marc sighed and shook his head. 'The stories we tell ourselves to make sense of chaos, even as kids huh?'

'Maybe, but he did stop drinking eventually, and I learned to cook and here I am. He went to meetings, got sober and got a job as lorry driver. Then we were okay and Dad spent the rest of his life trying to make up for that time. There were tough times and a few Christmases spent at the dining hall of a charity but I knew he was trying. That helps – when you can see someone is trying to change.'

Marc sighed. 'I wish I knew. So did he also buy you a present for Christmas?'

Christa laughed gently. 'He always did. Not expensive ones but always things he thought I might like. I mean he wasn't some redeemed soul. He was pretty rubbish sometimes. One birthday he gave me a copy of a book from my own bookshelf, as though I wouldn't notice. That was pretty rough but he tried in his own clumsy and broken way. But when he was sober, he always made an effort. So what if many of the presents were from charity shops? They showed he understood me. That meant more to me than anything expensive.'

Marc listened as she spoke, watching the kindness on her face as she thought about her father.

'So what happened after The Beginner's Cooking Set? How did you then decide you wanted to become a chef?'

Christa thought before she spoke.

'He gave me a book when I was sixteen. He knew I was getting good at baking. I cooked for us every night and I liked it. But then he gave me *The Cake Bible* – it's a famous cookbook for bakers – and that absolutely started me on my path to where I am now. He never got to see me graduate from Le Cordon Bleu but I felt his spirit every moment of the course.'

God she's so beautiful, he thought, *and not bitter at all*.

'Would you have forgiven him if he hadn't gotten sober?' he asked.

Christa looked him in the eye. 'What was there to forgive? He was in so much pain that he dulled it with alcohol. I didn't need to forgive him, I needed to love and support him, and I knew that even as a child. Was it ideal? No, but no life is. We all get a turn, don't we? It's just that some of us have the turn younger than others.'

Marc though about his life. He had grown up trying to keep the family together, trying to get his parents to change so he could have a childhood. All that energy and work and it didn't stop the outcome.

'I have a lot of anger towards my parents, still,' he admitted. 'I don't speak to anyone in my family.'

'Where are your brothers and sisters?' she asked him, looking confused.

Marc shook his head. 'I don't know. We were placed into foster care when I was fifteen. Split up and the younger ones adopted. I was older and angry so I got to live in a group home. I tried to find them years ago but they were all closed adoptions.'

'Oh that's awful. I'm so sorry. You must wonder and worry more often than you realise. You're probably used to living with it but I'm sure it's always there.' She sounded so sincere and sad he felt his throat tighten at her kindness. It was true. He did worry. He did look for his siblings in crowds, wondering if they were happy, hoping they had good lives.

He looked ahead, staring at the dark kitchen windows.

'It was pretty awful but it was still better than home,' he said.

They sat in silence for a while.

'Tell me about you getting into Le Cordon Bleu,' he said.

'Why do you want to know about that?' She laughed.

'Because I like hearing success stories – it fuels me,' he said with a smile.

She thought for a moment. 'I found out I got in the day of my father's funeral actually,' she said.

'Oh Jesus,' he said.

'That's life though isn't it? Endings and beginnings.'

'Maybe,' he said, 'but that's rough.'

'My dad had told me to apply before he was diagnosed with cancer but I didn't think we could afford the fees. It's expensive,' she said. 'Then he died and he had an insurance policy on him from his work, so I could go.'

'That would have been hard.'

She nodded. 'It was. Thank you for saying that.'

Their eyes locked for a moment and then Christa drained her cup of tea.

'I should head to bed,' she said, picking up his cup and hers, pushing her chair back and standing.

'Yes,' said Marc still sitting at the table. 'Oh, I forgot, we got you an ornament for the tree. The boys asked me to choose one for you.' He went to a shopping bag with lights and tinsel poking out of the top, rummaged until he found it and came back to the table and handed it to her, wrapped in tissue.

'You didn't have to do that,' she said.

'I know, but the boys wanted special ones. Seth chose Santa on a skateboard and Ethan chose a Christmas-themed milkshake decoration. Quite unusual selections but very them.'

Christa smiled as she unwrapped the tissue and turned the ornament over in her hand.

'A deer family,' she said, sounding surprised.

'Yes, I don't know why, it just appealed to me. I could have chosen something food-related but I guessed you would get sick of silly gimmick gifts like that.'

Christa looked at the ornament carefully. 'I have seen deer here a few times now. Once a huge stag when I arrived and then I saw a stag and a doe. They were just gorgeous.' She smiled at him. 'Thank you, this is really thoughtful and sweet.'

'It was nice actually. Thinking about what to get you.'

'Did you choose one for yourself?' she asked.

'I got a pudding,' he said, taking the ornament from the bag.

She took it from him. 'It's so sweet. It matches my pyjamas.'

He laughed. 'I suppose we should hang them on the tree.'

'My pyjamas? I don't think that's a good idea,' she teased.

Marc laughed louder than he'd planned to and quickly covered his mouth.

'No, these,' he said, holding his ornament up in front of her.

'Yes, let's,' she agreed and she followed him to the foyer of the house where the tree sat in all its glory.

The scent of the pine was one of the many favourite things about Christmas for Christa and the freshness of this tree and its pretty jewels and lights gave her a flutter of excitement.

'Gosh, where will I hang my little deer family?' she said.

'You can hang it anywhere,' said Marc, putting his

pudding on a side branch and adjusting it so it faced forward.

'No, I can't. I have to choose the right placement so the deer family can see the comings and goings and can see outside when the front door opens.'

She heard Marc laugh but not unkindly.

Finding a place in the centre of the tree, she carefully hung the family and moved some tinsel away from them, so they had a clear view of the room and beyond.

'I think that's just perfect,' she declared as she stepped back and looked about the area.

'The tree does look good,' Marc said.

'The boys did a great job.'

'I did some also. I did the lights. They nearly broke my spirit. I lost control of an end, and had to lay them out up the hallway to untangle them.'

Christa laughed, remembering her father's own battles with tangled lights.

'There is a saying that you can see what a person is really like under stress when they have to untangle Christmas lights. How did you go?'

Marc paused and looked at the tree. 'Let's just say, the lights and I have reached a mutual agreement that I will not be doing this task next year.'

'I think many Christmases have been jeopardised by poor lights management,' she said, giggling.

Marc crossed his arms and surveyed the tree. 'Lucky I'm not like that then.'

'Lucky you're not,' she agreed.

He turned to her. 'Thank you for the chat, Christa. It means a lot.'

She gave a gentle laugh. 'My pleasure. Baking and chatting are my specialties.' She paused. 'Goodnight, Marc.'

'Goodnight, Christa. Sleep well.'

She turned to give him a small wave goodnight from the top of the stairs but he didn't see her. Instead, he was staring at the tree, his face clouded in sadness that Christa understood only too well.

10

'Happy birthday dear Adam, happy birthday to you.' The song finished and Adam blew out the candles on the cake Christa had made. It was a twelve-layer chocolate cake with honeycomb and toffee shards on top and Chantilly cream on the side.

'This is incredible,' said Paul as Christa cut the cake and carefully placed it onto a plate.

'You should be a baker,' said Seth as he eyed the slice of cake she had handed to Adam.

'You think? I will look into that – thanks for the idea,' she said, laughing, but Seth looked at her with such confusion she felt bad for teasing him.

'I am a pastry chef actually,' she said to him. 'Pastry chefs make all the desserts in restaurants and people love desserts.'

'I love them the most,' said Ethan shoving a bite of cake into his mouth.

'That's not true, I love them more,' said Seth, putting a bigger bite of cake into his mouth.

'Okay, stop the competitive dessert discussion please,' said Marc. 'Who wants coffee or tea?'

Christa moved towards the kitchen to take over but Marc put his hand on her arm.

'Sit. You just made an amazing dinner and this cake; let me make you some decaf tea.'

Christa was unsure what to do but Marc gently pushed her in the direction of the table.

'Okay, boss,' she said and went to sit at the table.

Once everyone had cake, and Marc had made coffee and tea for the table and glasses of milk for the boys they sat in the kitchen.

Peggy had given up trying to make them sit in the dining room but she hadn't stopped being rude to Christa, including telling her that the food she cooked was not good for people's health and that the boys needed to stay out the kitchen and stop skating in the house.

Christa had ignored her and asked the boys to come and help with the cake.

They did and they enjoyed it, especially making the toffee and using the sugar thermometer.

'It's like science class but fun,' said Ethan.

'When do you go back to school?' asked Christa. 'Aren't you missing out on lots?'

Seth shrugged. 'School schmool. School is for suckers.'

'Who told you that?' asked Christa surprised.

'Joe Pesci,' said Ethan.

'You know Joe Pesci?'

'No, he was in a movie we watched last night – *My Cousin Vinny*,' said Seth.

Christa was totally confused but let it go. It wasn't her business why the boys weren't at school and Marc didn't seem to be worrying about it at all.

Now Christa sat next to Marc at the table, and she felt acutely aware of his leg next to hers. She imagined pressing her knee against his, wondering if he would push back and the thought of it gave her butterflies.

The boys took a second slice of cake into the sitting room to eat it and watch television, leaving the adults at the table.

'Paul, I was going to ask a favour of you,' said Marc.

Christa noticed Paul looked slightly terrified.

'Yes?'

'Can you organise some decorations for the house? The tree looks so alone in its glory without any of the extra trimmings around the house. I think you could do a great job. I mean, you know about that stuff. I know you won't do anything garish. I'm thinking traditional style you know?'

Paul gasped. 'Shut the front door, you didn't just ask me that?!'

Marc glanced at Christa who raised her eyebrows at him as she swallowed a piece of cake.

'He did just ask that,' she confirmed.

'Yes!' Paul clapped.

'Not tacky,' Marc reminded him.

'I am the very pinnacle of taste and class. I once convinced Lady Gaga to not decorate her house in the style of the catacombs with real skulls and to instead install a rainforest spa complete with a wall of rare moss flown in from South America. "Always choose life over death", I said to her. It really lifted her spirits.'

Christa burst out laughing. 'I don't know if you're serious or not, but I do love Lady Gaga.'

'She's divine – you'd love her,' said Paul eating more cake. 'You will need to stop making desserts like this though, otherwise I will be eligible to fit into the Santa suit for Christmas Day.'

'Shush,' said Christa. 'None of that, I don't like diet talk in my kitchen. Do you feel hungry right now?'

Paul paused. 'I do. It's the cold weather.'

'So, eat the cake, and when you feel full, which your body will tell you, don't eat any more.'

Marc looked at her. 'Not a fan of diets?'

Christa wasn't sure if he was being rude or serious. She knew she was curvy but she was fine with her body.

'I don't like diet culture. I like intuitive eating. If you know what your body needs then eat it. Eat when you're hungry and give it nutritious food. A slice of cake isn't something we have every day but when we do we should make sure we enjoy it.'

'My ex-wife would disagree with you. She's the food police for the boys, and for herself. So many rules about food and always new diets.'

Adam laughed. 'Remember when we went to Colorado and she asked for a glass of condensation at that health spa?'

Paul started to laugh with him. 'And when she said she could only have organic essence of anything.'

Christa inwardly rolled her eyes and sighed. This ex sounded like a nightmare and the exact opposite of herself.

'When is she coming?' asked Christa. 'I just need to know so I can catch the morning dew and forage wintry smoke flavours in the evening.'

The table burst out laughing and Christa felt Marc's hand on her forearm.

'Sorry, that was bitchy,' she said. 'I'm sure she's lovely.'

'God that's hilarious,' he said then, putting his other hand over his face, still chuckling.

His firm grasp on her arm wasn't too tight or too heavy. She swore she could feel every muscle in his hand, down to the tendons in his fingers. It sent a shiver up her arm and her skin prickled in response.

The sound of her phone ringing interrupted the moment and she grabbed it from the bench and saw Zane's name pop up.

'Excuse me,' she said to the table and walked out of the room.

'Hey,' she said.

'Hi, Christa, I hate to call at the last minute but is there any chance you can come and help tonight? We have two people out with colds.'

Christa checked the time. It was after nine. 'Can I meet you at the van after you've left?'

'That'd be great. We're going to be down on Coppergate if you want to meet us there.'

'Fantastic. Do you need me to bring anything?'

'Just yourself – that's more than enough.'

Christa put her phone in the pocket of her jeans and paused, trying to think of an excuse to leave. What would Marc say if she said she had to leave now and go and feed some homeless people? Maybe she should just tell him. Surely he would understand.

She walked back into the kitchen and saw that Marc had opened a bottle of dessert wine and the three men were drinking from elegant glasses.

'Everything okay?' asked Marc. 'Come and have a drink. This is a wonderful wine from a vineyard in France that I own.'

Christa didn't even know how to respond to that. Marc

was drinking wine from a vineyard he owned and she was being asked to help people who needed it most. It annoyed her deeply. He wouldn't understand. His childhood might have been troubled but he was so far removed from the everyday trials of people struggling she wanted to tip the wine down the sink and drag him to the food van and show him the reality for so many.

She started packing the dishwasher with the plates and cutlery and then put the pans and baking dishes into the industrial dishwasher in the butler's pantry.

'Don't do that,' she heard Marc say as she closed the door of the machine and turned I it on. 'Come and sit with us.'

'I can't.' She could hardly contain the anger in her voice as she replied. 'I have to head out. Do you need anything else done before I go?'

She pulled off her apron and threw it onto the bench.

'Are you okay? What happened? Who was on the phone?' he asked, his face concerned.

'I'm fine.'

She walked into the kitchen and pulled her coat and bag down from the hook.

'Happy birthday, Adam. I hope you had a lovely day and enjoyed the cake.'

Adam and Paul looked at her and her coat. 'Where are you going?' Paul asked.

'I'm meeting a friend,' she said.

'I sense a lover in York, a midnight fling. How perfect. Didn't take you long.' Paul laughed and Adam joined in his giggles.

Christa avoided Marc's gaze and grabbed her hat from

where it sat near the back door and headed outside to her car.

The air was crisp and she could hear frost crunching beneath her feet as she walked over the grass.

A vineyard in France? Who had a vineyard?

She started her car and let it warm up for a moment and then drove down the driveway towards town, wondering how she could be living between such different worlds.

The van was set up and people were milling around when she arrived. Soon she was serving soup and handing out sandwiches and some custard tarts a bakery had donated.

'Petey isn't here tonight?' she asked Zane as he came to help her.

'No, he's sick. He needs to take care; he's getting on himself.' Zane said. 'His wife died a few years ago. He runs the fudge company himself and runs the market stall alone most days.'

Christa made a mental note to call on Petey at the market the next day.

'Soup? Chicken noodle or pumpkin?' she asked, looking down from the counter of the van, to see a young girl of about eight or nine, in a thin jacket with a toddler in a stroller next to her. 'Hi.' She smiled at the little girl.

'Chicken noodle,' said the child.

'Where's your mum?' she asked.

'Talking to the nurse,' she said.

Christa looked at Zane who didn't seem surprised at the age of the children in front of them.

'Does your little brother want something to eat? Maybe some bread and butter or custard tart?'

Christa wished she had something more nutritious for the child.

'A custard tart would be nice,' said the girl shyly and Christa handed her four and a cup of soup with a lid on it and some bread and butter.

The child manoeuvred the stroller away with one hand while she held the soup after putting the other items in the basket below the child.

'Jesus,' she said to Zane, feeling shaken. 'It's so late, that child is clearly cold, and the toddler should be asleep. Why are they out here tonight? Is there a place their mother can get this support during the day?'

Zane looked at her.

'There is but what if she's working? What then? The mother is getting them food, good food, which is better than no food or eating rice for days. She's getting shopping from us. She's getting her wounds from her bastard ex-husband checked by the nurse and the children are together and safe with us here now. Is it ideal? No. But is she trying to do her best? Yes. Her best might not be what you and I might throw out to be the best but it's all she can do right now and all we can do is support her.'

Christa watched as the mother came back to her children and wrapped her arms around them, making a fuss over the custard tarts.

She wasn't a religious person but in the moment, she sent a little prayer up to whoever was turning this crazy world and asked if they would share a little magic with this small family doing the best they could on a cold winter's night.

II

Christa was tired when she came home from the food van and went straight to bed. Staying up late the night before talking to Marc had also taken its toll but when she woke in the morning she felt better and checked the time. It was only just seven and the house sounded quiet. She wanted to make some food for Petey and take it to him in the afternoon. She had his address from Zane and was planning on dropping it off and checking in on him.

Showered and dressed, Christa headed down to the kitchen where she put on the coffee, boiled the kettle and looked inside the refrigerator. No eggs.

Didn't the boys say there were chickens outside? Peggy hadn't arrived yet, so that must be why no one had collected the eggs.

Christa pulled on her coat and hat and opened the back door.

There was a glimpse of sunshine and the rain had stopped for a change. Christa saw a collection of wellingtons lined up by the back door and kicked off her shoes and slipped her feet into a pair, tucking her jeans into the boots. She looked around her and then took the gravel path lined with topiary trees that led to a brick wall. She followed the path around the wall until it opened up and she found herself inside a walled kitchen garden, carefully laid out, with winter vegetables in some of the beds alongside some of the empty ones. Presumably they were fallowing for the next plant. She had visited many organic farms and kitchen gardens when she was at Playfoot's. Seeing the ways the farmers grew the vegetables was wonderful and she would always come back with a new supplier of purple carrots or baby beets.

So many vegetables, she thought as she walked towards a crop of cabbages so fat even Peter Rabbit would have had trouble munching through them.

'Morning,' she heard and saw a man standing up from behind a crop of Brussels sprouts.

'Oh hi.' Christa waved. 'Are you the one responsible for all this beauty?'

'I am indeed. I'm Bill, head gardener.' He was a tall thin man, in his mid-sixties with a weather-beaten face and a green corduroy hat and boiled wool jacket with a long rain jacket over the top.

'Christa. I'm the chef here until just after New Year.'

'Peggy told me about you, said you were into all sorts of fancy things and you wouldn't like my vegetables.'

Christa gasped. 'That is entirely untrue, Bill. I would love to use these vegetables. I didn't know they were here. I came on an egg hunt and found this instead.'

Bill seemed pleased with her answer. 'You want to meet the girls do you? They are off the lay now it's getting colder. You might luck out with the odd egg but I believe Peggy has been buying them from town.'

'Has she? I didn't know. They twins talk about the chickens as though they're laying now.'

Bill shook his head. 'Come down and look anyway,' he said and she walked by his side through the grounds. He pointed out the different gardens on the way.

'That's the orchard. We have lovely pippin apples in there and there's the pond, which has beautiful water lilies in the summer. Shame you won't be here to see them.'

Christa looked up at the sky. 'Peggy thinks it will snow soon,' she said. 'Do you think it will?'

Bill shrugged. 'I don't know. The bees went into the hive early – that can mean it's going to be a harsh winter but I can't say when the snow is coming.'

Christa looked around the garden. It wasn't hard for her to imagine the beauty of the garden in spring and summer. Every edge of the pathway was trimmed so well there wasn't an inch of grass that dared to creep a toe over the edge. The yew trees that lined the pathway were perfect triangles, standing proudly surrounded by frost on the lawns.

'Have you cared for this garden for a long time?' she asked Bill.

'Since I was twenty. Came straight from horticultural school and stayed on. It's been through three owners but Mr Ferrier is the nicest one we've had at Pudding Hall.'

'Oh, how so?' Christa asked. She was interested to know what others through of Marc, since she couldn't always understand his moods over the past week. One minute he was saying he liked to help others and the next he was boasting about a vineyard in France. He spoiled his children yet he also neglected them. He was moody but could also be so attentive you felt like you were the most important person in the room.

'The garden needed work done to it when he came but

there was only me, and I didn't have enough hours in the day or the budget to fix what needed to be done. Mr Ferrier let me have some young people to come and work here and he did everything I recommended. We drained the pond and restocked the water lilies. He let me replant the iris garden, brought in twenty thousand irises from the Netherlands. They came up last year but this year there will be more. Some of the rare bulbs I never thought I would have the chance to plant and raise.'

Christa smiled at him as they came around the water and the sound of chickens murmuring came within earshot.

'It's a beautiful garden, Bill. You should be proud of your work.'

The chicken coop was large but not too big and the chickens were scratching at the ground and eating some vegetable leaves.

'I give the girls some scraps as there hasn't been much coming from the kitchen lately.'

'You will have all the scraps from now on in,' promised Christa. 'I didn't know they needed them but consider them first in line for the veggie soup remnants I will have today, provided I get some fresh veg from a gardener I know.'

Bill lifted the lid at the back of the coop and pulled out three eggs. 'Not enough for a family but enough for a breakfast,' he said.

'You keep them,' said Christa. 'I will get some tomorrow or ask Peggy to bring some in when she starts.'

Bill nodded and put the eggs carefully into the pockets of his wool jacket.

'Now how's about we get that veg for you. I have some parsnips that are ready to come out and some potatoes.

How about some leeks?' Bill seemed to be in his element sharing the bounty with Christa.

'I have some winter carrots and lovely chard also.' He listed more vegetables than Christa thought possible and she thought about the food van and how much they would like a nutritious soup. Not that the food they had was terrible but it needed more nutrients. The custard tart for the little toddler the previous evening was no doubt much enjoyed but it needed to be tempered with something to give the baby's body something to grow with.

Bill had harvested her a feast and put it in the wheelbarrow and walked her back to the house.

'Pudding Hall is a beautiful house,' she said, looking at the lines and windows and the grand roofline.

'Nothing like her for miles around here,' said Bill. 'There was talk that the house would become a hotel before Mr Ferrier bought it.'

'Is that a good or a bad thing?' she asked.

Bill snorted. 'No one wanted this to be a hotel. It's Pudding Hall. It's a grand home but it needs a family, not just drop-ins. This is the first time Mr Ferrier has stayed here and he bought it three years ago.'

'Really? If I had a house like this I would never leave.' Christa laughed. 'It's a dream come true isn't it? All these gardens and chickens and a pond and an orchard.'

Bill stopped, turned and looked around at the expanse of ground behind them. 'There're more but no one enjoys it. Sometimes I feel I'm keeping it alive just for me.'

Christa looked with him.

'How about this morning, I bring the boys for a wander? They would love it. They've been cooped up inside with video games and television. Could you take us on a tour? I could bring morning tea.'

Bill's face beamed. 'That would be grand, Christa, just grand.'

He helped her carry the vegetables inside the house and then carefully put the eggs on the bench.

'For morning tea – you might need them if you make something.'

Christa smiled at him.

'You're a star, Bill, thank you. See you at ten.'

12

Marc could hear the boys yelling from the kitchen as he walked towards it and he pushed open the door to hear one yell at the other, 'Go and bite your arse.'

'Give it back or I'll punch your face in.'

He was about to speak when he saw Christa come out of the pantry.

'No one will be biting bums or punching faces, and certainly not in my kitchen. Please treat each other with respect and kindness or you can't come on my adventure.'

He saw her hold out the coats for the twins and they sullenly pulled them on.

'Why do you say bum and not arse?' asked Seth.

'Bum is a much better word, isn't it?' Christa asked as she pulled their woollen hats onto their heads.

'Bum is a good word,' Ethan agreed.

'My aunt had a parrot that she taught to say to my uncle, "Bite your bum, Lester", whenever he passed. Used to drive him mad but it made my aunt laugh.' Christa said the phrase like a parrot and the boys roared with laughter and then copied her, repeating the phrase.

'Who is Lester and why am I biting his bum?' Marc asked, poking his head inside the doorframe.

The boys fell apart laughing again and he saw Christa join in.

Whatever happened to make her flee last night didn't seem to be a concern now.

'Good night?' he asked, wishing he hadn't when he saw her face. Her smile went steely. He had overstepped a boundary and he knew it.

'Sorry, none of my business,' he said.

'How was the wine from your vineyard?' she asked and he swore he could detect a hint of vinegar in her tone.

'Very sweet,' he answered.

'We're going on an adventure with Christa. Do you want to come?' Seth yelled.

'No need to shout, Seth.' Christa had her back to him and was fiddling with a large cane basket on the bench.

'Why not? Paul is decorating the house today and Adam and Peggy have been pulled in to assist, much to their horror.'

Christa turned to him. 'I was wondering why Peggy hadn't been in early.'

'She's in the woods with Paul and Adam scavenging for holly and ivy,' Marc said amusing himself.

Christa did laugh. 'I can't imagine Peggy out in the depths of the woods getting in touch with nature. I hope Paul can handle her.'

'Paul can handle anything. Peggy is a walk in the park compared to some of the big egos and demands he's worked with.'

'Don't you mean walk in the woods?' said Christa.

'Touché,' Marc said with a nod of his head.

She was clever and beautiful and talented and, he

realised, she was completely unimpressed by his wealth. The comment about the vineyard in France was meant to impress her but instead she'd left the house.

For some reason Christa's opinion of him mattered. Why did it matter when he hardly knew her? Yes he thought she was attractive and funny but there was something else. He felt he had to earn her respect, and Marc Ferrier hadn't had to earn anything in a long time.

'I will get my coat and gloves,' he said. 'Don't leave without me.' He wagged a finger playfully at his twins.

'Bite ya bum, Lester,' they said screaming at their own joke.

Sorry, Christa mouthed to him but he laughed with them and was still giggling when he came back to the kitchen all rigged up and ready to go.

'Ready and able,' he said to Christa, taking the basket from her hand. 'What's in here?' he asked about to lift the lid.

'No, don't look – it's a surprise,' she said firmly, putting her hand on his and pushing down the lid.

He felt a physical connection to her and he wished he could kiss her for a moment. Just a quick kiss on those soft pink lips.

'Righto,' she said and she opened the kitchen door. 'Let's go.'

Outside Bill the gardener was waiting, a small black dog by his side. A mutt who looked like a cross between a Yorkshire terrier and a Jack Russell.

'A dog,' yelled the boys.

'Mr Ferrier, Miss Christa,' said Bill formally.

'Marc, please,' he said. He had told him and Peggy many

times he preferred his first name but they refused to adhere to his wishes.

'Just Christa for me. I haven't been a "miss" since I was in school and in trouble.' He watched her get down on her haunches and tickle the dog under the chin. 'Who is this lovely lady?'

'Meredith,' said Bill. 'She's my assistant. She was sleeping earlier but is ready for the fun now.'

'Hello, Meredith,' said Christa and the boys joined her in patting the dog.

She stood up and smiled at them all.

'Let's get on with it then, and if you can't get on with it, you can bite your…'

'Bum!' Marc and the twins yelled in unison.

Marc had forgotten how beautiful Pudding Hall was. He had been thinking about selling the house after Christmas but now he wondered why he didn't live here permanently, except that the boys wouldn't want to stay. Their lives were in America and he still shared custody. Perhaps it was a fanciful idea. So many people wanted to live in the country but then when they stayed they became bored and restless, missing the luxuries of the city. But York wasn't so far away and it was a gorgeous place with everything he needed. He could work anywhere if he wanted to, he wasn't tied to a city or a country.

The boys ran ahead with Bill, peppering him with questions about the dog and the garden and whether he had ever owned a parrot. Christa and Marc walked companionably as their feet crunched on the gravel.

'So where are we off to?' he asked, swinging the basket by his side.

'We're exploring this wonderful garden,' she said. 'The boys don't know it at all. Have they been here very often?'

Marc felt ashamed. 'They're never been here actually. They're usually in California.'

'How many houses do you own?'

He felt embarrassed answering. He counted them in his head. The place in Gstaad that he never used. The one in Aspen. The penthouse in New York. The farm in New Zealand. The apartment in Paris.

'A few,' he said carefully.

Christa said nothing for a while as they walked. A peacock walked onto the path and opened his fan, much to the boys' delight.

They all stopped and watched him show his beauty to them.

Christa leaned over to him and whispered, 'Do you think he has a vineyard in France?'

Marc burst out laughing and the peacock, insulted, wandered off the path.

Christa turned and lifted her chin and gave a cheeky smile. 'Sorry, it was too easy. I had to take the shot. I hope you're not too badly wounded.'

'Not at all. It's funny and I did sound like an idiot. I don't know why I said it,' he admitted. But he knew why he said it. He wanted to impress her and he had failed.

Bill and the boys were a good way ahead now.

'We all say things that come out the wrong way,' she said.

They followed the path in a comfortable silence, as the sun shone down on them. There was no warmth in the rays but the light showed off the elegant lines of the deciduous trees that must have been over one hundred years old and counting.

'I can't remember the last time I was out in the country like this,' she said as the path meandered down and a large hedge loomed before them.

'Me neither,' he said. 'It's good for us, don't you think?'

She looked up at him. 'I do.' Her face was clear and bright. She didn't have on any makeup, synthetic fillers, false eyelashes, or expectations. Ever since his divorce, certain types of women were the only ones who approached him. The ones looking for a rich husband who were everywhere in parts of California. Perhaps they were lovely but it was hard to see under the exterior they had created, thinking that's what rich men wanted. Even his ex-wife had succumbed to fillers and Botox and eating next to nothing. It made him sad when he thought of her once-carefree face and attitude when they met before he became rich.

He found he suddenly wanted to kiss Christa, but then that would mean he'd be crossing boundaries and she would run away and that would be that. She was out most nights, probably seeing someone in town, he assumed. It made him wish he was something more than he was, so she would be interested in him, but she was not interested. She had made it clear she thought him shallow and silly at times. He saw her mouth part slightly and he leaned in a few millimetres.

'Dad, Christa, Dad, come find us,' he heard the twins yell, breaking the spell.

'Where are you?'

'In the maze. The first one to the centre is the winner; the last one to the centre has to bite their bum.'

Marc saw Christa run to the entrance and she turned to him before yelling into the maze, 'Challenge accepted.'

Marc put the basket down where Bill was standing. 'Do you mind looking after this?'

Without waiting for an answer, he stepped into the maze and looked ahead. There was a pathway surrounded by hedges, and all he knew was he had to find Christa who was somewhere inside the walls.

13

Christa walked through the maze, occasionally hearing the boys yelling out for each other or crowing like birds.

There was something eerie about the dense foliage and the scent of the rain from the night before that made her feel nervous but excited.

Marc was somewhere near. It thrilled her, like her own little private game.

She turned a corner and saw the leg of one the twins disappear ahead, then heard the crunch of gravel next to her behind the hedge.

She was silent and stopped walking. Was it a twin or was it Marc?

She started to walk again and turned right, coming to a dead end.

Why did she feel so nervous?

There was running and crowing from the inner part of maze while she turned right again and came to a small marble statue of some sort of goddess. Turning right again, she came to the fork in the paths. Which way?

She paused and then went right again. She had seen something on a television show years ago that if you ever wanted to get out of a maze, you had to keep turning in one direction. It could be right or left but to exit you had to stay committed to one direction.

She could hear the boys yelling. They were in the centre and she heard the sound of feet on the path next to her again.

Another fork and she waited.

To leave the maze she should turn right.

She turned left.

And there was Marc at a dead end.

She smiled at him, feeling her heart beating faster.

His gaze captured hers and he smiled in return. It was a lazy, sexy smile that she found truly knee-buckling.

'Are you lost?' he asked and she could have sworn he was flirting with her.

'Nope, are you?' She returned his sassy tone.

God they were flirting – so silly. Perhaps it was just in fun but Marc was looking at her in a way that she knew would get her into trouble.

'Should I leave?' she asked.

'Please don't,' he said.

Christa thought about what the next few weeks would be like if anything happened with Marc. There was a flirtation but he was teasing her, like he probably did all women. Men like him could have supermodels, actresses, heiresses. She would be nothing more than a Christmas fling and she would still have to cook for him.

God no, she thought, and she laughed at him.

'Last one to the centre has to bite the other's bum, remember.' She turned and walked in the opposite direction.

'Christa.' She heard him say her name but she kept walking towards the sound of the boys in the centre.

What would she have done if he'd kissed her? What if she had kissed him? What if she was mistaken? How embarrassing would it have been?

She worked for him. So many rules broken – it would have been a workplace disaster.

A phone rang and she heard him answer, saying Adam's name. Saved by the bell, she thought as she finally came to the centre, finding the boys looking into a pond with little fish darting about.

'There you are,' she said.

'Hey, I have to head back to the house – work emergency,' Marc called.

'Bye,' yelled the boys but Christa said nothing. It was better that way, she decided.

Keep it strictly professional. That's what she had always told the staff at Playfoot's. She and Simon never showed affection in the kitchen at work. It was professional and respectful at all times. In hindsight they probably took it too far when they brought that energy home as well but it was done now.

Christa and the boys found their way out of the maze, using her one direction theory, to where Bill was sitting patiently on a bench with the picnic basket and Meredith the dog next to him.

'Right, next stop please,' said Christa wishing Marc was still there but also grateful he wasn't. As they followed Bill through the garden, she began to think the conflicting feelings were a real pain.

Ahead was a large greenhouse, the glass shimmering in the sun.

'A greenhouse,' exclaimed Christa as they came closer. 'It's lovely.'

'One of only three like this in the country,' said Bill proudly. 'It used to be heated by coal but Mr Ferrier got us some solar panels and some natural heat so we have all sorts of things growing inside.'

They walked through the greenhouse while Bill pointed out the ferns and the tropical plants, including pineapples and even an avocado tree that was bearing fruit.

After the greenhouse tour, they sat inside and ate the lemon cake Christa had made and drank cups of hot cocoa that she had packed in a thermos with cups.

'This is the best time ever,' said Seth, a little chocolate moustache giving him a look of Charlie Chaplin.

'And Dad came and everything,' said Ethan and Christa wondered how they could be happy with less than an hour of his time.

Her own father wasn't a saint but when he became sober, he'd spent time with her. They went fishing, sometimes he would take her on bus trips to places she wasn't familiar with, or they would go window-shopping in Bond Street just for fun. He would watch television with her or read the paper while she did her homework. His company was enough.

After they said their farewells to Bill and Meredith and promised to be back, they walked back to the house, where Christa could see Marc standing in the kitchen doorway watching their return.

She wondered what could have been so important that he had to leave them for Adam but she wouldn't ask. She was setting up professional fences, she reminded herself as she kicked off her wellingtons and slipped on her sneakers.

'Let me take the basket,' he said, as the boys ran around to the front of the house.

'All fine, I have it,' said Christa with a firm smile and she pushed past Marc and into the kitchen.

'It was a shame you didn't stay. I saw your pineapples,' she stated as she started to unpack the basket onto the bench.

'My what?'

Christa laughed. 'The greenhouse has pineapples and avocados.'

Marc looked guilty. 'I don't see Bill's work enough.'

Christa said nothing as she tipped the remaining cocoa down the sink.

'Do you think I am a total idiot, a spoiled man who doesn't know what he has?'

Christa rinsed out the thermos. 'I don't think anything about your decisions,' she lied.

She heard Marc pull out a chair and sit at the table. She wished he would go away. He was distracting her and she needed to think about what was for dinner and if she should go into town for eggs.

'I told Adam to ask Paul to get some eggs when he was in town, as I saw we were out,' Marc said.

Dammit, he was thoughtful and observant at times. Then she remembered he was moody and quick to judge. Had Simon set the bar so low that she was impressed by even the slightest act of service?

'Thank you. I was going to get some, but that's good of you to organise,' she said.

Christa opened the fridge and saw all the food going to waste and it annoyed her so much, thinking of the children at the food bus the night before.

'There is a lot of food here that's going to go to waste,' she said. 'I need to cook with it or else it will have to go in the rubbish.'

Marc wasn't listening. He was staring at his phone.

'Perhaps I could donate it to a food kitchen or something?' she said, as though the idea had just come to her.

Marc didn't look up. 'Fine, sounds great. I have to find Adam. Issue with work.'

He stood up, still looking at his phone and left the kitchen, while Christa watched him go.

She had told him. He had agreed. While she wasn't completely sure if he had actually heard her or not, he had given her permission to cook the food and that was enough for now.

14

The next day Christa swung open the garden gate outside Petey's house with her foot, while carrying some potato and leek soup from Bill's harvest and some fresh soft white rolls she had made that afternoon.

She knocked at the door of the plain little house and waited.

Zane had given her Petey's address somewhat reluctantly but she promised she wasn't up to anything more sinister than trying to give the older man something nourishing to eat while he was ill.

The door opened a little and she saw Petey's face.

'Christa,' he exclaimed. 'What are you doing here?'

'Zane said you were sick, so I have some soup and bread and maybe a slice of chocolate cake. If you're hungry, of course, or you have it later when you're feeling better.'

Petey opened the door wider. 'Come in, come in. I could eat an oven door if it were buttered,' he said, his lilting accent making her smile.

Christa followed him into the warm house and down to the kitchen, which was neat as a pin.

There were signs of a female's touch in the house, with tea towels and oven mitts matching the yellow gingham curtains on the window above the sink.

'What a pretty kitchen,' she said, as she placed the bag of food onto the table.

'Oh, that's my Annie's doing, she was always good at the things to make a house a home,' he said as she sat down at the table with a sigh. His head still sounded as though it was filled with cold and he had a slight rasp to his voice.

'I'm sorry for your loss,' Christa said quietly.

'She's been gone a few years now. Cancer, terrible thing. She started making the fudge and did so well. All her recipes are the ones I still use today.'

He shook his head as though trying to remove the memories. 'Want a brew? I can make a pot.'

'Only if I make it. Now let me get this soup warmed for you and the bread buttered so the oven door is safe and then we can chat.'

Christa busied herself and soon Petey was eating his soup, giving a running commentary on the taste, the flavour, the viscosity. He raptured over the softness of the rolls and then finished his symphony of compliments with a rondo about the chocolate cake with the strong tea.

'You must have been a very good cook in London,' said Petey. 'Your little place must have been the place for everyone to go.'

Christa smiled. Usually she corrected people when they called her a cook because it was meant as a put-down but Petey's comment couldn't be further from that.

'I did okay,' she said. 'I ran it with my ex-husband, although he got most of the glory.' She scoffed thinking of Simon's excitement every time he was mentioned in a review.

'Men always do,' Petey replied. 'Even with my Annie's

recipes, and her name on the label, people still think it's all me. I stopped correcting them because then I have to tell them she died and that just makes me sad.'

Christa nodded.

'I understand. My dad didn't like to talk to people about my mum after she died.'

'So what are you going to do when you've finished cooking for the fancy man on the hill?'

Christa was surprised he cared but they had connected when they worked at the food van and at the market the way old souls do. Seeing the same values in one another about food, and compassion and doing what you can with what you have.

She thought for a moment. 'I think I want to open a place for people to come and eat for nothing. A free restaurant.' She laughed. 'Which goes against everything I worked for in London.'

Petey thought for a moment. 'So they don't pay nowt?'

'Nowt, nothing, nada,' confirmed Christa. 'But with good food. Nourishing food to help people's bodies and minds, not just sugary stuff donated, you know? I mean it's nice of companies and businesses to give it away but there's nothing in it to help the body. You need to balance it, you know?'

Petey nodded. 'Like this meal you make. Who wouldn't be happy after such a feast?'

'You are too sweet, Petey. Honestly, all these compliments will go to my head.'

She washed up the dishes and put them away according to Petey's instructions.

'Who is making the fudge for you, Petey?' she asked. 'Are you having a market stall this weekend?'

'I haven't made any,' he said. 'I might not head down this weekend – a bit cold. The air makes me cough.'

'You don't have anyone to help?' she asked, wondering if he had children or grandchildren.

'No, it's just me. Annie and I weren't blessed with littluns. Shame, too, would have been nice to have a bit of company now and then as I get on.'

Christa nodded sympathetically. 'Who do you spend Christmas with, Petey?'

'I help out with the van,' he said. 'It's fine. I like to help out, keeps me mind off my worries.'

Christa wished she could ease his loneliness and the loneliness of every other isolated person in the world. She knew what it was like to be lonely even when in a marriage.

'I would love to do a big Christmas lunch for families or people without families who were struggling or needed company. I would make beautiful turkeys and hams and vegetables and salads. And delicious fruits with puddings and cakes for a treat.'

Christa closed her eyes. 'I can see the space. Tall ceilings with individual tables of different sizes. I would have tablecloths, because we all deserve tablecloths and nice cutlery. And there would be Christmas crackers and presents for the children and little packs of sensible things for people like tooth-brushes and toothpaste and some vouchers and things people need and use. I think about giving cooking lessons for people, teaching them how to shop and buy smart at the super-market, making things go further and make them healthy.'

She opened her eyes to see Petey grinning at her.

'You know, you should look at the old pub on The Street. It's a grand place and hasn't had anyone in it for a year or so now. Pop by when you're on your way back today. I'll draw you a map.'

Petey pulled out a pad of paper and pen from a drawer behind her and drew a map of the streets from his house to the empty pub, describing each turn carefully and drawing little arrows on the paper. Finally, he finished and he pushed it over to Christa.

'Go on, have a look and let me know.'

'Even if it's perfect, I can't make something like that happen on my own. I'm not a social worker and haven't ever run a charity. I wouldn't know what to do. It's just a dream really.'

Petey crossed his arms, his face worn, but with a warm expression.

'Everything is a dream to start with. When Annie started making fudge she never imagined she would one day have a stall at Shambles, and yet we did. You can do if you think about it the right way.'

'What do you mean?' she asked.

'By thinking about why you want to do it. Annie wanted to sell fudge because she said everyone deserved a little treat. It wasn't about making money. I used to be a delivery man but eventually I gave up my job to help her. And that worked because I wanted to help her. If the reason is the right one, then it will happen. I'm not a rich man but Annie's and my success means I don't have to work but I like to. I like to meet people, people like you.'

Christa held his hand and squeezed it. 'You're a lovely

man, Petey, really. You remind me of all the good parts of my dad.'

'Then he must have been a fine fella to have a lass like you.' She saw his blue eyes glisten a little as he spoke. 'Now get out of here and let an old man have a nap. Don't you have a pub to inspect?'

15

Pudding Hall was becoming more festive under Paul's command. Even Peggy acquiesced to his vision, particularly after she saw the wonderful way he had used the holly and ivy and armfuls of spruce draped along the bannisters.

Ethan was filming every moment of the decorating of Pudding Hall, asking Paul about his vision and process, which Marc though was hilarious but which Ethan took very seriously.

But somehow Marc still had the feeling something was missing.

It was as though he had given the nod to the spirit of Christmas and it arrived in all its glory, throwing the front doors of Pudding Hall open and blowing magic everywhere and over everyone except Marc.

He couldn't understand why he felt so indifferent about the whole event. Granted he didn't have the general dislike he usually felt around this time of year but there was still a sense of distance from the excitement brewing in the house. He stood in the foyer of the house looking at the tree, splendidly dressed in all the silver and gold and red and green. The scent of the pine tickled his nose and he could hear the children chatting like magpies down the hall in the kitchen. What was wrong with him? Why couldn't he let himself feel it all? Enjoy it? He had worked for it and yet he was being a Grinch more often than not.

And then it came to him. He was lonely. He had brought the children to York to spend Christmas with them, saying no to tutors and nannies and yet he still hadn't spent enough time with them. He realised now he had brought Adam as an excuse to do business and avoid experiencing anything other than work-related activities. What he really wanted was someone to share this with. Someone to look at when the twins opened their presents and they could nod and feel smug at choosing the right thing. Someone who he could dance around the kitchen with as they organised Christmas lunch, someone who he could kiss at midnight on Christmas Eve and tell them he loved them and sit in front of the fire with them on Boxing Day and do the crossword or play charades with the kids.

God, he wanted all of that so badly it hurt. If he was honest with himself, which he had avoided doing for a long time, he had always wanted all of that, but his ex had not – and would never – want anything like that, and he hadn't made time to meet someone who did. Was it because he was afraid it would end up like his own parents? They once had dreams, before they had children, before they drank and gambled and ruined so many lives. No one sets out to mess up their life but when you don't own your pain then you put it onto other people, he thought.

The tree sparkled as a thin sliver of sun shone through the window and onto the deer ornament he had bought for Christa. No more passing on his pain, he thought. He'd brought the children here and he needed to be more present in every way. He went down to hallway and into the kitchen.

'Dad, you said you would help us,' said Seth as Marc walked in and started to make coffee.

The boys were sitting at the table with Paul, with plates of what looked to be coloured modelling clay.

'Yeah, Dad, you said,' Ethan echoed.

'Yeah, Marc, you promised,' Paul said, mimicking the boys, and Marc laughed as he kissed the boys on the tops of their heads.

Christa was rolling the gingerbread out on a marble slab, looking up briefly to smile at him and then back to her work.

'I did promise, I know, so what are we making?' he asked sitting down and moving his coffee to the side.

The boys didn't answer, instead Seth held up a green triangle-shaped blob.

'Does this look like a tree?' he asked him. 'We need one hundred and twelve trees for the driveway.'

'I don't think we need to do the whole drive,' said Christa. 'Just a few dotted around the house is fine.'

Marc looked at her and she made an alarmed face and mouthed the number of trees at him.

'That's probably the best idea,' said Marc looking at Paul's plate of coloured clay.

'Is this edible?' he asked, picking up what looked to be a fence that Paul had made.

'It's marzipan,' Christa answered.

'Don't break my fences, I spent ages putting that up,' Paul stated, taking the lopsided object from him. 'I did a lot of work with my therapist, highly recommended by Cher actually, to create boundaries, so I won't have some random billionaire crashing through them.'

Marc saw Christa giggling as she rolled some marzipan in front of her.

The kitchen was warm and cosy, and he took some brown marzipan and started to sculpt what he hoped would be a deer. It wasn't so bad when he finished and he let it stand on Paul's plate.

'Dad, that's so good,' Ethan cried.

Christa walked over and peered at the little creature. 'That's actually very good.'

'Actually? You're surprised?' he teased her.

'It's a hard thing to do, so yes, actually it's very good.'

She went back to the bench and he watched her put the gingerbread into the oven.

'Your dad is in charge of all woodland and farm creatures now, boys,' she said.

'We need chickens, and a peacock and some more deer and Meredith the dog,' Ethan instructed. 'Do you want me to text you a list?'

Marc laughed. 'No I think I can remember.'

Peggy walked into the kitchen then and stood in the doorway, staring at Paul. He held up a tiny marzipan fence. 'Boundaries must be respected,' he said and Marc watched as Peggy snorted and turned and left the kitchen.

Marc raised his eyebrows at him. 'What was that about?'

'She put my pinecones outside. I spent a long time collecting those.'

'Oh no, not Peggy and the Pinecones,' Christa said with a laugh. 'What did you do?'

Marc started working on more deer for the gingerbread display while Paul spoke.

'She put my pinecones outside and told me they were filled with creatures and that she wouldn't have creepy crawlies around the house even if it ruined the aesthetic.'

'She did not!?' Marc half teased. He knew Paul was passionate about his work and Pudding Hall was showing his skills off in all their glory.

'She did and when I told her it was me or the pine cones she went and complained to Adam because you wouldn't talk to her.'

'She scares me,' said Marc.

Christa burst out laughing. 'You two are out of control.'

As she spoke Peggy walked back into the kitchen and opened the refrigerator.

'I noticed the quails were gone. Did you use them, Cook?'

Marc noticed Christa's shoulders stiffen and her head raise. 'Yes, I made a stock for soup.'

'And you used the quail for soup – all of it? It must have been a large quantity of soup. Is there nothing in the freezer?'

Peggy opened the freezer and peered inside the shelves and opened the drawers.

'No leftovers?' She stood with her hands on her hips and stared at Christa. 'And I had a ham hock for you. Do anything special with that?'

Marc watched Christa's neck and face flush.

'We had the soup, it was lovely,' he jumped in. 'I think we should leave the ordering to Christa now. She is a chef after all – she knows what she's doing. One less thing for you to worry about, Peggy.'

Peggy snorted and he stopped himself from making a joke as he knew better than to antagonise an angry sow.

Christa's back was turned from him but he could feel her tension. Was there something happening with her and the food? Was food missing? He thought he remembered her saying something about excess food but he couldn't remember what exactly.

'Dad, make a monkey,' said Seth, interrupting his thoughts.

'A monkey? The only monkeys here are you and your brother.' He saw Christa looking at him now, her face unreadable but pink from the warmth of the oven.

He smiled at her, trying to convey that he didn't mind about quails and ham hocks and whatever else she was worrying about but a shadow had crossed her face. He would try and talk to her after dinner, he thought, as he made little monkeys for the boys.

Then they would sort everything out and Christa would smile again.

But after dinner he had a call from his team in New York and by the time he went back to the kitchen, it was clean and Christa's car was driving away.

She had been quiet during dinner, eating with them but sitting with the boys and not drinking any wine or making much small talk. She avoided his looks and picked at her lovely dinner of rack of lamb and baby potatoes and salad. How something so simple could taste so magnificent was beyond him.

And then she was gone. Marc thought quickly, grabbing

his coat and his keys. He headed out to his car and started it, turning it to follow Christa but with the lights low so as not to alert her to his presence.

Where did she go on these nights? He couldn't begrudge her a social life, because she would have sat around at night like Paul did, complaining about Adam's workaholism while Adam ignored him or occasionally patted his leg.

He was selfish to bring Adam here for Christmas, he thought. He should be with Paul and with their family.

Why was he so selfish and not thinking about other people's plans?

He rang Adam from the car.

'Where are you?' Adam asked.

'I'm heading into York for a bit. Can you keep an eye on the boys? Sorry to ask but something's come up.'

'Sure, Paul is with them anyway. They're watching *Hairspray*. It's his favourite film.'

Adam paused. 'I need to ask you something.'

'Yes?' Adam sounded wary and Marc's guilt soared.

'Did you want to head back to the States for Christmas with Paul? I feel bad about you being here when you should be with your friends and family. We can do our meetings by Zoom if you go home. I'd understand. I was being selfish when I demanded you come.'

Adam said nothing for a moment and Marc waited as he saw Christa's car reach the main road and turn right. He hung back a bit and then turned, seeing her lights ahead.

'You know, I am enjoying it, and so is Paul, even though he complains a lot; but the house is great, the kids are fun and the food is terrific. If I go back home it will be for Chinese food. I'm Jewish, so it's no big deal.'

Marc laughed. 'Okay, I was just thinking that I shouldn't have assumed you didn't have a life, that's all.'

'I appreciate you calling and asking. But we'll stay, if it's okay? It's nicer than we thought it would be. And Paul has pinecones to protect.'

'I am glad you're here then – it means the world.'

He finished the call and followed Christa into York. He wished he wasn't in something as large as the Bentley but he was hanging back and saw her park in a side street.

He parked and turned off his lights, watching her from a distance as she took large bags from her car boot and then locked the car and started walking up the street.

Jumping from his car, he shoved his hands into his pockets, wishing he had remembered his gloves and hat. The wind was bitter and his face felt tight from the ice he was sure was forming on his skin.

Where was she going? She turned and walked up a hill to the front of the library, to where there was a group of people crowded around a van, who all waved and shouted her name. She went to a handsome man and handed him the bags and he saw him put his arm around Christa and give her a squeeze.

He wasn't sure if he was jealous of the man but he didn't like how it made him feel. He didn't like how any of this made him feel.

And then the side of the van and the back doors were opened and people were putting on aprons and setting up small tables with food on them and what looked to be shopping bags of things and Christa was taking out containers from the bags and putting them onto the benches.

A man came from the shadows and nodded to Christa

and she handed him a package of her food and then a shopping bag of something. He took a cup of what looked to be soup ladled into a mug and some bread and sat away from the van as he ate.

A woman approached him and asked him some questions and then he saw her take his temperature and listen to his chest.

A man and his son came to the van next for soup, shopping, a smile, and some chat with Christa who beamed at them like a snowflake in the darkness.

A woman with a dog came for shopping and then bustled back into the night. People without enough food, not enough warm clothes, without support besides this van.

Marc forgot his chill and stood against a wall, watching them for the hour, and then the stream of people trickled away until there was no one left and they started to pack up.

He walked towards the van, arriving as Christa was taking down a foldable table.

'Anything left?' he asked.

'I'm sure I have something,' she said, looking up at him.

Her mouth dropped open.

'I believe you owe me some quail and ham hock,' he said with a smile and she promptly burst into tears.

16

'I will finish up tomorrow,' she said. 'And pay you back the money you gave me.'

'Why? That's ridiculous,' Marc said as he set their hot drinks down in front of them. The only place open was a fast food chain with Christmas carols playing and the smell of grease in the air. 'I am pretty sure I agreed to you doing something with the excess food.'

Christa couldn't look at him.

'But I should have been more open, transparent about it all. I might as well have stolen it. I've been underhanded,' she cried. She had stolen it. No matter how she tried and convinced herself otherwise, she had stolen the food and handed it out to people for free.

'You used what would have gone into the trash and you gave it to people who needed it more than me or you. There is nothing devious about it. You mentioned it to me and I said yes. Why are you so upset?'

Christa sipped her watery tea and grimaced.

'Is that face because of the tea or me?' he asked.

'Both.'

Marc smiled. 'Why are you so upset about this, Christa?'

She shook her head. 'I don't know. I feel like I should

have been more honest with you.' She sighed and slowed her breathing down. 'I think I was embarrassed to ask, like I was some chugger, leeching off the largesse of my boss.'

'What? What the hell is a chugger?' he asked.

'A charity mugger. Like those people who harass you in the street about famine somewhere or other while shaking a tin at you.'

Marc laughed. 'No, I don't think it's the same.'

Christa rubbed her temples and then looked at him.

'I'm a hypocrite,' she said.

'Why?'

'Because I was glib about your success and your wealth, yet I used it to help others without being totally honest with you. I turned up with meals for the people and didn't tell anyone they were made with your goods. I took the credit and didn't mention once that it's your food I'm using to feed people.'

Marc shook his head. 'It doesn't matter where it comes from though, and it doesn't matter who "owns" it, as long as it gets to the people who need it.'

They were quiet for a moment and then Marc spoke again. 'So, do you make a habit of being a food-driven Robin Hood?'

She thought for a moment, wondering how much she should tell him and then decided she had nothing to lose, not since he had caught her red-handed.

'I have always tried to help people the way I know how. Which is with food. I did it when I had the restaurant in a casual way, feeding people out of the back door of the kitchen.'

Marc leaned in, listening.

'And it made me happy to feed people – you know, with good nourishing food.'

'Okay.' He nodded in agreement. 'We help with what we have, I get it.'

'Then I came here and I finally had the time to help, really help. I had some time at night. So I did. I met this lovely old man at the market who made the fudge. He told me about the charity so I called, and next thing you know, I'm making vegetable soup and breadsticks and pasta and little delicious lemon cakes that are actually really healthy. They were very popular.'

She saw Marc smile at her and she smiled back.

'You know I spent time in soup kitchens and refuges as a kid. The food was a lifesaver when Dad wasn't well but the food was mostly donated or cooked for quantity not quality because that's all they could afford. I wanted to make people food that would help them from the inside.'

Marc was nodding. 'And you want to do that once you finish at Pudding Hall?'

She thought for a moment. For most of her adult life she had been overlooked, with Simon taking the credit for talent, but now her future was so clear, she could feel it.

'I do, I want to help people. I want to open a place here and make it low cost or no cost for people to come and get food. I want to give cooking lessons to people who haven't been taught how to shop and how to make meals that nourish and are affordable. I want people to be able to volunteer and chat and provide support for mums and dads and children. I want it to be the place where anyone can come and they will be fed, respected and supported.'

She finished her speech and then took a sip of her tea and was reminded it tasted like hot dirt water.

Marc sat back in his chair. 'And you want me to fund it?' he asked.

She looked at him and frowned.

'Not at all. I didn't ask. You asked me what I wanted to do and that is it. It was the first time I've actually been able to clarify it for myself but that's it; that's what I want to create. It might not happen soon – it might take ten or twenty years – but I will work towards it and hope it will happen. And meanwhile I will keep cooking for those who pay well and save what I can.'

Marc's face was unreadable.

'I'm not asking for your help at all, Marc. I am really sorry about the food. I will pay it back. I will replace the ham hock and quails tomorrow.'

He shook his head. 'I don't care about them. I don't. I get it. I get why you did it.'

He leaned back in his chair and ran his hand though his hair and then clasped his hands behind his neck.

'I had a shitty childhood. It was tough and we didn't have any help until the night my mother tried to kill my father.'

'Jesus,' said Christa.

'She failed,' said Marc. 'But we were taken away from our parents and then ended up in the system. My whole life, I have run away from my past, avoided doing anything that might make me feel anything other than successful and yet you, with your own shitty upbringing, you run towards it now. You're not afraid of it. You want to help.'

Christa said nothing as they looked at each other.

'So why do you run towards it when I run away? What are you looking for and what am I avoiding?'

She shrugged and smiled a little. 'I told you I'm not here to be your therapist.'

'I know, but it's interesting, isn't it? We have had similar struggles and yet we're coping with them so differently.'

She pushed her tea away.

'The difference is love,' she said.

'How so?'

'Because even though my dad struggled with alcohol, and we ate at refuges and used the food bank, I knew he loved me. I knew he hated himself but he loved me more and that was finally enough to make him stop drinking. But you, it sounds like you had terrible parents who didn't care for anyone but themselves. You weren't loved.'

She saw Marc's eyes fill with tears and she felt terrible for saying what she'd said.

'Sorry, that's not my call to say that. I shouldn't have said it.'

But he shook his head. 'No, you're right. They were narcissistic nightmares. They hated having children. We were a burden yet they kept having more. I sometimes wonder why people have kids if they don't like them.'

'Why did you have children?' she asked him.

'I wanted children and so did my ex-wife. It was exciting to find out we were having twins. But I wasn't a great parent. I haven't been but I'm trying to get better. Pudding Hall has been great for me to see them and do more with them. That's why I didn't worry about school while they're here; I just wanted to let them have a proper break. I mean, I know I'm full of shit because I've been working so much, but that's to avoid feeling stuff. I know I need to work on that more.'

Christa gave him a small smile. 'They boys adore you,' she said.

'They also adore you,' he replied. He waited for a moment and then leaned over the table. 'Can I come out with you tomorrow night? I'd like to help.'

'Sure, I think Zane said they're still a few people down so he would be happy with the extra pair of hands.' She stifled a yawn.

'Come on, home to bed. Want a lift? I can get someone to pick up your car tomorrow.'

Christa thought about the drive home in the dark, worrying that a deer might spring out from behind a tree and into the path of her car.

'That would be great actually,' she said.

The drive back to Pudding Hall was smooth in the large car and, in the silence, Christa felt her eyes heavy from the work and from crying. She shouldn't have cried in front of her boss. She told herself off as she watched the shape of the trees flash by her. Soon her eyes closed and she leaned her head back for a moment.

'Christa, Christa.' She heard her name whispered and she opened her eyes.

God, she had been asleep in Marc's car and she was pretty sure there was dribble running from one side of her face down onto her coat.

Seriously? She was a mess.

'God, sorry,' she uttered, as she undid her seat belt and wiped her mouth.

Marc held her hand as she stepped out of the car.

'Not really my best Princess Di moment,' she said, feeling herself hot with embarrassment.

'I was never into Princess Di,' he said. 'I was more of a Demi Moore fan.'

'Oh?' Christa was still holding his hand, wondering why she felt flickers of delicious anticipation inside her stomach.

'You know in *Ghost*? The short hair, big eyes, that laugh.'

Christa nodded, trying to think if she did know any of Demi Moore's traits and could they possibly be traced back to her.

Was she still dreaming? Was she still dribbling in the car?

And then the moment finished. Marc dropped her hand and turned away from her and closed the car door with a thud.

'Right then,' she said. 'I better get to bed. Pancakes in the morning, if you're up early enough.'

'I have a phone call at five am so I will be,' he said as they walked towards the house.

Inside they took off their coats and Marc locked the front door as Christa went upstairs.

'Goodnight, Marc,' she said. 'Thanks for being so understanding and supportive.'

He looked up at her. 'My hocks are your hocks; now Hammy Christmas to you and to all a good hock.'

Christa stifled laughter. 'That makes no sense.'

'I'm tired – throw me a bone,' he said as he climbed the stairs.

'I have a ham hock I could throw you tomorrow,' she said as she walked backwards down the hallway.

Marc walked backwards in the opposite direction.

'That's truly hocking,' he said.

'I aim to hock and awe,' she said.

'You're a hock star,' he answered and she giggled loudly.

'Goodnight, you big ham,' she said as she got to her door and smiled at him.

'Goodnight, Christa, the Robin Hood of Hocking Forest.'

She stepped inside her room and closed the door, taking a deep breath. She had no idea what was happening but it was fun and silly and wouldn't lead anywhere. She'd forgotten how much she loved to flirt and tease and play.

She lay on her bed and looked at the ceiling. Marc was great company when he stopped trying to take over the world and he listened when she spoke about her dream and didn't dismiss it.

She could imagine Simon explaining all the ways she would mess it up and how it wasn't viable and people should just get a job and pull themselves up out of the rut and get some control.

This from the man who had never had to want for anything; but Marc, she knew he understood. There was a look on his face when she spoke about being in soup kitchens as a child that she recognised. He'd known what it was like to be hungry once. He knew her dream mattered.

And she hadn't asked him for money. It hadn't occurred to her to ask him. She didn't have a plan or any experience in undertaking such a mammoth task. But she could learn and when she knew enough she could do it, one day.

Maybe Pudding Hall wasn't such a terrible idea after all. She could keep helping at the van and now that Marc wanted to help her, she could prepare even better food and wouldn't have to hide it.

When she was curled up in bed, about to drift off to

sleep, Christa remembered when she had dribbled in the car and groaned.

Seriously. She really wasn't the sort of woman Marc would like anyway, so why did she think there had been a moment between them? Why on earth would he want to kiss a ham-hock-stealing, quail-poaching, dribbling cook?

Sometimes she really didn't understand herself at all.

17

In the morning, Christa was prepared for the dressing-down she knew was coming when Peggy arrived for work.

The kitchen was prepared for pancakes and Marc was drinking coffee at the table and reading on his iPad.

'Morning, Mr Ferrier, Cook,' said Peggy as she took off her coat and hung it on the hook by the back door.

'Morning, Peggy,' said Marc and Christa together.

Peggy was about to leave the kitchen when Christa spoke.

'You mentioned the quail and the ham hocks,' she said and she saw Peggy's chin lift, as though ready for a fight.

'I forgot to tell you I made soup with them and then I took the leftovers to the St William's food van.'

She saw Peggy glance at Marc who didn't look up from his reading and then back to Christa.

'St William's you say?'

Christa nodded. 'Yes, there are many needy people this time of the year.'

Peggy nodded and looked at Marc again who finally lifted his eyes from the iPad. 'There were many out last night, weren't there, Christa?'

'Many. Hard times for good people.'

'You were there, Mr Ferrier?' Peggy cleared her throat

halfway through speaking, as though her tongue was tied in knots.

He nodded and sipped his coffee. 'And I'll be there again tonight,' he said.

'Tonight?'

'Yep.'

Peggy's mouth opened and shut for a moment.

'I meant to ask you what your recipe for shepherd's pie is. It would be a good healthy and filling dinner I can put it into containers, if you don't mind sharing?' Christa asked.

Peggy shook her head slowly like a carnival clown and Christa felt like popping a grape into her mouth from the fruit bowl.

'I will get the cleaners ready and then I will come and walk you through it,' she said as she walked to the door that led out into the main part of the house. 'I am pleased you asked me, Chef, very pleased.'

And with that Peggy had melted into a softer version of the iced character she had been minutes earlier. She left the room.

Christa looked at Marc who laughed. 'You now have to try and make her recipe into something edible. The boys said it was like paste.'

Christa held up her hands. 'Don't you worry about a thing. I have worked with some of the most egotistical chefs in Europe. Peggy will be a walk in the park.'

Marc stood up and put his coffee cup in the sink.

'Well, have a good morning,' he said.

'I'll try,' she answered and she wondered why she sounded like she was flirting.

Marc walked out of the kitchen and she adjusted the jug of maple syrup on the bench.

'What's for lunch?' she heard him ask and saw his head pop around the corner of the doorframe.

'Tomato soup and cheese baguettes.'

He nodded and then disappeared as she felt herself smile like a loon, alone in the kitchen.

'Anything for morning tea?' he asked, peeking around the doorframe a second time.

'Let me know if there's anything you would like. I can make anything you want.'

He was grinning at her. 'Anything?'

'Anything.'

He held her look and she raised her eyebrows at him, challenging him.

'Madeleines,' he said proudly.

'Madeleines?'

'Yes. I don't know what they are but I heard about them once from somewhere and that's what I would like for morning tea with coffee. Can I pre-order that, like a soufflé?'

'You can. See you at eleven.'

He disappeared again and she waited until she was sure he wasn't coming back and then she wondered if there was a madeleine tray in the house.

She searched through the tins and by some sort of miracle, there were two unused madeleine trays with the price tag still on them.

Oh, this was too much fun, she thought as she peeled off the stickers and washed the trays. If Marc wanted madeleines then he would get madeleines. All of them.

★

Marc sat at the table with Adam and Paul and the boys.

Along the centre of the table were beautiful serving plates of fine china in all shapes and sizes.

'Are these mine?' he asked Peggy, who was putting the coffee accoutrements on the table.

'Yes, Mr Ferrier, you have an expansive range of china for all occasions.'

Marc was nodding and looking about the table. 'Good to know,' he said.

Christa came to the table and smiled at him.

'You requested madeleines but you didn't state what sort of madeleines you wanted so I took the liberty of making a selection for you.'

Marc could see a glint in her eye as she used a clean wooden spoon to point a plate out.

'Do you know where madeleines originated?' she asked the table, doing her best schoolteacher impersonation.

'No, Miss Christa,' said Paul in a little boy's voice. The twins roared at his impression and copied him.

'Buckle up then, you're in for an exciting ride.'

She tapped the first plate. 'These are a classic madeleine, made by a young baker named Madeleine for the Duke of Lorraine. Yes, the same originator of the name of the quiche, which the duke was also a huge fan of. This duke loved his baked goods and he adored madeleines, so he took them to the French court where King Louis XV tried them and also adored them and, making them a part of the royal menu.'

She tapped on a pink scallop-edged china platter.

'There are madeleines filled with lemon curd, made with lemons from Pudding Hall's tree. They are delicious with tea.'

She saw the boys' hands creeping out and she whacked the wooden spoon onto the table, making them jump and then laugh.

'Madeleines became popular again in France after Marcel Proust wrote about dipping a madeleine in lime blossom tea and having a memory come back to him of being a child at his aunt's house and doing the same.'

She looked at the boys. 'Have you ever eaten something and had a memory of another time you ate it and what was happening back then?'

Seth frowned, his face in thought. 'Yes. I remember when we were eating oat pancakes and they made me gag and Mom and Dad were fighting. Now I can't eat oat pancakes.'

The table was silent.

'Okay, that went south,' muttered Marc but Seth was still thinking.

'I also think I will always remember the hamburger you made the first night you came here.'

'Oh? Really?' she asked, thankful they had moved on to happy food memories. 'Why is that?'

'Because Dad ate with us,' said Seth, smiling happily at Marc.

Marc grimaced in shame and he pulled Seth to him. 'I will always eat with you, buddy, especially Christa's hamburgers and chips.'

Ethan put his arm around Marc's neck. 'What are the other ones?' he asked.

Christa pointed to a yellow plate with little bees on it. 'These are honey and orange. And these—' she showed them a white plate with pink madeleines on top with icing sugar scattered across the plate '—are strawberry and lemonade flavoured. These are my favourite; I have a terrible sweet tooth.'

'Which one?' asked Ethan.

'Pardon?'

'Which tooth is sweet?'

Christa laughed. 'All of them.'

Peggy poured tea and Christa made coffees with the machine and soon they were sitting around the table, sharing cakes and chatting.

Perhaps this would be her madeleine memory, she thought, as she watched the way Marc moved the hair out of Seth's eyes while they were talking. It was a small gesture but so tender that Christa had to look away, moved by the intimacy between parent and child.

Sometimes she wondered what it would be like to love a child the way her father had loved her. Because even when he was unwell, she knew he loved her.

'It's nice to have you at the table, Peggy,' said Marc and Christa knew he meant it.

Peggy preened under his attention. 'I know I can come off a bit prickly at times but I mean well and I am thankful for you keeping me on here, Mr Ferrier.'

Marc sighed and shook his head. 'You're never going to call me Marc, are you?'

Peggy shook her head gravely. 'There will be a snowstorm in Tahiti before that happens, Mr Ferrier. I am very traditional and I like things the way I like them. I have never addressed any of my employers any other way than simply as it should be.'

After morning tea, Christa set about making the soup for lunch and cutting the bread while Peggy peeled the potatoes for the shepherd's pie. The two worked in synchronicity, not getting in each other's way, and Christa was grateful for the company in the kitchen.

There was some robust discussion about putting garlic into the pie until Christa told her Gordon Ramsay always put garlic into his pie, which convinced Peggy.

Not that Christa minded terribly. Peggy was so old-fashioned that Christa knew she thought only men should be chefs, which is why she called Christa a cook instead – apart from her brief concession earlier. It wasn't a hill Christa was prepared to die on; after all she would be gone soon and Peggy would have the kitchen and the rest of Pudding Hall back to herself again.

Christa's Madeleine Recipe

Ingredients

2 free-range eggs
100g/3½oz caster sugar
100g/3½oz plain flour, plus extra for dusting
1 lemon, juice and zest
¾ tsp baking powder
100g/3½oz butter, melted and cooled slightly, plus extra for greasing

Method

1. Preheat the oven to 200°C/400°F/Gas 6. Brush the madeleine tray with melted butter then dust with flour to coat, tapping out the excess.
2. Whisk together the eggs and the sugar in a bowl until frothy. Lightly whisk in the remaining ingredients. Leave to stand for 20 minutes before carefully pouring into the prepared madeleine tray.
3. Bake for 8–10 minutes, or until the mixture has risen a little in the middle and is fully cooked through. Transfer the madeleines to a wire rack and leave for a few minutes to cool slightly. These are best eaten within an hour of cooking.

18

This time Marc was prepared for the cold with a warmer jacket, a wool cap and gloves, and even thermal underwear on under his clothes.

Still, the wind hit him like a slap when he opened the car door for Christa.

'Thanks,' she said, moving around to the back of the car as he opened the boot where they had stored the food containers.

Marc picked up the bags with Christa's shepherd's pie, inspired by Peggy, the extra madeleines she had made and some healthy chocolate muesli bar slices.

'All set?' he asked and Christa nodded, carrying some extra shopping bags of supplies that she had picked up at the supermarket on the way into town: sanitary items, shower items and packaged food that could be eaten without a stove or an oven.

Marc had paid for everything even though Christa had tried to go halves.

'It's the least I can do,' he'd said, taking her purse from her hands and placing it back in her bag.

The van was setting up when they arrived and Zane met Marc with a firm shake of the hand, setting him to work serving stew and soup inside the van.

They worked for a few hours, occasionally chatting between waves of people coming to the van. Sometimes he saw her glance at him and he smiled at her and she seemed embarrassed to be looking but he knew he was doing the same. When she didn't notice him, he could watch her talking so easily and kindly to everyone she met. Her laughter with some of the people was like a bell and when she rubbed people's arms, in sympathy or empathy, he saw in her face her compassion was true.

He saw her hug an older man who kept patting her on the shoulder, and she took his arm in hers and guided him over to the van.

'Marc, this is Petey, my friend who makes the fudge. Petey this is Marc, who owns Pudding Hall.'

Marc put out his hand to shake and then realised he had a disposable glove on.

'Don't worry about it, young fella,' said Petey. 'I have been poorly for a few days but started feeling better when Christa brought me soup and cake. She's a keeper.'

'She certainly does like to feed people up,' he said. 'I've put on two kilos since she started.'

Zane called out to Christa and she left Petey with Marc.

'She's the most generous girl, and really wants to help people,' said Petey, smothering a cough.

'She does,' agreed Marc. 'I only found out she was doing this last night.'

Marc served a man some stew while Petey stood to the side of the doorway of the van.

'Did she show you the old pub I mentioned?' Petey asked.

'No, is she planning on going there or buying it?' he joked.

'It's where she should run her dining hall. She has a whole thing planned in her head. I told her about the pub and how it might be the right place, but I don't know if she's seen it yet.'

Marc tried to remember if she had mentioned a pub to him when she'd been talking about her dream but he was sure she missed that part.

'Where is the pub?' he asked, handing out some soup with a smile to an older woman.

'Down at the end of The Street, on the banks of the river.' Petey pointed in the direction of the river. 'Nowt been in it for a few years. Would be a fine place.'

Before Marc could ask any more, he saw Peggy walking towards the van, rugged up and ignoring everyone but Marc as she came closer.

'Soup or stew?' he asked. 'Or can I tempt you with some shepherd's pie – not sure where the recipe is from but it's getting good early press.'

'Oh you think you're a laugh don't you, Mr Ferrier?' Peggy scoffed. 'Since you said you and Christa were here, I thought I might be able to help out now and then.'

'Then you should talk to me,' said Petey. 'Peter Chandler, fudge stall owner at Shambles Market, widower, also part-time volunteer here.'

Peggy seemed to assess him from top to toe.

'Peggy Walker, housekeeper, divorced, and shepherd's pie maker for tonight's takeaway contribution.'

Marc wished Christa could see this moment but she was busy talking to Zane. He watched her laughing at something Zane was saying and he wished he could be the one making her laugh right now.

Petey was now showing Peggy the shopping bags of items they were giving out, chatting away while Peggy seemed to inspect everything with an eagle eye.

Christa came back to the van then. 'You okay?' she asked.

'Fine. What were you and Zane chatting about? He seemed to be making you laugh a lot.' As soon as he said it, he knew he sounded churlish and stupid and tried to fix the sentence.

'I should chat to him more – he seems like a nice guy.'

But Christa didn't seem bothered by his comment. 'He is – he's lovely. You should definitely get to know him better.'

Christa came into the van and stood by him, helping to serve as the next wave of people came by for supplies and company.

Finally, the people trickled off as rain began to fall. Petey and Peggy had said their goodbyes to each other and to Christa and Marc.

By the time everything was packed up and put away, and Christa and Marc were in the car, he was exhausted.

'It's intense work, isn't it?' he said as he started the car. 'And finishes so late.'

Christa took off her gloves and held her hands against the heater vents on the dashboard. 'It is but it's important. I don't mind it. I'm used to the late nights.'

Marc drove through the streets and then down towards the river where Petey had directed him. He had looked up the pub and the address on his phone during a break and saw the potential that Petey had seen.

'Where are we going?' asked Christa, looking around the area as he pulled up outside the pub.

'Why are we here?' she asked.

'Petey told me about this pub, said he had told you to look at it for your dining hall idea.'

Christa shrugged. 'Yes, I did look at it but I don't have the money or the experience to run such a big project. It would be irresponsible to think I could.'

'Why couldn't you?' Marc challenged. 'Anything is possible.'

Christa twisted her body towards him. 'I looked up how many charities fail. People have great intentions but don't have the infrastructure to do it successfully.'

'I could help you,' said Marc. 'I can fund it.'

'It's not about money.' She sighed. 'I know what I am capable of and I have limits. I can feed people and care for them and support them but this sort of work requires a really strong infrastructure with policies and processes. We are dealing with people's lives and mental and physical health.'

They sat in the car and looked at the pub, the moon high above them, shining a spotlight on the old slate roof.

'It's a great building,' he finally said. She was right of course. If she was to do this it needed to be done right. This was more than just funding some endangered trees, which was the kind of philanthropy he usually engaged in.

'It is,' she said quietly.

The need to hold her hand was overwhelming and he didn't stop himself. He took her hand in his and squeezed it gently.

'I have no doubt you will do this, Christa. You are a truly powerful woman.' She held on to his hand and squeezed back.

'And you are a very rich man who means well but has

to understand that money can only go so far, though I do appreciate the interest and support. It means a lot. My ex-husband didn't always think my ideas were good. Actually, he didn't like any of my ideas unless he was a part of them.'

The car was still running, and he felt warm and safe with Christa, just them against the world under the moon.

'Insecure people do that,' he said. 'Just so you know, I think your ideas are brilliant. In fact, I should offer you a role as my Chief Ideas Officer.'

She laughed but he noticed she didn't take her hand away. The need to kiss her was intense but he knew that was too much. She hadn't given him any signal she wanted to be kissed and holding hands didn't mean anything more than support in the moment. Anyway, what would happen after they kissed? he thought.

Yes he was interested in Christa, but it would have to wait until after she finished working for him. Only then would he ask her out on a date. Hopefully that was something she was interested in.

'Have you dated much since you split with your ex?' he asked.

She shook her head. 'No, I'm not much of a catch at the moment. Pretty jaded and angry with him and with myself for being so stupid.'

'Why? What did you do that was stupid?'

She pulled her hand away and crossed her arms.

'I let my ex take care of the business and I ended up with next to nothing,' she said. 'I was wilfully ignorant because I wanted to be looked after. I needed a break but it came at a cost and left me nearly broke. All those years of looking after my dad, paying the bills, making decisions when he was sick and drinking. Helping him back on his feet again only to have him die before I started at Le Cordon Bleu meant I wanted a break from being a parent to a parent. I did this to myself; it was a choice.'

'But still, what a prick.' And he meant it. He gave his ex the world and more when she asked for it when they split. Anything to keep her comfortable and the boys well cared for, though his ex had proven to be a less than present mother.

'It's okay; it is what it is. But I know I can't do any business again with a partner. It has to be me alone because I lost my power, my self-worth and my confidence and I miss it. I miss how I used to be.'

He saw her wipe a tear from her cheek and his heart ached for her.

'If I can do anything, Christa, I will, okay?' His promise sounded futile but he meant it. He would do whatever he could to make this pain go away.

'Just talking is good. Thank you.'

She took his hand again. 'After this is all over, this Christmas thing, and I don't work for you anymore, maybe we could be friends.'

Marc held tight and looked at the moon. 'I couldn't think of anything I would like more. Let's go home.'

There was some sort of energy between them he couldn't place. It wasn't just attraction but connection at a deeper level than he had ever felt with a woman before.

He cleared his throat, trying to find the right words.

'Actually, I would like to see you when Christmas is over, like properly, for dinner or something, one you don't have to cook.'

He heard her take a fast breath. Dammit, he shouldn't have asked.

'I would like that. I would really like that,' she said slowly.

He turned her hand over and traced the callus at the base of her forefinger. 'The chef's mark,' she said. 'From chopping.'

He touched a scar on her wrist. 'Burn mark from when I was an apprentice.'

'And this?' A feathery scar up the side of her hand.

'A fall off my bike when I was nine.' She smiled.

Marc held her hand up to his mouth and kissed the palm.

'I can't wait till Christmas is over,' he said in a low voice.

'Me neither,' he heard her whisper and he had never wanted anyone more than her in this moment.

'Let's go home,' he said and he drove them back to Pudding Hall still holding hands.

The lights were on when they arrived.

'It's two in the morning. Adam must be up,' he said as he turned off the car.

And then the front door opened.

'Are you fucking kidding me?' Christa said.

'What?' He looked at the people walking towards the car.

'That's my ex, Avian – no idea who the guy is though. Probably her new boyfriend.'

'That's my ex, Simon, oh God. Set me on fire and bury me under the house. Seriously, I cannot do this.' Her breathing was becoming shorter and faster, her voice tight. Simon and Avian were approaching the car and waving.

'Your ex-husband?' Marc asked.

'Yes, my stupid, selfish ex, who is the host of a new

cooking show – that's how he met her.' They were nearly at the car.

'Avian is producing it,' he said. 'I'm funding it for the new streaming network I'm buying.'

Avian knocked on the window. 'Hi,' she said, trying to peer into the dark car interior.

'I resign,' said Christa. 'Effective immediately.'

MAIN COURSE

19

Selene always answered Christa's calls, no matter where she was and who she was with and the two-in-the-morning call from a sobbing Christa was no exception.

'Sweetie, tell me what happened again? Simon, a pudding, the bird lady – it sounds like a fever dream or you ate too much Stilton.'

Christa took a deep breath. 'That woman at the restaurant, who was with Simon, she's the producer of the TV show. And she's Marc's ex-wife. And she brought Simon for Christmas.'

'Oh, okay, yes, that's bad.'

Christa tried to forget the moment she jumped from the car and ran inside, ignoring Simon and Avian, while Marc called her name and she heard Simon laugh. It was a mean laugh, one she knew too well.

Then she heard Marc come to her door and knock several times but she refused to open it, instead throwing her clothes into her bags and calling Selene.

'So now I have to go and live in Siberia and make pinecone jam for a living.'

'Pinecone jam? Is that even a thing?'

'In Siberia it is.'

Christa thought about Paul's attachments to his pinecones and started to cry again.

'And I think I like Marc, like, *like like* him' she admitted, sitting on the bed.

'Oh, that's intense. And how does he feel?' asked Selene.

'We held hands and agreed to not do anything until after Christmas.'

'Somewhere Jane Austen is nodding her approval.'

Christa lay back on the bed. 'I can't stay with Simon here. It's humiliating.'

'You like Marc and he likes you and yet you want to leave because of Simon. When are you going to stop letting this idiot control your life, Christa?'

Part of her wanted to hang up on her best friend and the other half knew she was right.

'He forced you to leave the restaurant. He gave you nothing. He took credit for all your signature dishes. Why don't you ask him if he wants to date Marc and then you can just get it over and done with? Since you've given him everything else in your life.'

Christa covered her eyes with her hand. 'Ouch, that hurt.'

'It was meant to,' said Selene. 'Do what you have to do but please stop changing your life to suit Simon's agenda. You're better than that and better than him. Okay?'

'Yes, okay,' she mumbled.

'Call me tomorrow and let me know what you have decided to do but you know what I think and you know I am right because you wouldn't have called me and asked otherwise. You knew the answer all along.'

After hanging up, Christa pulled on her pudding PJs and was sat on her bed thinking about what Selene had said when there was a knock at the door. She opened it, expecting Marc but instead it was Adam in a dressing gown and with tousled hair.

She hadn't had much to do with Adam. He was intimidating with his business-like manner but when he drank a glass of wine and laughed, he was almost fun. But she liked Paul and she knew Paul liked her.

'Hi?'

'Marc tells me you want to leave,' he said, rubbing his eyes.

'Come in, I don't want this broadcast to the house.' She opened the door for Adam to step into her room.

'Sit,' she said, gesturing to the sofa while she sat on the end of the bed.

'Are you here to ask for the deposit back?' she said. 'I can arrange it. I haven't spent anything.'

'Not at all. Marc said I should pay you in full if you want to go.'

Christa frowned. 'Okay?'

'Marc doesn't know I'm here, but I want to talk to you about him. About Avian. I am overstepping boundaries but there are things you should know.'

Christa sighed. 'This is where you tell me that Marc is still in love with Avian and I am merely a pawn in their shitty toxic marriage and Simon is being used a decoy and I should be aware that I will never win and nothing is real.'

Adam's face was shocked. 'What the hell are you talking about?'

'Isn't that why you're here?' Christa was so tired she honestly did think she was having a fever dream now.

'No.' Adam started to laugh and tried to quiet himself. 'What sort of cheesy romance novel storyline have you just concocted?'

Christa couldn't help see the funny side also. 'I don't know, it seemed legitimate when I was saying it.'

Adam shook his head. 'If this chef thing doesn't work out then become a romance writer, okay?'

She giggled and then became serious. 'So why are you here then?'

Adam waited for a moment, as though gathering his thoughts.

'Marc is falling in love with you. I have no doubt about it and neither does Paul, and we have known him for twenty years.'

'He hardly knows me,' said Christa. 'And besides, if he is falling in love with me, why is he sending his lawyer to tell me? That's not your story to tell.'

'That's the thing, he doesn't know he's falling in love with you, so I don't want you to go.' Adam took a deep breath. 'Avian is a stone-cold bitch who uses people and then discards them when they're done being useful to her. Marc was useful because of his money but then she was tired of being a parent, tired of being a wife, tired of being nothing – according to her – so she left Marc and the boys. He does ninety per cent of the time with them. He's not perfect but he tries. But since you've been here, he's actually spending quality time with them and working less, which I could take or leave, but still, he's present. And it's because of you.'

She shook her head. 'Me spending time with him and the twins doesn't mean he's in love with me.'

Adam crossed his arms. 'I challenge that statement and I put it to you that he can't keep his eyes off you. That he talks about you when you're not around and that he looks at you in a way he never looked at Avian.'

Christa was silent.

'Do you know the number of women who throw themselves at him?'

Now she looked up. 'I don't care. Are you trying to suggest that I should be grateful that the rich handsome American is even looking at me, the round, nearly broke, pastry chef?'

Adam stood up. 'No, it means that he chose you and I want you to wait and find out if you want to choose him, because he's a helluva guy and you're a great woman and together you could be amazing.'

He walked to the door and put his hand on the door handle.

'If you want to go, message me in the morning and I will arrange payment, but I hope you don't because more than Marc, the twins will be devastated. They also adore you. You have won the Ferrier men's hearts.'

He left then, closing the door quietly behind him, and

Christa fell into bed, closing her eyes, where she prayed for dreams about anything other than Marc and Pudding Hall as she drifted off to sleep.

20

The sound of the twins laughing echoed down the hallway as Marc walked towards the kitchen.

Could he hope that Christa had stayed?

As he pushed open the door that was already slightly ajar, there she was.

Wearing a cream woollen knit and pink lipstick, she glowed as she served the boys strawberries and fresh yogurt on their pancakes.

'Morning,' she said cheerfully and he caught her eye and saw her smile at him like she had before this all happened.

'Mom's back,' said Seth, his mouth full as he spoke.

'And she brought a total douche with her,' said Ethan as Christa turned away from them, trying to stifle laugher.

'Don't say douche,' said Marc half-heartedly.

'Pancake? Scrambled eggs and bacon? Omelette?' she asked as she turned on the coffee machine.

Marc walked behind the kitchen bench and came to her side, taking down two cups from the cupboard above him and placing them on the bench.

'You stayed,' he whispered.

She was silent but he felt her hand on his, lingering for a moment, as she took a cup before making him an espresso.

'You look beautiful today,' he said. 'The pink suits you. I also like your pink coat when you wear it – it makes me happy.'

She blushed and handed him the coffee. 'Someone once told me I looked like a blancmange when I wore it.'

'I don't know what that is but I am assuming it's not a compliment, and I can guess who said it,' he said, shaking his head.

As though he'd summoned the devil, the kitchen door opened and Avian waltzed in wearing exercise clothes and a smug expression.

'We went for a run,' she announced, checking the watch on her wrist. 'Five miles, pretty good considering we have had zero sleep.'

Simon staggered through the door behind her, gasping for breath.

'Here comes slow coach,' said Avian. 'He's on a diet. He needs to lose weight so I am working with him to get him camera-ready. You can't be fat for TV – the camera puts on ten pounds.'

Christa's back was to them but Marc saw her shoulders square defensively.

'So, he has to lose weight so he can eat food on TV?' he heard her say. 'That sounds ironic.'

'Yes, it is ironic I guess,' said Avian as Christa turned around and Marc saw his ex laugh a little at Christa as she looked her up and down.

'Babe, can I get an egg-white omelette with wilted spinach, thanks,' she said and sat at the table, glancing at the boys.

'Pancakes? I hope that's a treat and not every day.'

'It's not,' said Ethan.

'Yesterday we had French toast made with... Christa, what was the bread?'

'Brioche,' she answered with a sweet smile at the boys. 'With caramelised bananas and whipped cream.'

Avian made a disgusted face. 'Can you not feed my children that crap?'

'Hey, Ave, don't call it that, and it's their holiday so they can have some treats,' Marc said.

'I just don't like sugar, or carbs,' Avian said looking Christa up and down. 'They make you fat.'

Marc wished they could go back to before Avian and Simon were here, when it was just him and the boys and Christa.

'Mom, do you want to come and see the chickens after breakfast?'

'You might see some of your birdlike friends,' he heard Christa mumble to herself and he tried not to laugh.

'Chickens? No thanks. I thought we could go into town and you can choose your Christmas presents.'

The boys looked at each other and Marc was sure he saw a hint of disappointment.

'Finish your breakfast, kids, and I'll go down with you. I wanted to see more of the garden anyway.'

Avian was already on her phone, tapping and scrolling like her life depended on it while sipping hot water that she had demanded from Christa.

Simon was sitting at the table now, his breath recovered.

'This is funny – seeing you here, Christa. Never saw you as a house chef. Must be good pay.'

Christa put two plates of egg-white omelettes in front of

Avian and Simon, which looked as appetising as a bowl of drool.

'Perhaps if you hadn't cheated me out of my share of Playfoot's, I wouldn't be here,' she said and Marc glanced at her.

'Don't be bitter. My parents invested more than us – they deserved a bigger pay-out.'

Christa went to the stove and plated up pancakes and bacon for Marc. She handed it to him and then looked at Simon. 'I am not speaking to you about this here, or at all, actually. It's done.'

Marc sat opposite Avian and he noticed she looked at his breakfast with a longing he had never seen during their marriage.

'Do you want some?' he asked, cutting off some bacon and pancake and dipping it in syrup. He held it out on the fork for her to taste.

She shook her head and took a forkful of her omelette.

'No thank you,' she said, but he saw she watched every mouthful he took.

They ate in silence, including the boys, who seemed to read the room and figure out that this wasn't a group meant to be together for any amount of time.

Paul walked into the kitchen and looked around. 'Nope,' he said, turning back around and then Marc heard him call, 'Adam, we're going out for breakfast.'

Christa was banging pots and pans about the sink when Peggy came in the back door and took off her coat.

'Morning, all,' she said and then looked at Avian and Simon.

'You must be the boys' mother. Hello, Mrs Ferrier, I am Peggy, the housekeeper.'

Avian didn't look up from her phone. 'Great, can you get me some tampons, organic preferably, and get me a hairstylist to come to the house for the dates of the twentieth, twenty-fourth, twenty-fifth, and twenty-sixth. The water here screws my hair so I will need it washed and dried every day.'

Marc looked at Peggy. If he could have taken a picture at that moment, he would have titled it, 'Disgustedly astonished in situ'.

He saw that Christa noticed it also, and she was hiding a smile.

Peggy looked at Marc as though waiting for permission and he gave it, nodding slightly.

'I don't buy women's intimate health items and I do not believe there will be a hairdresser who will give up their Christmas and Boxing Day for you. You can try but I don't know anyone here who can assist you with that. I am the housekeeper; I am not a concierge. Though if you can't wash and dry your own hair by now, I am happy to give you a lesson. A woman your age should know these basic life skills. Now if you will excuse me, I have to go and supervise the window cleaners.'

She turned on her heel and left the kitchen, with Avian's jaw flapping in shock.

Marc handed her the fork with some bacon and pancake on the end, dripping in butter and syrup.

'Taste?' he coaxed and Avian, unthinkingly, took the fork and ate the food, chewing slowly.

'Who the fuck was that?' she spluttered at Marc.

He stood up from the table and pushed the plate towards her to finish it off.

'That was Peggy, the one woman you don't want to make a bad impression on, but sadly I think that horse has bolted.'

'Christa, boys, let's see what Bill has in the garden for us today, shall we? You in?'

The boys jumped up and ran to get their coats and hats, while Marc took Christa's pink puffa from the hook and held it out for her to slip her arms into.

'Thank you,' she whispered as she turned to face him and he smiled at her.

He still wanted to kiss her and he wished this Christmas was over, but this time it was for different reasons.

'Come on, Dad, let's go,' yelled one of the boys, opening the kitchen door, and the cold air came inside with a rush.

'Let's go,' he said, recovering from his moment with Christa. 'First one to the maze is the winner.'

21

Avian and Simon's self-absorption knew no boundaries. After offending Peggy, Avian then told Paul the decorations were upsetting her allergies and that she thought the styling of the house for Christmas was too busy. Simon was always in the kitchen telling Christa how to cook whatever she was cooking and speaking loudly when Marc was around about the reviews for the restaurant and how Avian had seen his potential during a small appearance he made on a travel show talking about English food.

Christa spent three days hiding in the pantry whenever Avian came into the kitchen, demanding Christa make her fresh almond milk or kefir or sweet potato crisps. Not that Christa was against any of the food Avian asked for; it was the way she asked.

'I don't think she knows the words please or thank you,' Peggy agreed as they chatted over a pot of tea during the afternoon.

'She won't stop calling me babe,' moaned Christa.

Pudding Hall was temporarily peaceful.

The boys were out with Avian, choosing their own Christmas presents, which Marc had argued against over dinner the night before, saying it ruined the surprise.

They boys hadn't argued but were also unenthusiastic when they headed out in the car to York, with Simon driving Marc's Bentley.

Now Marc and Adam were upstairs working and Paul was antiquing in some of the surrounding villages.

'He's an odd fellow your ex-husband,' said Peggy, as she poured the tea into the fine china cups. Christa had also made them a simple teacake with cinnamon and sugar topping, the butter dripping down the side into little caramel rivulets that pooled on their plates.

Christa scoffed. 'That's a kind description.'

Peggy pushed a cup to her. 'I mean he's an odd choice for you.'

'I suppose. He's very charming. I think I was initially seduced by his charm and confidence.'

'Charming is as charming does,' said Peggy with a scowl. 'I was married to a man like Simon.'

'I didn't know you were married,' Christa said.

'Because I come across as an old spinster?' Peggy answered, with a small laugh but it wasn't a bitter laugh, Christa thought.

'No, maybe, I don't know,' Christa said. 'You're very guarded. It's hard to know you.'

Peggy stirred her tea, the spoon making a sweet chiming sound as she tapped it lightly against the side of the cup.

'Before I worked here, a long time ago, I owned a hotel in Manchester with my husband.' She paused, as though dragging up the memories to the surface from the deepest parts of her mind. 'Oh, he was handsome and charming, just like Simon, but how he lied. That man couldn't lie straight in bed. Always another woman, gambling, debt, and even a child I didn't know about until we were married.'

'I'm sorry, Peggy,' said Christa, hoping to hell Simon didn't have a child she didn't know about.

Peggy shrugged. 'It's been ten years since we divorced, and I ended up with nothing but that was enough. I had my freedom and my truth. I was sick of being told I was the weak one in the relationship, that I would have nothing without him.'

Christa nodded, understanding where Peggy was heading with the story.

'That man you married is a chameleon, becoming what people want so he can get what he needs. He sucks you up and then turns you into ashes, taking all your fire and spark.'

Christa felt her eyes burn with tears ready to spill, and Peggy put her hand on her arm.

'Don't let him take anything away from you now, not when I see the light around you when Mr Ferrier is nearby.'

The tears fell then and she looked up at Peggy, her unlikely friend. 'Can you see it?'

'That you like each other? Yes.' She smiled.

'But I'm just a cook and I'm working for him.'

Peggy shook her head and ate a piece of cake and then wiped her mouth with a linen napkin.

'No, you're a chef and a very good one. You're probably twice the chef your ex is.'

Christa didn't answer, though she knew it was true. Everything Peggy said was accurate and more.

'Also, I wanted to thank you for introducing me to Peter. We're seeing a film on Thursday night.'

Christa was shocked. 'You aren't! That's amazing.'

'It's a film, not a trip to Paris – no need to overreact,' said Peggy.

'I'm not overreacting, I'm happy he and you are friends. You're both lovely people.'

'He's lovely; I'm less so but somehow we get along.'

Christa giggled. 'Perhaps that's the key. Balancing each other out. Like good food, the flavour is all in the balance.'

They finished their tea and cake in comfortable silence.

Finally, Christa stood up. 'Speaking of which, I need to start cooking. I have to do a meal for Avian and Simon and a different one for the rest of the family.'

'Surely she can just have some chicken feed in a bowl. It's organic, vegan and good for birds,' said Peggy with uncharacteristic humour.

Christa laughed, thinking of serving Avian the food as a healthy snack. Part of her wanted to do it but she never would. Avian was a nightmare but she was also the mother of the boys, whom Christa adored.

While peeling potatoes for dinner, stuffing chickens and preparing the salads and vegetables, Christa thought about what to make for Avian and Simon. She knew roast chicken was Simon's favourite meal, especially this recipe where she had brined the chickens the night before so they were so tender and ready for roasting.

This was one of their signature dishes at Playfoot's, and one Simon had taken the credit for over and over again.

Kale and tofu would suffice for Simon and Avian, with some cauliflower rice on the side.

Of course, she would try and infuse flavours to make it more enticing but she laughed to herself at the thought of Simon watching everyone else eat the delicious chickens while he ate the tofu, which she knew he loathed.

Once dinner was prepared, Christa thought about dessert. Now this was becoming fun, she decided. Making things she knew Simon adored eating, knowing Avian wouldn't let him have them was almost like a sport now.

Oh she knew what it would be that would absolutely ruin him. She checked the pantry for the ingredients and then closed the door, feeling pleased with herself.

Tonight's dinner would be fun, and she could show Marc some of her best cooking while also showing Simon what he was missing.

Brined Roast Chicken

Ingredients

> 1 x 1.6kg/3½lb chicken
> 2 lemons, sliced
> 1 tablespoon extra-virgin olive oil
> Sea salt and cracked black pepper

Brine

> 1 small bunch fresh bay leaves
> 2 tablespoons black peppercorns
> ½ cup/150g/5.3oz rock salt
> 1 cup/175g/6oz brown sugar

1 cup/250ml/8fl oz malt vinegar

3 litres/100fl oz water

Method

1. To make the brine, place the bay leaves, peppercorns, salt, sugar, vinegar and water in a large saucepan over high heat.
2. Bring to the boil and cook, stirring, for 4 minutes or until the salt and sugar have dissolved. Remove from the heat and set aside to cool completely.
3. Tie the legs of the chicken with kitchen string and place, breast-side down, in the brine. Cover and refrigerate for 4–8 hours.
4. Preheat oven to 200°C/390°F. Place the lemon slices onto a large oven dish lined with non-stick baking paper. Remove the chicken and bay leaves from the brine, discarding the brine liquid. Place the chicken, breast-side up, on top of the lemon with the bay leaves. Drizzle with the oil and sprinkle with salt and pepper. Cook for 45–50 minutes or until the chicken is golden brown and cooked through.

22

'Wow, that looks incredible,' said Marc as she placed the platter of chickens onto the table.

It wasn't a full Christmas dinner but a practice run, she and Peggy had told each other but when she had mentioned to Peggy that she had wanted to show Simon what he was missing out on at dinner that night, Peggy had risen to the occasion. She had set the table in the dining room for eight, with napery and silver cutlery and some sprigs of holly and ivy in the centre of the table. The fireplace was crackling at the end of the magnificent room and the glassware sparkled under the chandelier and candles on the table.

Soft white rolls waited patiently to be torn apart in silver baskets at either end of the table. Pats of butter with the Pudding Hall crest pressed into them lay in cold glass dishes. Salads in glass bowels and crisp, roasted potatoes in silver serving bowls. There was a dark gravy and bottles of red wine already decanted.

And then there was the bowl of kale and tofu with the cauliflower. There wasn't anything wrong with it. Christa had tasted it and it was all fine, tasty in fact, and probably Avian would be more than happy with it, but she knew Simon would struggle with the choices being made for him.

She was surprised Simon hadn't bitten back at Avian and her running and food regime so far. He must really want to be camera-ready and famous.

'This is like something from a magazine,' said Paul. 'I should get *House and Garden* or *Architectural Digest* here and do a shoot after you go back to the US, Marc. Christa, Maybe you can come and cook for the shoot. We can do a set-up like this.'

Christa looked at Marc who didn't look up at her. Going back to the US? Is that what was being discussed and she didn't know about it?'

'Sure,' she said, trying to keep her voice light.

Simon sat scowling at the end of the table with Avian, looking at the platters and bowls in front of him.

'Perhaps you can be an on-set caterer for film and TV, maybe Avian can get you a gig,' he said. Christa wanted to throw a bread roll at him for being so condescending.

Thankfully Avian shook her head. 'No, I don't think so; besides, you couldn't have this sort of food at craft services. No one I know eats like this.'

Christa sat next to Adam who gave her a look of sympathy.

'Eat up then,' she said, trying to maintain some sense of self-esteem under Avian's withering gaze.

'What did you get in town today, boys?' she asked.

Seth and Ethan were very quiet around their mother, watching her adoringly but also careful, as though she might vanish at the slightest sudden movement from them.

'Um,' said Seth. 'We got some Lego, video games, nerf guns and bikes.'

'Bikes – that's great, what a good idea,' she said.

'That was my idea,' said Simon looking at Marc. 'Kids

should have bikes for a place like this, otherwise it's pretty boring.'

Marc raised his eyebrows and Christa saw his jaw twitch. 'Thanks for the advice. They were on the list for Christmas from me but I will have to get something else now.'

'Anytime, old fellow – if you need more ideas let me know. I had a very happy childhood; parents didn't let me want for anything.'

'Explains a lot,' whispered Adam to Christa who smiled as she handed him a bowl.

'Roast potato? They were cooked in duck fat, so they are very decadent. Delicious with the gravy. And make sure you take a roll to mop up the gravy at the end. Such a good thing to do.'

Christa swore she could feel Simon's eyes boring holes into her as she handed the potatoes to Marc who thanked her and smiled.

She felt her stomach flip and then fall when she remembered Paul's comment about them returning to San Francisco.

Marc poured the wine for them all and offered some to Simon and Avian.

'We can't,' said Avian. 'Makes me bloat.'

Simon's face was thunderous. 'I can have half a glass,' he muttered, toying with some tofu on his fork.

'No you can't. We shoot in a month and I showed you how jowly you looked from the trailer shoot.'

Christa looked at Paul who made a face, and mouthed the word *ouch* at her.

'You don't need to bring up my jowls here,' Simon snapped.

'That reminds me,' said Christa, knowing she couldn't help herself – it was just too easy a pass to make. 'Do you remember that lovely lemongrass pork jowl we had in Thailand?' She looked at Avian. 'In Thailand, pork jowl is similar to the pork belly that's so popular in China. Fatty and tasty.'

'He could work on his belly also,' said Avian meanly.

For a moment she felt sorry for Simon, being fat-shamed by Avian in front of everyone but then she remembered he was just as mean, albeit much subtler about it.

The dinner was delicious, and Christa thanked Adam and Paul for keeping the mood light at their end of the table, interrogating the boys about Lego and challenging them to a building competition another night.

When they had finished eating, Christa stood up.

'Now if you can assist in clearing the table, I will get dessert ready for us. It will take fifteen minutes but it will give us time to let this meal settle.'

Simon was sneaking a potato while Avian was looking at Christa. 'Dessert? No thank you. Simon and I don't do that.'

'Hang on,' said Simon, trying to swallow the potato whole so Avian couldn't see his duplicitous act.

'What is it?' he asked.

'Chocolate molten lava cake with raspberry coulis and Chantilly cream with a scoop of French vanilla ice cream I made today.'

'Get out of town,' exclaimed Paul. 'I will have Simon's if he can't eat it.'

Avian stood up. 'Thank you but no thank you. Simon?'

Reluctantly Simon stood.

'Thanks for the kale and tofu,' he said, glaring at Christa.

'If you want yours later, I will leave it in the refrigerator. You can heat it up in the microwave.'

'No, he won't. It's bad for you,' Avian instructed. 'I will come and see you after dinner,' she said to the boys, who were looking from adult to adult like it was a tennis match.

'Go and play, boys, and I'll call you for dessert,' said Marc.

Adam, Paul and Marc cleared the table, laughing in the kitchen about Avian and Simon.

'He looks hungry,' said Adam.

'He is hungry,' said Marc. 'He looked at that chicken like he was about to propose to it.'

Christa laughed. 'He is starving, I know he is. I'm betting that that molten lava cake will be gone in the morning.'

'Avian will probably put a lock on the fridge,' Paul said.

'I feel a bit mean,' admitted Christa. 'But Avian's approach to food is so damaging. I'm not sure the boys should be indoctrinated by her weird rules and phobias.'

'What do you mean?' Marc asked.

'She calls food good and bad all the time. Food is morally neutral. You can't eat like this all the time as it's not healthy but you can have a meal like this and enjoy it and know it's a sometime event.'

The men listened keenly as she spoke.

'If you are given choices with every meal, you will find kids choose a balance. A plate of fruit with some good quality chocolate will be taken from equally. The children will take a strawberry and chocolate. A few berries, a little watermelon and so on and then maybe some chocolate again. If weighed in the balance it would be equal.'

She paused, choosing her words carefully so she didn't upset Marc about the boys.

'Being too rigid in anything can be damaging, is all I'm saying.'

Marc sat at the kitchen table.

'Avian is rigid, that's for sure.'

'And Simon will rebel. It will start with the lava cake and then explode into something bigger. It's only a matter of time,' Christa said as she put the individual ramekins into the oven.

Adam and Paul left the kitchen to drink their wine in front of the fire.

Christa avoided looking at Marc as she set up the items for dressing the cakes when they were out of the oven.

'Are you okay?' Marc asked. 'It must be really awful for you with them being here.'

Christa stirred the berry coulis. 'It is what it is.' She said but the truth was every moment around Simon was unbearable. Her anxiety was back, and she kept waking in the night in a sweat, and had started to twist her hair at the crown when she didn't realise, only to stop when she felt some of it coming out in her hand. But she wouldn't say that to Marc, he would think she was fragile and useless.

She thought about what Adam said about Marc and her, and she looked at him.

'Are you going to go back to America after Christmas?'

Marc was silent for a moment. 'I don't know, to be honest with you. The boys have friends there and I share custody with Avian.'

She nodded, and looked down at the bench.

They were talking about things that seemed so far away

but so important and yet they didn't know anything about each other. It was silly.

'Would you come to America? To visit?' he asked.

She shrugged. 'I don't know.'

They looked at each other until finally Christa broke away.

Everyone was living in a fantasy, she decided, and the only reality was the people on the street who needed help, who didn't have a choice of which country to live in, or which wine to drink.

'Probably not,' she said as she turned on the oven light to check the cakes. 'America doesn't interest me. I think I will stay here and see if I can't get a job working somewhere that helps make a difference. That's what interests me.'

But she knew she was lying. She would have gone to America if she loved Marc but it was too much of a risk to assume anything anymore. She wasn't about to give up her new freedom for another man and lose herself again.

She turned around to gauge Marc's reaction but he was gone and she was speaking to an empty chair.

I guess he didn't want to find out, she thought as she started to clean up the bench. Not that she blamed him. Who would wait for her anyway?

23

Adam turned the laptop screen around to show Marc the figures.

'If we buy the network with *Blind Baking*, then the price goes up enormously.'

Marc sat in thought.

'Does Avian know you're thinking of buying the service?'

Marc shook his head. 'No, she doesn't.'

'Or you can buy without the show, cut them loose and save a bunch of money and still meet your goal.'

He rubbed his temples and then sighed. 'I don't want to pay that much, to be honest. The show isn't worth it; it's a risk. We already have *The Great British Bake Off* and *MasterChef*. Has Avian signed with Cirrus?'

'She said she has but I haven't seen the papers yet,' admitted Adam.

Adam looked back the screen.

'Find out if you can.'

Marc stood up and went to the window where he saw the boys riding their bikes around the paths. It looked freezing but their faces were red and healthy and he could hear them yelling out instructions to each other. He was glad they had them early, even if they were Simon's idea. It was good to see them outside and being active instead of being in front of the screen playing video games.

'Christa asked me if I was going back to the States,' he said.

'And your answer was?'

'I said I didn't know,' he answered honestly. 'I like her, I would like to get to know her but my life is there, not here. I can't see how it would work and I don't want to uproot everything for it not to work out.'

He turned to Adam who was leaning back in the chair listening intently. Having worked with Adam for ten years, he knew that his counsel would be wise and considered and always put Marc's interests first.

But Adam said nothing.

'Well, what do you think?' Marc felt frustrated at the lack of response from his friend and business adviser.

'What does it matter what I think, you will do what you need to do.'

'What sort of a stupid answer is that?' Marc was frustrated now. He wanted Adam to tell him what to do so that he didn't have to make the decision himself. And Adam always chose business, which would mean Marc would be back in San Francisco for the start of the next year.

'You are asking me if you should go back to America or stay here and pursue the spark you have with Christa?'

'Yes, yes I am,' Marc said.

'I am not telling you what to do about that. That's a personal issue,' said Adam.

'You had no qualms four years ago, when you told me that you thought Avian and I should separate.'

'Because she's abusive – to you, to the boys, to people she

works with. She's an awful person who hasn't changed at all since you divorced. In fact, I think she's become worse. You see how different the twins are around her compared to when it was just you and Christa spending time with them.'

Marc was quiet now. Everything Adam said was true. Avian was toxic and nasty and he might have escaped it but the boys hadn't. They had changed and he worried for them.

'I can't take them away from their mother.'

'I'm not saying you should, I am merely pointing out you have an opportunity to explore things with Christa and can keep the boys here for a while longer and let them decide where they want to be.'

Marc sat back at his desk and stared at his computer screen.

Adam was right, as usual.

'Did you look into the other thing I mentioned, in town?'

Adam nodded. 'Yes I emailed the papers to you this morning.'

'Great, now let's get back to this deal. I want it sorted by Christmas, which is only a week away.'

After Adam had finalised the paperwork for the offer for the network, Marc walked through the house looking for Christa but she was nowhere to be found, and we looked outside he saw her car was gone.

He wondered where she was and called Peggy, even though it was her day off. What if Christa had gone?

'Mr Ferrier?' Peggy answered. He could hear music and talking in the background.

'I am sorry to call. I know it's your day off but do you know where Christa is?'

'She said she was going to the Shambles Market.'

Before she could say any more, Marc had shoved his phone into his pocket, pulled on his coat and grabbed his keys.

He had no idea where Shambles Market was but he could find it, he was sure.

York was busy when he arrived and he saw people milling around with baskets and trolleys of food and more.

'Excuse me, which way is the market?' he asked a man with a baby in a carrier on his chest.

The man directed him while his hand caressed the baby's head and Marc tried to remember whether he had been that tender with his sons. They had been raised largely by nannies because he was working and Avian was working on a career, which he respected, but he wished he could do it all again and make it better. Love the twins better, tell Avian to be a better parent. Tell himself to be a better parent.

He walked the streets towards the market, noticing every family, every couple of every age. People enjoying their time together, having coffees and laughing and looking at the market stalls. He wanted to be a part of it all and he wanted one person with him.

As he walked past a stall, he saw Peggy in an apron offering a plate of something to passers-by.

'Peggy?' he said.

'Hello, Mr Ferrier, you found it I see.'

Petey from the van waved at him. 'Fudge?' asked Peggy, holding the plate in front of him.

'No thanks, I need to find Christa. Have you seen her?'

Peggy shook her head. 'Have you called her?'

'I don't have her number,' he said, feeling stupid. He'd never had any reason to call her until now.

Peggy pulled her phone out of her apron pocket and handed him the platter of fudge.

'Hold this,' she said, and scrolled through her phone and pressed send and he felt his phone vibrate in his pocket.

A market goer walked up to Marc and took a piece of fudge from the plate, then stood there chewing at him.

'What's the flavour?' asked the man.

Marc looked at Peggy. 'Flavour?'

'Peppermint and dark chocolate,' said Peggy, slipping her phone back in her pocket and taking back the platter.

'There's a lovely strawberries and champagne one also, if you like something lighter.'

Marc called Christa's phone while he watched Peggy sell several packets fudge to the man.

She was a truly a gem, underneath her disapproving disposition.

Christa's phone went through to voice mail and he hung up without leaving a message.

What would he say? He didn't even know what he would say if he saw her in person; he just wanted to see her.

As if he'd manifested her, he spotted her pink jacket, then her white wool hat with the pom-pom on top and he called out.

She turned and looked around and then saw him and

smiled, a tentative smile but not a scowl, nor did she turn away.

He made his way through the crowd and came to her side.

'What are you doing here?' she asked, her face pink with cold and her nose red. He wanted to kiss the tip of it but instead he took the bags of shopping she was carrying from her.

'I wanted to see you,' he said.

'Why?'

People passed them in the market but he felt they were all spinning around them and only he and Christa were still.

'I don't know, I just wanted to be with you.'

She bit her lip, as though trying to stop herself from smiling.

'Was there something you needed to tell me? Something I needed to buy? Rhubarb, perhaps? I could make you a lovely apple and rhubarb strudel. I know how much you would love that.'

'No, thank you,' he said. 'I would prefer something else,' he said.

'What would you prefer?' she asked and he knew they were flirting now.

'You,' he said and he saw her take in a sharp breath and then she breathed out slowly.

'What do you mean?'

'Christa, we like each other, perhaps it's more than like for me. I want to know you and I want you to know the boys. I'm going to stay here after Christmas so we can get to know each other like normal people. I'm not going to go back to America. I can put the boys into school here for a while. It would be good for them.'

Christa looked down at her feet and scuffed her boots on the cobblestones. 'It's impossible to get to know you when both our exes are in the house with us.'

'I know but we can ignore them until they leave, can't we?'

Christa laughed but there was no joy in the sound.

'This is sport to Simon. He is constantly baiting me, needling me, making me feel less than adequate. I thought I left that when we split but no, it seems I am still in his web.'

'He can't make you feel anything you don't want to, and you shouldn't listen to him,' he said. 'I can tell Avian to go if you want?'

But she held up a gloved hand.

'I can't tell you to tell Avian to go because she's the boys' mother, but you have to understand, I can't stand Simon being here. It's exhausting and stressful.'

Simon interjected. 'Then I'll tell her to tell him to leave. If she wants to see the boys then she'll stay. I have no idea why he's here anyway. I had no idea they were even dating.' He put his hand on her arm but she pulled away

'Please don't. You don't owe me that. She is the boys' mother, that means something. We are just an attraction that would probably never happen if I wasn't in the close confines of the house with you. Our worlds would have never crossed otherwise.'

'Don't say that, I sound like some sort of horrible emperor.' He shook his head at the thought

But Christa had stepped back away from him.

'I just want this whole thing to be over. I can't do this

game-playing with Simon and Avian using us as pawns in their emotional chess match.'

'I'm not playing games, I'm just telling you I like you. I want to get to know you better.'

Christa paused, and he could see her choosing her words before she spoke.

'I can't tell you what to do with your ex-wife, but I know I can't be around Simon for any longer than I have to. I don't want to tell you about my marriage yet but there is pain that is real and raw and I'm not strong enough to see him like this, day after day.'

Marc wanted to hold her and keep her safe from whatever that man did to her during their marriage but he knew that wouldn't heal anything.

'I'll ask Avian and Simon to go then,' he said.

'And then the boys don't get to spend Christmas with their mum. That's not fair on them or on her,' she answered.

He looked down at the ground and tried to think of a solution. He should be good at this. He was successful in business with a mind for strategy, so why was it so hard to work out how to keep everyone happy?

'Christa, tell me what to do,' he pleaded, but instead she took the shopping bags from his hands.

'I'm not your therapist,' she said, walking past him and into the crowd of Christmas shoppers.

He watched her go and wondered if he should follow her but he knew it would be pointless. There was something there he couldn't heal. It had to come from her when she was ready and he could only hope it would be soon.

24

Christa drove her car to the pub by the riverside, wiping tears from her cheeks with her gloved hands.

She wanted Marc to tell Avian to leave but she would never ask that. She never understood why some men couldn't see mean girl behaviour in women. Avian was the ultimate mean girl, whose main purpose in existing was to make other people feel bad about themselves, but Christa also knew that people like Avian had stuff happening in their lives to make them like this. She tried to cut Avian some slack but it was hard.

Avian didn't seem to really care about the boys the way Christa expected her to. She treated them as though they were an accessory, making them pose for photos with her and then telling them to go away. Then other times she could see her looking at her children wistfully, lovingly. Christa never knew what the woman was thinking and didn't care enough to ask but she prayed she would leave sooner rather than later.

But deep down this wasn't about Avian. She could blame her all she liked but this was about Simon. How he bullied her through their marriage. Belittled her and gaslit her constantly until she doubted her ability to even choose her own clothing. Nothing she did was enough for Simon and he was still in her life chipping away at her self-esteem.

She parked her car and looked at the pub. At least she could still dream about what she would do with the place. She had even thought about bringing Zane down to show him her vision.

And then she saw the sign.

Sold.

She started to sob. She knew it wasn't the only place to build her vision but she had been so attached to it because Petey had told her about it, and because she had shown Marc.

Putting her head on the steering wheel, she cried properly for the first time since she and Simon had split. She cried for her choices and naivety. She cried for her dad. She cried for losing herself to Simon. She cried because she wanted something different than this right now and she cried because she wanted to be with Marc and the boys but Avian would never let that happen. Not when Avian and Simon were a couple. Avian would always be in Christa's life if she was in Marc's life.

There was no way she could escape the mother of the boys and nor should she.

When her sobs finally subsided, she wiped her face and looked in the rear-view mirror. She looked like she had run into a wall but that would go. She would lie down when she got home but first she had a call to make.

'Peggy? Can I ask you a favour? I'm not feeling well, and I'm wondering if you can make a shepherd's pie for the house. Really? You have one in the freezer? Amazing thank you.'

At least dinner was sorted, she thought as she drove home.

Dinner conversation was non-existent as Christa served Peggy's shepherd's pie to the table.

'Is this your version of a shepherd's pie? Or Peggy's original?' asked Marc, looking at the dish.

'Peggy's,' said Christa not looking at him as she handed a plate to Seth.

'It's gluggy,' said Seth, poking it with his fork.

'Shhh,' said Marc. 'It looks very hearty.'

'Hearty makes me farty,' said Ethan, putting extra emphasis on his complaint with a huge pretend fart.

Seth laughed and then joined in.

Christa spooned two servings of the potato topping into bowls then handed them to Avian and Simon.

'Pie, no shepherds,' she said.

'I can't eat this,' said Avian.

Simon, however, looked thrilled to be having carbs. He poured tomato ketchup on top and started to eat like a Siberian prisoner.

'Excuse me? What is this shit?' Avian pushed the bowl away.

'It's Peggy's dish, so if you don't like it I suggest you speak to her,' Christa said and went behind the kitchen bench and wiped the surface with extra gusto.

'Marc, what is going on?' asked Avian. 'You shouldn't let the staff speak to you like that.'

Marc looked at the boys.

'Boys, you can go and order a pizza and eat it watching some TV, okay?'

'Thank the Pope,' said Ethan.

'Where did you learn that?' asked Marc, looking around the table.

'Peggy,' said Adam and Paul at the same time.

'Can we also go and order a pizza?' asked Paul. 'No offence, Christa, but I think my dinner is forming a gelatinous skin.'

Marc nodded as Adam and Paul fled the kitchen, while Simon took their bowls and shoved the food into his mouth.

'Why did you bring Simon here?' Marc asked Avian.

Avian looked unfazed.

'We're in a relationships,' she said.

'You have dated other men and never even bought them to coffee, let alone Christmas. Did you find out Christa was cooking for us?'

She said nothing.

'Did you?' asked Simon, pausing for a moment from the great shovel fest he was having.

'I heard she was good,' said Avian. 'The boys mentioned her and I recognised the name.'

Avian seemed to suddenly be very interested in her cuticles.

'Simon, did you know?' Christa asked.

'Yes,' he said, wiping his mouth with his napkin. 'But I didn't think it would be a problem since you are only the help.'

'The help?' Christa heard her voice become louder but

she couldn't stop the fury from exploding inside her. 'You absolute classist wanker.'

'Don't be so pissy Christa, it's not a class thing.'

Christa looked at Marc. 'Anytime anyone in Britain says it's not a class thing, it's a class thing.'

'I wanted to find out more about you,' said Avian suddenly.

'Why?'

'Because the boys won't stop talking about you. Because all Simon does do is talk about you, constantly. I had to see what I was up against.'

Christa looked at Simon who seemed to be nonchalant about the revelation. 'I do talk about you but not in the way you think,' he said to her.

Christa shook her head in disbelief.

'I don't love you, so don't worry about that,' he said to Christa.

'That's fine. I don't love you either,' she said, speaking truthfully.

Simon kept speaking with his mouth full, shoving in potato.

'I talk about you because I saw great potential in you but you never met it,' he said. 'I tried to push you but you couldn't do it. That's why we divorced, because I couldn't keep investing in potential with no reward. I was tired of carrying you.'

The fury Christa felt was unlike anything she had ever known.

'Oh. My. God,' she yelled. 'Me? You carried me? Are you kidding me? All I did was let you take credit for everything

I did. The menu, the desserts, the sommelier we brought on, the soufflé that got us the hat.'

'That soufflé was my recipe,' he said to Avian and then turned to Marc and continued to speak. 'We're using it in the TV show. The contestants have to recreate it and I'll blind-taste it and chooses the best one.'

'It wasn't your recipe, it was mine, and carefully designed; it was a project to make that as perfect as it was,' Christa said, trying not to cry from frustration.

'No, it was my recipe,' Simon insisted.

'No, it was mine. My soufflé was always better than yours. That's why you made me make it for A.A. Gill when he came in once.'

'I didn't make you, you wanted to impress him.'

Christa gasped. 'The way you bend the truth to suit the way you want the wind to blow is astonishing. I made the better soufflé and you can't admit it.'

Simon laughed meanly. 'Christa, just admit I was better and then we can let it go.'

She glared at him and then she put her hands on the table.

'Then we will both cook, in tandem, and Marc will decide. He will be the blind-baking judge of Pudding Hall.'

'That's ridiculous,' scoffed Simon.

'Is it? If you believe you are the better chef then prove it. Marc won't know who cooked what and then we can just let it go and you can rest knowing you beat your ex-wife in the final round of our relationship.'

Simon stared at her. 'Fine, bring it on. I look forward to

proving my point to you and you finally seeing you would never even be here, cooking for a billionaire, if it wasn't for me. I also look forward to your apology when Marc chooses my soufflé. And the sight of you waving goodbye when you leave Pudding Hall.'

'You want me to leave if you win?' she asked, incredulous at his nerve.

'Yes.' Simon sneered at her.

'So you agree to leave if I win?' she said.

'Absolutely.'

'Fine,' she said. A warm feeling of satisfaction knowing he would soon be gone came over her body. 'Bring it on.'

He stood up from the table and drained the wine that Adam had left in his glass.

'I'm going to bed. Goodnight,' he said and he left the kitchen with Avian scurrying after him.

Marc looked at Christa. 'Why the hell did you rope me into judging this? I don't even eat soufflé. I always choose the affogato.'

Christa felt her blood start to simmer down with Simon's departure.

'I needed someone more powerful than him. He's easily impressed by money and success; your word would be final. He's actually really chauvinistic.'

Marc scoffed. 'You think so? He's like something from the 1950s; it's kind of bizarre to see such old-fashioned ideals.'

Christa sighed and leaned back in her chair. 'He makes me so furious. I shouldn't have taken the bait.'

'I get it. They know us and they know where to place the cuts, because they know where the old wounds are.'

They were quiet as they sat in thought.

'So, can you win?' Marc finally asked.

Christa looked him in the eye and a knowing look crept over her face. 'Absobloodylutely.'

25

The next day Simon charged Peggy with buying the ingredients for the soufflé bake-off, which would take place that evening.

'Of course, he's too lazy to go into town,' said Christa as she finely chopped chives for the mushroom soup she was making for Avian.

'This air in this house is so tense I could carve it up and serve it for lunch,' said Peggy as she folded napkins and wiped down the table from breakfast.

Christa had not spoken to Marc as he seemed to be hiding in his office. Simon was also missing in action but not Avian who had announced she needed selenium and mushrooms would be the only remedy.

'If Mr Ferrier chooses the other soufflé, then I will have to make my shepherd's pie for their Christmas lunch,' said Peggy.

Christa slammed her knife onto the bench and turned the cutting board around.

'He will not win. Trust me on this. He never gets the egg white consistency right. He rushes it like he rushes everything. He's half-arsed, lazy, selfish.'

She chopped furiously, thinking about all the times Simon put himself first.

'You know, the thing with Simon is...' Peggy stopped speaking, as though catching herself.

'Tell me. What where you going to say?' Christa asked.

Peggy's opinion mattered to her because it was hard-earned. The respect Christa had for the no-nonsense woman was strong and the more she saw her work ethic the more she liked her, especially since she knew she and Petey were becoming friends.

'I don't know you well enough to say anything that you don't know yourself.'

'Tell me,' Christa said. 'I want to know what you think.'

Peggy straightened the pile of napkins on the table.

'I think we can pretend things are okay because we want them to be okay. We can overlook and overlook until finally we can't ignore it anymore.'

Christa listened.

'If your ex-husband hadn't asked for a divorce, would you have stayed in the marriage?'

Christa couldn't speak because she knew the truth.

'Stability means a lot to a girl like you, I see that. Whatever happened to you in your childhood has meant you stay places now because you are afraid of not knowing what will happen next. But the familiarity can eat away at you until there is nothing left, my love.'

Christa felt tears fall. She had never been so fully understood by anyone.

Peggy reached across the table and held her hand.

'You have one life, Christa. Chase after what you want. No matter what it is.'

She nodded, unsure what exactly Peggy was referring to but she knew Peggy saw something in her was smouldering.

KATE FORSTER

'Do you mean Marc?' she asked.

Peggy shrugged. 'Marc, York, the van, the restaurant. Peter told me. Whatever it is or if it's all of them, you have to trust your talent and ideas and capacity to love.'

Christa nodded, feeling herself about to weep.

'I might go for a quick walk,' she said. 'Just to clear my head.'

Peggy nodded. 'And I am off to change the sheets in Avian's bedroom because she says they are too hard. Princess and the Chick Pea, I tell you.'

Christa took her coat and hat from the hook and slipped her feet into the boots by the back door.

'I won't be long,' she said and she smiled at Peggy through her tears. 'You're the best part of Pudding Hall,' she said to her friend.

Peggy tilted her head to one side and made a thinking face. 'So far,' she said, and then she walked out of the kitchen, clearly proud of having the last word.

A peacock passed Christa on the path, ignoring her and pecking at the wet grass. Bill wasn't anywhere to be seen and the garden was quiet apart from the occasional sounds of the birds.

Of course, Peggy was right. She was so busy trying to be safe in her life after her dad died that she forgot to take risks. The last risk she had ever taken was going to Le Cordon Bleu and asking them to take a chance on her. Then Simon took over their life and her talent and she let him.

She walked further than she had before, down through the manicured paths, until she came to what looked like

218

a dell. Nothing was blooming and the naked trees were sleeping but it was still beautiful. She sat on the woven willow seat, thankful for the length of her coat against the wet wood.

A crack of sticks made her turn and she saw the stag on the edge of the wood.

She stayed still. The stag watched her for a while and then decided she wasn't any risk to him.

He walked about the dell, occasionally munching on bark and then moving on to the next tree or the grass on the ground.

He was magnificent. Proud, so big. The antlers were works of art and the red coat glowed in the winter light.

She thought about the little deer she found in the Christmas cracker when she was a child, and the night she saw the deer when she arrived and then the deer family Christmas decoration that Marc gave her.

She wasn't a superstitious person but surely this had to mean something?

'What do I need to learn from you? From this?' she whispered.

The deer ignored her and she felt silly for asking a creature who could easily kill her what it was there to teach her.

Fear, she thought, it was here to teach her fear. But she knew fear. She had been afraid all her life. Of what people thought of her. Of taking risks. Of claiming her ideas and pulling back from Simon and asking for support and recognition. But when she looked at the animal, she wasn't afraid.

As though understanding her, the deer ambled away as slowly as it had come into her view.

She had to stop being afraid of her possibilities. Anything was possible if she wanted it and worked hard enough for it.

Standing up she brushed off her coat and straightened her shoulders.

She would win the soufflé competition and Simon would go away and she would tell Marc exactly how she felt and everyone would live happily ever after.

She just had to have a little faith and the best cultured butter and bittersweet chocolate she could find.

26

Seth stood on a kitchen chair. He wore a red plastic top hat while Ethan stood next to him wearing a green glittery top hat.

Paul had bought them from the pound shop as a joke but the twins loved them and insisted on wearing them for their roles as scrutineers for the soufflé competition.

While the twins through it was great fun, Christa had never been more determined to win at anything in her life.

Even her finals at Le Cordon Bleu didn't raise her adrenaline like this moment.

Everything was set out on the benches.

Exactly the same metal bowls. A double-boiler saucepan. Ramekin. A handheld mixer each, which Peggy had bought new so they had the same one of the same make. And the ingredients.

These were the only differences.

Christa had chosen a different butter and chocolate. She had kept her eggs at room temperature while Simon's were in the refrigerator. She was surprised he did this but maybe he forgot that cold eggs don't get the same peaks as room temperature ones.

'The soufflés will be made at the same time. They will

be taken into the judge's room by us, and the tasting will be done. The decision will be made. And the winner of the soufflé competition will be announced.'

Christa took a quick breath in and then let it out slowly, trying to calm her nerves.

Marc wasn't in the room. He was sitting alone in the dining room, at the insistence of the boys, who said he needed to be far away so he couldn't cheat.

'The judge will choose his favourite dish and only then will we discover whose is whose,' said Seth, reading from the paper of rules that Adam had helped him write.

'Is there a prize?' asked Ethan and Christa saw Avian and Simon glance at each other.

'We will decide that after,' said Avian, sneering at Christa.

'The soufflés will be served on the same plates so there will be no disting, disting, disting...'

'Distinguishing,' prompted Adam.

'Between the dishes.'

Seth turned to Christa and Simon.

'Chefs, your ovens have been heating, so you may now start your soufflés.'

Christa went to work.

First she buttered the soufflé dish with the cultured butter that Peggy had found from a farmer nearby. Then she sugared the inside of the dish, making sure she didn't miss a single part of the china, knowing the best rise came from a complete coverage of sugar.

Putting the dish aside, she started chopping up the dark chocolate she had found in Petey's kitchen.

He told her he had the best bittersweet chocolate and he was right. She took a block of Belgian but he gave her another. 'Just in case,' he said. 'Not that you will need it but you will feel safer.'

He was right: she did feel safer with the extra block.

She chopped up the chocolate as fine as she could, wanting it to melt smoothly and at the same time.

She saw Simon tipping his dark chocolate buttons into the double boiler saucepan and putting the water on to simmer.

You wouldn't get the same melt with buttons, she thought but she wasn't about to tell him he was making his first mistake.

While the water was simmering, she separated her egg yolks and stood them aside with the whites.

Simon was now melting his chocolate buttons while Christa waited for the water to be at a gentle simmer and then she gently poured the chocolate into the top of the saucepan, sitting over the water. She stirred continuously, while she noticed Simon letting it sit for a moment, separating an egg and then stepping back and vigorously stirring the chocolate again, breaking down the lumps.

If she was supervising him as an apprentice, she would have told him to throw it all out and start again.

Focus, Christa, she told herself. *Put into the soufflé everything you feel and love.*

She stirred slowly, coaxing the chocolate into a smooth stream, watching it dissolve with each turn of the spoon.

She thought about Marc and the boys. She thought about when Marc's hand held hers or when the boys told her she looked pretty in her woollen hat. She thought about Petey and Peggy and their friendship and she thought about the old pub. Even though that hadn't become hers, everything else was beautiful and special. Whatever happened with

Marc, she knew she would stay in York now. It felt like home more than London ever had.

After taking the saucepan off the heat, she let the chocolate cool slightly while she put cream of tartar into the egg whites and then turned on her beaters. As the soft peaks began to form she put in a tablespoon of sugar as she beat the mixture, and then rested it for a moment.

Then she went back to the chocolate and tipped in the eggs yolks and salt and whisked them together.

'All okay, Christa? Need a hand?' asked Simon and she resisted the urge to throw an egg at him.

'Fine, thanks,' she said. 'I hope you have your bags packed already.'

Simon laughed as though she had just told the greatest joke in the world.

'I should pretend I'm on the show already, shouldn't I? I could talk my way through what I'm doing for you all.'

'Please don't,' said Christa. 'You voice will make my egg whites drop.'

Christa heard Paul laugh but she ignored it and Simon went back to whipping his eggs whites.

When the sugar was dissolved in the egg whites, she then brought the chocolate to the bench. She whisked in some of the egg whites to lighten the mixture and then gently folded in the remaining egg whites. *Light touch, light touch*, she thought as she remembered the times Marc had held her hand, touched her arm, the looks she saw him giving her when he thought she didn't notice.

She then carefully put the mixture into the prepared dish and expertly ran her thumb around the inside of the dish to create a small space between the soufflé and the dish.

'Ready?' she asked Simon who was now pouring his mixture into his dish.

'Any moment,' he said and she turned down her oven to the baking temperature she needed for such a delicate dish.

She opened the oven and took the baking sheet from the floor of the oven that she had placed there earlier and put the soufflé onto a baking tray, as did Simon.

And then she slid it into the oven, and closed the door.

'Twenty-five to thirty-five minutes,' he announced to the kitchen.

Christa suddenly felt sick. She wasn't sure if it was the close proximity to Simon's ego or the nerves she felt.

'I need to go outside,' she said. 'I need air.' She pushed past Simon and out the back door.

The boys and Paul and Adam rushed out behind her. 'Do you need a doctor?' asked Adam, pulling his phone out of his pocket.

'No, I just need air,' she said and sat in the cold, on the bench by the back door.

'I'll get you some water,' said Paul.

'It's okay, I promise,' Christa said, as the boys sat on either side of her.

'It's cold out here – go inside,' she said to them but Seth took her hand and Ethan the other one.

'Do you want some Skittles?' whispered Ethan, pulling out a packet and shaking them at Christa.

'Your mum better not see those,' she said.

'Peggy got them for me,' whispered Ethan. 'She lets me have things, just like you do.'

Christa pulled him to her in a little hug.

'Thank you, Ethan,' she said.

'Boys, come inside,' she heard Avian say as she tapped on the window behind them.

Reluctantly the boys stood up. Christa felt the packet of Skittles being put into her hand and Ethan looked her in the eye.

'Take one every fifteen minutes, and you will feel better soon, I promise.'

27

Marc sat alone at the dining room table. He felt stupid and nervous. This idea of Simon's was ridiculous. But he knew Christa would win. Simon was one of those men who thought near enough was good enough, and he was sure that Simon wouldn't put in the same hard work that Christa brought to everything she did.

He had watched her and the boys work on the gingerbread house of Pudding Hall, meticulously icing all the window frames and the front door and then individually icing the slate roof, each slate shingle outlined and then filled in one by one. He wasn't sure how much he and the boys had helped but she was encouraging of them all.

Hi phone rang and he answered it.

'Marc Ferrier,' he said, not recognising the phone number.

'Hi, Marc, it's Trent Blake from *The Hollywood Reporter*.'

'Okay?' he asked carefully. He and Adam were trying hard to keep their takeover of the streaming service quiet until the sale had gone through.

'I heard that your ex-wife and producer of *Blind Baking* has sold her show to Netflix, will this affect the deal for Cirrus?'

'I don't know what you're talking about,' he said and hung up the phone. He called Adam from his phone.

'We need to talk,' he said and he soon heard Adam coming into the dining room.

'Shut the door,' he said.

'How's Christa going?' he asked, not being able to help himself.

'She's okay, had a little turn and we had to take her outside.'

Marc stood up. 'I need to see her. Did you call a doctor?'

'She doesn't want one, just said it was the masculine toxicity from Simon's ego that was upsetting her balance.'

Adam smiled and Marc felt somewhat better.

'I just had a call from *The Hollywood Reporter*. They said that Avian has sold the show to Netflix. If that's true, Cirrus will lose most of its value.'

Adam sat down. 'Shit? Really? I thought she had signed. She said she had signed.'

'I need you to look into this, because if we lose *Blind Baking*, we lose a huge drawcard for onsell.'

Adam was already tapping on his phone. 'Let me send some emails and make some calls.'

Christa couldn't understand it. She had done everything perfectly for the soufflé but the rise wasn't there. It smelled okay but didn't have the same richness that Simon's was emanating when they had taken them from the oven.

'Look at that,' said Simon proudly as he carefully took the dish from the oven.

Christa followed suit and nearly cried at her soufflé. She had put everything into it and this was all she could manage. It was okay, it was passable but it wasn't anything like she had expected.

'I hope your bags are packed,' Simon sang as he dusted the dish with icing sugar and put a small bowl of cream on the side.

Christa felt tears prick her eyes as she dusted hers with sugar and put some cream on the side. The dishes were moved to serving plates and the twins stepped forward to take them to Marc.

'Off you go, boys,' said Avian, looking smug.

Christa leaned against the bench and sighed.

This was the worst soufflé she had ever made and she simply couldn't understand it at all.

She had cooked with love, with the best ingredients and had been detailed in every way in her technique and measurements and she had a soufflé that wasn't half of what Simon had produced.

She untied her apron and put it on the counter.

'You off to pack?' asked Simon and she turned to him. 'Wasn't one of your finest ones,' he said.

She looked at him, wondering what she had ever seen in him.

'Oh bite your bum, Simon,' she said and she went upstairs to pack.

The knock at the door came and Adam opened it for the twins who were standing solemnly with their plates.

Each one with a soufflé and cream and the name of the twin carrying it was written on a piece of paper in their handwriting, taped to the plate.

'Come in,' Adam said and Marc watched them carefully carry the dishes to his side.

'We can't tell you whose is whose,' said Seth.

'I know,' said Marc. 'You can go now.' He smiled at the boys as they left the room.

He looked at the dishes. One was considerably taller than the other and the scent was delicious.

That was definitely Christa's he thought. He tasted it and then took another bite. And then another.

'Don't eat all of it – you will feel sick,' reprimanded Adam.

'This is seriously good.' He gestured to the soufflé. 'Do you know who cooked which one?' he asked but Adam shook his head.

'I didn't see them come out of the oven,' he said. 'And I wouldn't tell you anyway. It's attorney-client privilege.'

'She's not your client,' said Marc.

Adam tilted his head and raised his eyebrow. 'She might be if she murders Simon. I don't think I've ever seen anyone loathe someone the way she loathes him.'

Marc took a spoonful of the other soufflé. It was okay but not amazing. He tried the other one again and then one more spoonful of the smaller one.

'My decision is made,' he said and he pushed back the chair.

'Should I call the contestants?' he asked Adam, unsure what the protocol for this situation was.

'I'll ask them,' he said.

Marc walked out into the foyer of the house and saw the tree, the light hitting the deer family that Christa had placed proudly on the branch.

He saw some red and green wrapped packages under the tree. He bent down and saw the gift tags.

To Marc, Merry Christmas from Christa. One for Seth, Ethan, Adam and Paul and even Peggy and Bill and Meredith. When did she put these here?

He heard voices and Simon and Avian came from the kitchen, laughing and kissing like teenagers.

Christa was standing at the top of the stairs, her bags by her side.

'What are you doing?' he asked her as Adam and Paul came to the foyer.

'I'm leaving. My soufflé was a failure,' she said and he heard her voice break.

'No, yours was amazing. I chose yours,' he said looking up at her. 'I would know your cooking from anyone's. You cook from the heart.'

'Which twin's name was on your plate, Christa?' asked Simon but Christa was already walking down the stairs.

Marc looked at Adam to do something but he threw his hands up in surrender. He clearly didn't know what to do any more than Marc did.

Christa was lugging her suitcase and another travel bag with her, and she dropped them with a thud on the floor when she came to the bottom of the staircase.

'I just need to get my knives and a few things that are mine from the kitchen and I will go,' she said to Marc.

'But, Christa, I chose yours,' he said, wishing he could just hold her and have the rest of the watchers leave them alone.

'You didn't. You chose the one with Seth's name, didn't you?' Her eyes searched his face and she saw the truth.

'Yes,'

Simon jumped up and down, doing fist pumps into the air. 'Yes, yes, winner. I'm the winner,' he hissed at Christa and then tried give a high five to Avian who, to her credit looked embarrassed by her boyfriend.

'Shut the hell up,' Marc said to Simon.

Christa walked to the kitchen and Marc followed her.

'You don't have to leave. I don't want you to go. It was a stupid deal made by Simon – you don't have to follow it.'

Christa turned to him, her eyes streaming tears.

'I made the deal. I agreed to leave, just as he did.'

'You don't have to go,' he pleaded but she shook her head angrily.

'I do. I agreed with Simon and besides, I can't deal with him anymore. You don't think he will lord this over me like some psychopath? He will, trust me. He's horrific and abusive in his small pathetic way. And if I stay, then Avian leaves and the boys don't get to see her for Christmas. I can't do that to them.'

She went to the bench, collected her knives, pulled out a leather roll and put them each in their place and then rolled and tied it up.

'Avian won't leave. I'll talk to her,' he said.

Christa stopped looking through cupboards and looked at him.

'I don't want you to talk to her. I want to be as far away from her as I can. She's as bad as him.'

Marc was silent. He had let Avian get away with so much during and after their marriage because it was easier than asking her to be a better parent when he knew he was also found wanting.

Christa had small crepe pan and her knives in her hands.

'That's me then,' she said. 'Don't worry about the balance of the money. I don't want it.'

She walked out of the kitchen to the foyer where Marc followed and saw everyone standing looking upset except for Simon. Even Avian looked concerned but probably because she knew that Marc would be furious, he thought.

'Boys, I have something under the tree for you but you can't open it until Christmas morning, okay?' Christa said.

Seth's lip trembled as Ethan openly started to cry.

'But we haven't finished the gingerbread house,' Seth said.

'Your dad can help; he's a dab hand at it now,' Christa said and she hugged the boys and then stood up.

'Paul or Adam, do you mind helping me with my bags?'

Marc rushed forward but she waved him away.

'Thanks but Adam has it,' she said and she turned to Avian and Simon.

'Merry Christmas. Well done on the win, Simon. I guess you were the better cook all along. Thank you for teaching me this lesson. I needed to remember some humility.'

And then she was gone, out the front door and into the cold.

'At least she finally saw the truth,' said Simon to the room and Marc simply couldn't help himself; he turned and punched him as hard as he could, sending Simon flying into the Christmas tree. The decorations scattered and smashed across the marble floor.

'Now you've ruined Christmas,' Seth yelled at his parents.

'Don't look at me,' said Avian with her arms crossed. 'I had nothing to do with any of this.'

'You're both douches,' screamed Ethan.

'Bite your bums,' added Seth, his face red with fury and the boys ran outside as Marc heard Christa's car speed down the driveway away from Pudding Hall.

Christa's Chocolate Soufflé Recipe

Ingredients

½ cup/114g/4oz unsalted butter softened, plus more for coating dish

4 tablespoons/50g/1¾ oz granulated sugar, plus more for coating dish

225g/8oz bittersweet chocolate (60 to 65 per cent cacao), finely chopped

6 eggs, separated, at room temperature

Pinch fine sea salt

½ teaspoon cream of tartar

Method

1. Remove wire racks from oven and place a baking sheet directly on oven floor. Heat oven to 400°C (390°F). Generously butter a 1-litre or 6-cup soufflé dish. Coat bottom and sides thoroughly with sugar, tapping out excess. For the best rise, make sure there is sugar covering all the butter on the sides of the dish.

2. In a medium bowl, melt chocolate and butter either in the microwave or in a bowl over a pot of simmering

water. Let cool only slightly (it should still be warm), then whisk in egg yolks and salt.

3. Using an electric mixer, beat egg whites and cream of tartar at medium speed until the mixture is fluffy and holds very soft peaks. Add sugar, one tablespoon at a time, beating until whites hold stiff peaks and look glossy.

4. Gently whisk a quarter of the egg whites into the chocolate mixture to lighten it. Fold in remaining whites in two additions, then transfer batter to prepared dish. Rub your thumb around the inside edge of the dish to create about a ¼-inch space between the dish and the soufflé mixture.

5. Transfer dish to baking sheet in the oven, and reduce oven temperature to 190°C (375°F). Bake until soufflé is puffed and centre moves only slightly when dish is shaken gently, about 25 to 35 minutes. (Do not open oven door during first 20 minutes.) Bake it a little less for a runnier soufflé and a little more for a firmer soufflé. Serve immediately.

28

'We're going back to America,' Marc told the boys as they came inside after Christa left.

'No,' the boys cried and tears followed but Marc didn't listen to their protestations.

Simon had stumbled to the kitchen and Avian followed him.

'I'm calling the police,' she screamed at Marc.

'Good, please do, tell them I said hi,' he answered her as he took a packet of frozen beans from the freezer and put them on his knuckles.

'You go with Avian and I'll stay with Marc,' whispered Adam to Paul who had followed them to the kitchen but Marc heard him.

'I don't need babysitting,' he snapped at Adam as he took the stairs two at a time to his study.

'I'm not babysitting you, I'm seeing if you're okay,' Adam replied. 'You did just hit someone and screamed at your children and...'

'And?' Marc stood in his study and crossed his arms.

'Nothing,' Adam said.

'Bullshit, what were you going to say?' Marc demanded.

'Forget about it.'

Adam sat on a chair. 'So you want to go home? Want me to organise a plane?'

Marc didn't answer as he sat in his desk chair and looked outside at the grey day.

'I'm sick of it here anyway,' he said. 'I need some sun.'

He couldn't believe that wasn't Christa's soufflé. He swore he could have tasted anything she cooked and known it was her. There was something special about her food; it was thoughtful, not flashy yet elegant, just like her.

'Actually,' he said, not looking at Adam, 'you can put this place on the market. I don't think I'll come back here again.'

'Oh for God's sake,' Adam said. 'Stop this crap. Go and see her, talk to her. It was a stupid bet; it doesn't mean you won't see her again.'

Marc spun around in his chair, staring down Adam. He was furious at his feelings for Christa being so exposed when they were so new, so he did what any man would do: he denied and deflected.

'What the hell are you talking about?'

'Christa!' Adam cried.

Marc turned away from him again. He could see Bill in the distance, riding the mower towards the top fields.

'This isn't about her,' said Marc. It was mostly true but there was one thing he couldn't get over. That he was wrong. He was never wrong but apparently he was this time, about someone that meant more to him than anything else.

Adam sat in silence while Marc gathered his thoughts into something that wasn't a volcano that resulted in him using his fists on Simon again.

'She didn't have to go,' he said to Adam finally.

'She did,' said Adam. 'How can she stay here with that idiot around?'

Marc knew Adam was right but he didn't know how to fix it. He wanted to leave but he wanted the boys to have their mother here on Christmas Day and if he kicked Simon out then Avian would go too and the boys wouldn't have their mother for Christmas Day. If he asked Christa to come back he would be exposing her to Simon who was one of the worst men he had ever met – and he grew up in Las Vegas. There was always someone around with his father, making a deal, selling something at the pawn shop, talking up a new opportunity, wearing their flashy clothes and using their smooth patter and his dad was one of the worst of them.

He would sell his grandmother for a deal and he had no doubt Simon would sell Christa out for his own benefit.

'You know,' said Adam slowly, as though choosing his words carefully, 'this is the first time you haven't asked me to do a background check on a woman you're interested in.'

Marc laughed a little. 'I never even thought about it,' he admitted. 'I just wanted to get to know her in time, began to look forward to seeing her and getting to hear her opinions or learn about her life.'

There was a knock at the door and then Paul put his head around.

'Come in,' said Marc and Paul closed the door behind him.

'Simon is lying down in bed with a pack of frozen broad beans on his nose.'

'What the hell are broad beans?' he asked Adam.

'The opposite of string beans?' Adam answered, shrugging.

'Where are the boys?' asked Marc. 'I need to speak to them.'

'They are in their room, saying they won't leave and that they are writing a letter to Adam to ask for a divorce from their parents,' Paul said.

'Definitely. I can sue said parents also, if the boys want?' Adam offered but Marc ignored him.

He walked through the corridors of Pudding Hall, decked in boughs of holly and pine, with pinecones and red ribbons. Paul had done a lovely job on the decorations, maybe he could bear the next few days until Christmas and then head back to San Francisco for New Year's.

He knocked on the door of the boys' bedroom. They had one each but always ended up together planning grand schemes and whispering into the night.

'Go away,' he heard one of them say.

'Can we talk?'

'No,' the boys said in unison.

Marc waited for a moment and then leaned his head against the wall.

'I'm sorry I said we would leave,' he said. 'We can stay until the New Year.'

There was silence for a moment and then whispers that he could hear but not make out.

'Can Christa come back?'

He closed his eyes. 'She can't.'

More furtive whispering was heard and then a note was slipped under the door.

Marc stepped back and picked up the piece of paper.

'Bite ya bum, Dad.'

He tried not to laugh and he carefully folded the paper and put it in his pocket. He wished Christa was there to see it and he wondered how he could solve this enormous mess three days before Christmas.

29

Christa drove to the only person she really knew in York. Petey was walking down the street pulling a wheeled shopper of food, and singing to himself when she arrived. She jumped out of the car and watched him. She called him but realised he couldn't hear her, so she waved and then he stopped, smiled broadly and took two earbuds out of his ears. 'Was listening to a bit of Burt Bacharach. I love him,' he said.

'Earbuds – that's so modern of you,' said Christa. She had trouble setting the clock in her car so a seventy-odd-year-old man using Bluetooth technology was impressive.

'What are you doing here? Come in for a cup of tea?' he said as she walked with him to his gate. He pushed it open and she followed him and his little cart of supplies inside.

'I've resigned from Pudding Hall,' she said.

'What?' Petey turned to her and frowned.

'Let's go inside and I will tell you – it's freezing out here,' she instructed.

Once inside Petey turned on the kettle and Christa helped unpack his groceries. He bought many of the same items her dad used to buy.

Yorkshire tea, HP Sauce, cherry Bakewells, white bread, cheddar cheese, some apples, and a few bananas.

'I will make the tea while you tell me what happened,' said Petey bustling about the kitchen.

Christa told him the whole sorry story, from her marriage to Simon, to the restaurant, and up to now, over three cups of tea, two cheese sandwiches and a Bakewell tart.

Petey sighed and shook his head when it was finished.

'You had to leave. You can't stay there with him, no matter how much you like Marc and the boys.'

Christa nodded. 'Thank you for saying that. It's exactly what my dad would have said. I needed to hear it.'

Petey patted her hand. 'Now, you can stay here until you get sorted. It will be easier for you and I would enjoy the company.'

'I can't do that, Petey. You have your life; I have to find mine.'

'Let me help you for a while,' he said. 'You don't have anyone else here and you're a friend to me. I hope I'm one to you also.'

Christa grabbed his worn hand. 'You are a friend. A real friend, Petey.'

'Come on then,' he said. 'I can show you to the little guest room. It's not much but it's clean and warm.'

She followed him through the small home to the bedroom next to his, which housed a small single bed with a yellow chenille bedspread and daisy wallpaper.

A white bedside table sat next to the bed and a matching wardrobe.

'The sheets might need changing, been on there for a while, but it's all yours until you figure out what to do next.'

'Thank you, Petey,' she said feeling her throat ache and eyes sting from the tears threatening to fall again.

'It's no Pudding Hall but it's mine,' he said.

'This is better than Pudding Hall,' she said. 'I'm calling it Petey Hall.'

He chuckled. 'Petey Hall – I like that,' he said.

That night Christa tossed and turned in the small bed. Not from lack of comfort – it was warm and soft and cosy – but from the vision of her soufflé and its failure to rise like Simon's. Perhaps she had overthought it, or overwhipped the egg whites. Maybe she was too arrogant and this was the little-known God of Soufflé reminding her she wasn't as good as she thought she was.

Was there a God of Soufflés, she wondered, staring at the daisy wallpaper.

She thought about the day she had been accepted into Le Cordon Bleu. Marc had asked about it as though he cared; he had thought she was successful. She didn't know why so many memories had sprung up since she'd been in York. Perhaps she had time to listen to what they had to tell her now.

The day she found out she was accepted into the course, she had woken up and forgot for a few seconds her father was gone. When she'd remembered, she'd cried. She had cried for the previous four months but always in secret, using the shower to weep or the storeroom at work, amongst the flour and grains.

But that day she'd cried wrenching sobs until finally she was out of tears. Walking to the kitchen to get a glass of water, she'd seen the letter on the table.

She had picked it up, headed back to bed and lain down,

placing the letter on her stomach, trying to divine what was inside it based on her gut.

Her stomach wouldn't tell her anything though. She would have to open it and find out for herself.

Sitting up in bed, she'd turned on the light and opened the envelope, careful not to rip the paper. She hadn't known why she'd felt she needed to be careful but the emblem and words on the crest made her respectful of the process.

She'd pulled out the letter and opened it and her eyes scanned over the words.

Congratulations.
We are pleased to inform you.
Accepted for the Grand Diplôme of Cuisine and Pastry.
£30,000.

'You got what you wanted, Dad,' she'd said looking out the window at the snow.

He had told her to apply before he was diagnosed but she'd told him they couldn't afford it. Then, when he'd was told he was dying, he'd announced that he had a life insurance policy. It wasn't much but it was enough to put her through the course and help her live in the rented flat for a year or so.

'Dad, I can't think about that now,' she had said to him, as she had helped him into bed.

'You have to think about it. You love cooking and you love caring for people.'

'So I can cook in a nursing home or something,' she'd said.

He had gently swatted her hand. 'Go and learn all those

techniques I see you watching on the television and the computer. Your croissants would make the French jealous.'

As she lay in the small bed in the house of an old man whom she hardly knew, she wondered what her dad would make of her success now. He would have hated the way she gave her life up for Simon to control.

'I'm sorry, Dad,' she whispered into the darkness.

She wondered what Marc was doing. Just thinking about him made the shame rise inside her and she closed her eyes and sighed. What must he think of her?

The vision of Simon's gloating was burned into her memory and she wished she could get him out of her mind and think about all the nice things about Marc instead.

His hand in hers, the shared glances, the laughter, the teasing, the flirting.

Who was she kidding? Marc was never going to stay in York and Avian and the boys would return to America. Why was she pretending this would be happy families forever and ever?

She looked at her phone next to the bed. Ten missed calls from Marc. More texts. She didn't read them or listen to the messages. She was too embarrassed.

Closing her eyes again she lay on her back and took some deep breaths, slowing down her racing mind by thinking about the garden at Pudding Hall. The orchards and the maze, the dell with the shared company of the fantastic stag.

She didn't know what she was going to do next but she had to choose a future that spoke to her heart and soul; one that helped her put good into the world.

The selfishness she had seen from Simon and Avian

and even Marc at times wasn't anything she wanted to be around.

She'd enough of the self-involved. She wanted to make a difference and even though the pub was now sold, she could work towards that, couldn't she? She would speak to Zane in the morning to find out what was needed and how she could help beyond the van. She would get out of her head and into the world.

30

'Dad?'

Marc looked up from his laptop in his study.

'Not now, Ethan, we're busy.'

Adam was sitting opposite him, tapping furiously at the screen.

'No, Dad, we need to talk to you.'

Seth's face appeared now.

'If it's about Christa, I can't get her back here. She isn't returning my calls or my texts, so you will have to deal with shepherd's pie until I get a new chef.'

'Dad, it's not about Christa,' said Ethan.

'Well, it's kind of about her but it's also about the douche,' Seth added.

Marc didn't bother to correct them because Simon was a douche and had been so unbearable since he won the soufflé competition the day before that Marc and Adam and Paul and the twins went out for a very sombre dinner at the local pub.

Marc sighed. 'I know he's annoying but he will be gone after Christmas.'

The twins were in his study now and they closed the door behind them.

KATE FORSTER

'Dad, I need to show you something,' said Ethan, his face troubled.

Marc closed his laptop and pulled the child to him. He had been distracted and he had been rude. He would have been furious with the boys if they had ignored him like he had ignored them. They deserved better than that dismissive side of him.

'Okay, buddy, what is it? I'm sorry I tried to brush whatever it is away. Tell me, what's up?'

Seth put the video camera onto the desk.

'Dad, you need to watch this.' Seth looked at Adam. 'Can you plug this into the monitor?'

Adam took the cable from the camera and did as Seth instructed and then Ethan pressed some buttons and the Pudding Hall kitchen came into the view and there was Christa.

'When was this?' he asked, his heart aching to see her again.

'It's the soufflé competition,' said Seth as Ethan fast-forwarded through the footage, giving Marc a view of what had been happening when Marc was in the dining room waiting to judge the final dishes.

He watched Christa and Simon cook. He noticed her concentration and precision even on fast forward. She barely looked up while Simon seemed to be performing as though he was on camera.

'Did they know you were filming this?' asked Marc, still watching.

'No,' Ethan answered. 'I set up on the mantelpiece so I could edit it later. I wanted it to be natural, so I didn't tell them.'

Marc nodded as they kept watching. He didn't know

248

what was coming but he was pretty sure it wasn't good for someone who was cooking.

Ethan stopped fast-forwarding and Marc saw them put the soufflés in the oven and then Christa's knees buckled. She spoke and then rushed outside and Adam and Paul and the boys followed her.

'What happened? Why didn't you tell me she was upset?' He turned to Adam, furious.

'She said she needed air. We offered her water but she said she was just nervous.'

The camera was still filming Avian and Simon who didn't seem bothered by Christa's near collapse and instead he could see them talking by the bench. Avian was gesturing wildly and Simon was shrugging and throwing his hands up at her.

And then it happened.

Simon went to the oven while Avian watched the door and he swapped the soufflés.

'You slimy mother fu—' Marc started to say.

'We can sue him. We can sue him for fraud, for misleading you, and anything else I can think of,' said Adam his face bright red.

Marc turned to the boys. 'Thank you for showing me this,' he said and he hugged both of them.

'I think you might have just saved Christmas, boys.'

The boys looked pleased with themselves but Adam stepped in.

'You cannot tell your mom or Simon about this, okay? It's now up to us to deal with it.'

The boys nodded and Ethan looked downcast.

'I wish Mom didn't do it.' His son's words made Marc

remember what it was like to be so disappointed in a parent. How many times he had hoped his own parents would step up and pull through, only to be let down again and again.

'I know, buddy. I will talk to her – but later, okay? Let me find Christa first and then I can talk to your mom.'

Ethan and Seth went to the door.

'And can we finish the gingerbread house later?'

'We sure can,' Marc promised, meaning it, as the boys closed the door.

'I'm going to text Paul and show him and then get him to take the boys out for the rest of the day. That okay with you?' Adam asked.

Marc nodded as he wondered what to do.

Paul watched the video, his face shocked as the deception became apparent. 'The audacity of those two. I am shook, as the young people say,' he said. 'I'll take the boys far away today to the Viking Centre. There is an enormous fossilised Viking turd they can look at. That will entertain them. We could put Simon on display as real-life human shit but it might be harder to sell tickets.'

Marc laughed despite himself as Paul left him and Adam.

'Wow. I am shocked but not surprised,' Adam stated.

'Me neither. I knew Christa had cooked that soufflé. I could tell.'

Adam looked at him. 'What will you do about it then? And make sure it's legal, okay?'

Marc leaned back in his chair.

'I need to tell Christa but I also need to deal with Simon and Avian. If I kick him out and Avian goes with him then that's on her. I will tell her she can stay for the boys and then let her decide.'

Adam nodded. 'And Simon? Surely you're not just going to give him the boot and then forget it happened?'

Marc shook his head. 'No, I am going to kick him right where it will hurt him most.'

Adam made a face. 'That sounds like a police charge.'

'No, I'm going to kick him right in his ego,' Marc said. 'Make the deal with Cirrus TV, buy today.'

'Are you sure? With *Blind Baking* going?'

'Oh yes, buy it,' Marc said feeling surer than ever. 'I am going to make my own cooking show, one that will blow *Blind Baking* out of contention. Get me a time to speak to the guy from *The Hollywood Reporter*. I need him to write a story for me.'

'On it,' said Adam.

He stood up and grabbed his phone.

'And now I have to find Christa. Wish me luck.'

'Ask Peggy,' said Adam.

'Peggy?'

'She said she saw her this morning in York. Says she's devastated.'

Marc rushed to the door. 'Why didn't you tell me?'

And without waiting for an answer he rushed through the house calling Peggy's name.

Seth and Ethan's Gingerbread House Recipe

Ingredients

250g/8¾oz unsalted butter

200g/7oz dark muscovado sugar

7 tbsp golden syrup
600g/21oz plain (all-purpose) flour
2 tsp bicarbonate of soda
4 tsp ground ginger

For the icing

2 egg whites
500g/18oz icing sugar

Method

1. Heat the oven to 200°C/180°C fan/gas 6. Melt the butter, sugar and syrup in a pan. Mix the flour, bicarbonate of soda and ground ginger into a large bowl, then stir in the butter mixture to make a stiff dough. If it won't quite come together, add a tiny splash of water.

2. Cut out a template. You can find these free online. Put a sheet of baking paper on a work surface and roll about one-quarter of the dough to the thickness of two £1 coins. Cut out one of the sections, then slide the gingerbread, still on its baking paper, onto a baking sheet. Repeat with remaining dough, re-rolling the trimmings, until you have two side walls, a front and back wall and two roof panels. Any leftover dough can be cut into Christmas trees, or monkeys for the trees around your house.

3. Bake all the sections for 12 minutes or until firm and just a little darker at the edges. Leave to cool for a few minutes to firm up, then trim around the templates again to give clean, sharp edges. Leave to cool completely.

4. Put the egg whites in a large bowl, sift in the icing sugar, then stir to make a thick, smooth icing. Spoon into a piping bag with a medium nozzle. Pipe generous snakes of icing along the wall edges, one by one, to join the walls together. Use a small bowl to support the walls from the inside, then allow to dry, ideally for a few hours. Ask Christa to do this part as it's really hard.

5. Once dry, remove the supports and fix the roof panels on. The angle is steep so you may need to hold these on firmly for a few mins until the icing starts to dry. Dry completely, ideally overnight, and then decorate as you wish.

31

'You have to make the chicken house,' said Seth to Ethan.

'I can't make the chickens,' Ethan stated. 'But I can make the eggs.'

Seth considered it for a moment. 'Eggs could work. We can pile them over by the trees.'

'What are you doing, boys?' asked Avian as she came into the kitchen.

'Making a gingerbread house,' said Seth.

'Gross. Make sure you don't eat it – it's bad for you,' she said, taking a bottle of water from the refrigerator and leaving again.

Ethan said nothing as Avian left but Seth groaned.

'I want Christa back,' he said.

'So do I,' Ethan answered. 'Mom said she's going to make broccoli burgers. Disgusting.'

Seth made a face. 'What if we made a maze?'

'We can't cook any more gingerbread, not without Christa,' said Ethan.

'We could make it from cardboard?' Seth suggested.

They found cardboard in the recycling and used the

kitchen scissors to cut it, even though they knew Christa wouldn't like them using them.

There was green paint from the arts and craft set they had never used and glue and sticky tape. It was quite a process as they worked, waiting for the paint to try and then sticking things down so they stood up.

Ethan drew a shape and then cut it out.

'What's that?' he said.

'Dad,' he answered as he drew all the keys on the laptop. 'He's doing business.'

Seth looked at it closely. 'Where are you going to put him?'

'In the maze,' Ethan answered.

Seth thought about it for a moment and then nodded.

'You better make a Christa then. She can go in the maze with Dad.'

Ethan finished the effigy of Marc and put it down on the table and started work on Christa.

'I saw them holding hands,' he said to Seth.

Seth giggled. 'They're in love,' he said in a singsong voice.

He took his pen and wrote in fine writing on the face of his dad.

Ethan looked at it and laughed and then wrote on Christa's face and showed Seth.

The roared with laughter at their own jokes as they finally stuck Marc and Christa in the centre of the maze.

'Now we just have to make a spell to bring her back to us,' said Seth. He was serious.

Ethan laughed as he wiggled his fingers at the gingerbread house in what he hoped was a mysterious manner. 'Come back to Pudding Hall and feed us,' he said. 'No more broccoli burgers.'

'We need saving from the broccoli burger monster,' Seth joined in and when they finished laughing they sat and looked at their work.

'It's finished,' Ethan said. Seth adjusted the last monkey Marc had made that was hanging in a marzipan tree and Ethan made sure the antlers of a lopsided deer were stuck on securely.

They sat glumly at the table looking at their handiwork.

'I hope Dad can get her back,' was all Ethan said and Seth started to cry.

Seth was always the ringleader and the instigator of trouble, so for Ethan to see his brother, older by a few minutes, so vulnerable was unnerving.

'I just want her back because Dad did stuff with us, and talked to us more and we ate dinner together and now we won't.'

Ethan nodded and felt his own sadness well up and he wiped a tear away.

'Wanna go to the maze?' he asked Seth.

'Nah,' said Seth looking downcast and then, as though a bolt of lightning hit him, he looked up and smiled. 'Wanna get some of Meredith's dog poo and put it in Simon's shoes?'

Ethan gasped. 'Yes, let's go.'

And the boys pulled on their coats and hats and, taking a plastic container and a pair of kitchen tongs, they went to seek their own form of revenge.

DESSERT

32

Christa helped tie the last of the Christmas ribbon on the fudge packets in Petey's kitchen. She had been wrapping and cooking all morning but they were happy with the amount they had produced.

'It will be a bumper market for us,' said Petey happily. 'I haven't had this much to sell in a long time.'

'And I can't wait to sell it all for you. Peggy said the last market before Christmas is always so busy.'

Peggy had called in to see them after Christa had texted stating she wouldn't be at Pudding Hall. Peggy arrived early, before she went to work, to find them already up. Christa had barely slept, and Petey regularly rose with the first birdsong.

'What do you mean you left?' Peggy had said.

'I can't stay there with Simon,' Christa replied then started to cry and Peggy tutted at her.

'That mother of those boys has a thing or to work out,'

she said. 'You can't put a man before your children, I will tell you that much.'

Christa had cried again at the thought of the twins.

'I think maybe I am overreacting. I mean, Marc and I weren't really anything. We sort of liked each other but I am probably reading too much into it,' she had told them, but mostly she told herself. 'It's probably a rebound crush, the first one you get with a new person when your relationship ends.'

Christa had noticed the glance between Petey and Peggy.

'I don't think it's anything like that,' Peggy had said. 'I think there's something there but it will be you two who have to work out if it's worth pursuing knowing Avian and Simon will be a part of your lives.'

Christa had groaned and put her head on the table.

'No thanks,' she had said and she'd meant it. Nowhere in her future was Simon included, especially not her personal life.

Peggy had gone to work then and Christa and Petey had started to cook.

'Let's do a Christmas-themed line for the last market,' Christa had suggested. They'd worked out what they needed for the ingredients and Christa had popped down to the shops and returned with beautiful Christmas ribbon in different colours.

There was peppermint swirl, cranberry and walnut, almond and cherry, and candy cane fudge.

Christa had bagged them all and tied them off with the pretty ribbons and had printed little cards inside listing the ingredients, using Petey's state-of-the-art home printer.

'You are remarkable for your age, Petey, which I know

can be taken as a backhanded compliment but I mean it. You still work, you take of yourself, you can manage technology better than me – not that that's hard but seriously, you're a catch,' she said as she put the last bags into a box and wrote the flavour on the side.

Petey laughed. 'I don't know about that,' he said, 'but I am interested in lots of things. I think that's why I come across as interesting, but I'm just interested,' he said.

'What about Peggy?' she prompted.

He paused. 'Peggy is a lovely woman, and very smart but I have only ever loved one woman in my life so I'm not sure I know how to love another. We are grand friends though.'

Christa listened. 'I wonder if your wife would have wanted you to be alone all these years though,' she said gently.

'Well I'm not alone now – you're here. You're like a lovely daughter to me,' he said.

The doorbell rang and Petey checked his wristwatch.

'I'm not expecting anyone. You?' he asked.

Christa shook her head. 'Only Peggy knows I'm here,' she said. 'Want me to go?'

Petey was already leaving the kitchen so Christa finished tidying up as she heard the door open and she looked up and there was Marc.

'Hi,' he said. She felt her knees go and she sat at the table.

'Hi,' she answered.

Petey was nowhere to be seen and Christa wished he would come back and make small talk so then she could run out the back and climb the fence and never let Marc see her shame again.

'We need to talk,' he said.

She was silent for a moment.

'I don't know what to say to you. It was stupid bet and one I thought I would win but I was arrogant and it showed me I have been kidding myself my whole life. It always was Simon who was the star and I hid behind him because I was too afraid to do anything myself.'

Marc went to speak but she put her hand up to stop him.

'And whatever we had, whatever attraction we had has gone since I made such an idiot of myself, but that was because of Simon, not because of you. I have some pretty serious thinking to do about myself and where I'm going in life.'

Marc put his hands up now. 'Sorry, I have to stop you there,' he stated. 'Here's the thing, Christa. You won.'

She shook her head. 'No I didn't, you chose Simon's soufflé.'

Marc pulled out his phone and played with it. 'Are you texting someone?' she asked. 'It's considered rude to do that in the middle of a conversation.'

He handed the phone to her and pressed play on a video.

She saw herself leave the kitchen and then she saw Avian and Simon arguing and then him swap the soufflé from her oven to his and his to hers.

'Oh. My. God,' she said, replaying it and watching it several times.

She looked up at him.

'God, I knew it. I put everything I had into that soufflé for you.' She started to cry. 'I did everything right and he did everything wrong. I had the eggs at the right temperature and his were cold. Everyone knows you get stronger peaks with room temperature egg whites.' She threw her hands up and then slammed them down on the table.

'I didn't know that but go on,' he said.

'And he didn't cool the chocolate before putting the yolks in. It would have tasted too eggy.'

She paused, trying to stop crying but she couldn't stop now she had unbottled her pain.

'I wanted it to be the best – the best chocolate, butter, eggs – everything was so carefully chosen...' She hiccupped from crying. 'And then when I stirred the chocolate as it melted I thought about you.'

He took her hand. 'What did you think?' he asked softly.

Christa sobbed, feeling every injustice Simon had ever put on her during their marriage. The gaslighting, the dismissive comments, the gloating when he got mentioned in a review, his teasing that was supposed to a joke about her weight, her clothes, her background.

'I thought about love,' she said, not self-censoring anymore. If she wanted to be brave in life, then she had to start right now.

'I thought about the way you look at me sometimes, and the touch of your hand, and what it would be like to kiss you,' she said. 'And I know that probably won't ever happen but I put love into that dish and I wanted you to know it, to taste it.'

'To look at you like this?' he asked and she lifted her eyes from the table to his.

'And to touch you like this?' he asked and swept her hair from her forehead.

She sat very still.

'And to kiss you like this?' He paused and she smiled a little at him, unsure if he was serious or not.

The touch of his lips on hers showed his sincerity and as they melted into each other, sitting at Petey's table, Christa wondered if she was dreaming until there was a knock at the kitchen door.

'Come in, Petey.' She laughed, wiping her eyes.

'Just got to get my bits and bobs and pop down to the pub,' he said.

He looked embarrassed as he took his wallet and keys from the bench.

Christa looked at Marc and she saw his eyes searching her face.

'If you need me to pick you up, call me,' she told Petey, and she felt Marc's knee press against hers.

Petey chuckled as he closed the door and Marc kissed her again, this time more insistent. Christa thought she had forgotten what desire felt like, but now she couldn't stop grabbing his clothes, his hair, his face, his arms, his back.

Finally she pulled away. 'We cannot do this here,' she said.

'Come back to Pudding Hall,' he said, his voice husky, his eyes sparkling.

She shook her head. 'I can't go back while he is there,' she said and she stood up and went to the sink and poured a glass of water.

Turning to Marc she looked at him where he was sitting at the table of Petey's humble home.

He seemed entirely out of place in his fancy puffa jacket and expensive haircut.

'Simon might seem silly and ineffectual to you but to me

he was abusive. He made me doubt myself over and over instead of building me up. He was truly a horrible husband and even though I don't like Avian, I worry he is a part of her life, because then he will be a part of the boys' life.'

Marc nodded. 'I have thought about that with the boys. But I can't tell Avian who to date – just as she can't tell me.'

They were silent for a moment.

'I will sort it out,' he said and he stood up. 'I promise.'

'Sort it out for the boys not for me,' she said and Marc leaned in and left a lingering kiss on her lips.

'What if I did both? Would you come back then?'

Christa laughed in spite of herself. 'If you can do that then you'd be performing a Christmas miracle.'

'Then get ready to be awed,' said Marc and he left Christa in the kitchen, surrounded by boxes of fudge and the taste of him on her lips.

33

Marc sat through a dinner of takeaway pizza, watching Avian and Simon bicker and complain while they ate a kale salad and sunflower seeds. Simon kept eyeing the pizza and Avian kept hitting him on the arm.

'Looking at it won't make it come to you,' she said and he laughed.

'It did with you,' he said and Simon wanted to punch him again but he felt Adam's hand on his shoulder as he poured him a glass of wine.

Adam had managed to convince Simon to not press charges, saying it would be bad for his image with the show coming out soon, considering Avian was the producer. Avian and Simon had reluctantly agreed and Marc had given them each five thousand pounds as a sweetener.

'I saw Christa today,' Marc announced, watching Simon's reaction.

Simon didn't seem interested at all and Avian rolled her eyes.

'God, she was a drag wasn't she? She had such a huge crush on you, Marc. She was like a sad teenage cow, her gaze always following you around, wide eyed and moon-faced.'

Simon seemed to bristle a little at the news he wasn't the centre of Christa's longing.

'She was doing that to me also,' he said.

'No she wasn't,' said Avian, adjusting her hair. 'It was only at Marc.'

'I saw her look at me a few times also,' said Simon and Paul coughed into his wine.

'Anyway, she was really sad about the soufflé. Said she couldn't understand how hers could be so flat since she had done everything right. She said the room temperature was perfect for the eggs, which helps them to get a good peak. Said yours were in the refrigerator.'

Simon scoffed. 'She will be trying to figure out for the rest of her days why it didn't work for her the way mine did and the answer is some people just have it and some don't.'

Avian nodded in agreement. 'This is why you are the judge on *Blind Baking* and not Christa. You can't teach instinct.'

Adam stood up with his plate. 'I might join the boys in the other room. They're watching *Britain's Got Talent*. I'm always fascinated by the ones who don't have it and who still win anyway. It's almost enough to make you think it's rigged or something.'

'I'll join you,' said Paul.

'Oh, Adam, before you go, did you finish that agreement today we talked about this morning?'

Adam smiled at Marc. 'Just waiting for the final contract. Should come through anytime from nine, New York time.'

'What are you buying now, Marc?' Avian picked at some seeds and ate them, and Marc nearly laughed at her attempt at nonchalance. 'A movie studio? A radio network?'

Marc smiled at her and finished his wine.

'Can't say too much yet but I think you will be excited,' he said and Avian clapped her hands.

'How thrilling,' she said as Marc left the room.

'Can you clean up for me, Simon? Appreciate it,' he said and went to sit with the others, thinking about what to do next.

The sound of Avian's yelling woke him.

'Marc, you fucking prick. You motherfucker, wake up and tell me what the fuck you have done!'

He opened one eye and saw her in a robe, her hair mussed and with a sleep mask on top of her head, clearly pushed up in a hurry.

'Please don't swear. The boys will hear you,' he said and he rolled away from her.

She pushed his back with her little bird hands.

'You're producing your own cooking show? I just saw it in *The Hollywood Reporter*,' she screamed. 'You've bought Cirrus TV and now you have a celebrity cooking competition? With Gordon Ramsey, and Nigella and Marco Pierre White as some of the competitors? How the hell can we go up against that?'

'You can't,' he said, keeping his eyes closed.

'Why did you do it then? Why? Do you hate me that much you want to ruin my career?'

Marc sat up. 'I don't hate you, Avian. You're the mother of my kids. You're a terrible mother but you're all they have.'

'How dare you say I am a terrible mother,' she gasped.

'But you are a terrible mother and I'm a terrible father. At least I'm trying to get better. That's the difference between you and me. I know I'm shit but I'm trying to be and do better. You, however, don't actually care about what the boys think about you or them in general. You only care about yourself and whatever is happening in relation to you.'

Avian's mouth was opening and shutting in shock and anger.

Marc pulled on some sweat pants from the floor and then pulled on a clean T-shirt and sat on a chair.

'I saw what you and Simon did with the soufflé, so you can't deny it. It's on film,' he said.

Avian sat on the end of the bed.

'Why?' he asked. 'It wasn't just about winning for you, was it?'

Avian stared at the floor, her legs crossed and her arms wrapped around herself.

'Simon is a pretty terrible person. I don't know why you're with him but I'll tell you this: if you keep seeing him, you won't see the boys. And I think, even under all that self-absorption, you love them.'

She looked up at him. 'I do. I do love them,' she said quietly.

He nodded. 'So Simon goes and you can still do *Blind Baking* for Netflix but please find a new judge, a woman please.'

'How can you tell me what to do with my show?' she spat as she spoke.

'If you get rid of Simon, then I will drop the cooking show from Cirrus TV,' he said.

Avian was silent for a moment.

'Do you want me to hire Christa as a judge?'

He laughed. 'No, she wouldn't do that.'

Avian immediately went on the defensive. 'Because she's too good for the show and for TV?'

'No, because she doesn't want to do that sort of stuff. She has other plans and she's really shy.'

Avian's face was stony as she uncrossed and crossed her legs again.

'You can't tell me who I can and can't date,' she said.

'I can, because I know Simon is abusive and narcissistic, and he will use you and hurt you, Ave, and underneath your armour I know you just want to be loved, like we all do, and he won't do it.'

'Did Christa tell you he was abusive? I mean, her perspective is tainted,' she started to argue.

But Marc laughed. 'I didn't need Christa to tell me. I saw it in him from the minute I met him. He's exactly like my father. A self-absorbed lying piece of shit who will sell his kids for a good deal, which is exactly what my father did to me and my siblings. You know this about my family, Avian. So don't let Simon Playfoot make you sell your kids for a good deal that benefits him and him only and leaves our boys fucked up like I've been.'

Avian was silent but he saw her shoulders drop.

'You love her,' she said as she looked up at him.

He said nothing.

'I know you do because you look at her in a way you never looked at me.'

'And she looks at me in a way you never did,' he replied.

She stood up and walked to the door. 'So you will drop your show if I dump Simon from mine?'

'And from your life. Honestly Avian, you know he's a shit.'

She paused. 'He is pretty annoying; he's been getting on my nerves lately. He talks about himself constantly, and he's not that interesting.'

Marc laughed a little. 'Will you tell him or will I?'

'Which part? That he's not interesting or that he's being dumped?'

'Any of it, I would enjoy it,' he said.

But Avian shook her head. 'No. I'll do it. I'll tell Simon they want a new direction.'

She was quiet for a while. 'I might head back to LA; the boys can come over later. I think I need to sort a few things out back there, mostly myself.'

He nodded. 'What will you tell the boys?' he asked.

'The truth. That I need to work on being a better person, that Simon and I aren't together, that I want to be able to be there for them and be the best I can be. I don't know. What do you think?'

He saw her insecurity and fear and he felt sad for her.

'That sounds pretty great to me,' he said. 'Just so you know, they were the ones who filmed the soufflé incident so you will have to deal with that also.'

Avian closed her eyes for a long while. 'I really need to get myself together,' she said finally. 'I work so hard to make people think I'm invincible, that I know everything, am in control of it all but I'm not. It's hard trying to do it all.'

He nodded. 'I know it is. I'm not any better than you, losing myself in work, avoiding being a parent, avoiding my past and the feelings I struggle with daily.'

She stepped forward towards him and when he held out his arms she leaned into him.

She felt so frail and tiny.

'And, Avian, eat something and stop pushing food rules onto everyone else, especially our kids. You can't produce a cooking show and hate food. I only say this because I worry about you. You used to love food; now it seems like a punishment.'

She cried a little into his chest.

'I know. I need some help. Thank you. You were always right about this stuff. I miss these reality checks.'

She pulled away and wiped her eyes. 'And you need to deal with your family. Look for your siblings, go to therapy, do the work. We both need to do the work to be better parents.'

He nodded. She was right. They were both right.

Avian walked to the door and held the door handle and then looked at Marc.

'Can you ask Christa who she would recommend as a new judge?' she asked.

'Of course,' he said and Avian left the room.

Marc sighed with relief. He didn't like hurting anyone but he also knew Simon couldn't be around his children, or Avian for that matter.

He thought about calling Christa but saw it wasn't even six yet so he climbed back into bed and thought about everything he had to do to convince her and prepare for her return.

But first he picked up his phone and called Adam.

'Sorry to wake you so early but expect some calls from Gordon Ramsey, Nigella Lawson and Marco Pierre Whites' people today about a red herring story in *The Hollywood Reporter*. Just deny it and say it is a false rumour and then send the reporter a new Tesla will you? In the black, with extra cup holders.'

He pulled the covers up and gave a sigh of relief. Now he could finally look forward to Christmas.

34

Peggy and Petey finished counting the cash and adding up the bank payments and then Peggy circled the number and pushed the notepad to Christa and showed her the final tally.

'Wow,' she said, looking at Petey in amazement.

'It were them Christmas fudges that everyone liked. We haven't got a single bag left,' he said to Peggy.

'You did very well,' Peggy said to him and patted his hand.

'We all did,' said Petey and Christa noticed he held on to Peggy's hand.

She wasn't sure when the tune changed for Petey but for the past two days Peggy had been over when she wasn't at work, and this morning Peggy was already in the house, stating that it was easier to leave for the market from Petey's place.

Christa didn't comment but she was sure to send a text message to Marc informing him of the news.

They'd loved gossiping about Peggy and Petey and their burgeoning romance, which seemed to have gone from zero to one hundred overnight. Part of Christa was jealous about Petey and Peggy's intimacy but she knew not to rush things with Marc, and certainly not with the boys at the house.

She didn't want to disturb Marc while he was wrapping things up with Avian. All she knew was that Simon had been banished from Pudding Hall and she hadn't heard from him, thank God.

Besides, she was she was enjoying the space from Marc while she worked things out for herself.

She had worked at the soup van for two nights and had asked Zane how she could get more experience. He had said she just needed to volunteer and that they could talk about it after New Year's.

She was excited to see what would happen next but she was also terrified. When they spoke on the phone Marc told her that this was normal and healthy and that he was terrified before every deal.

'If you're not scared then you're not outside your comfort zone and that's where the good stuff happens.'

But he hadn't actually invited her back to Pudding Hall and she didn't want to push in case Avian was still there. She could have a nice Christmas with Petey, but she felt sad that she couldn't cook the meal she had planned.

Maybe she could volunteer, she thought, but Petey told her there wasn't an actual sit-down Christmas lunch that he knew of, though he could ask around if she wanted.

'Christmas is only two days away,' she said. 'This is why I want to create the dining hall one day. It would be wonderful.'

The doorbell rang and Christa, who was closest, went to answer it and when she opened it she gasped.

The twins stood tall in their puffy jackets, looking pleased with themselves.

She looked around for Marc and saw him in the car.

She hadn't seen him since they had kissed in the kitchen and she felt a longing deep inside her.

'Hi,' she said. 'Come in.' She stepped back from the door for them but they shook their heads.

'We can't, we have to give you something,' Seth said and he unzipped his jacket and pulled out a large envelope with her name written in a child's writing on the front.

'This is for you,' said Ethan.

'Thank you,' she said and looked at Marc in the car, who smiled at her and she felt herself blush.

'Open it,' demanded Seth, so she did.

It was a large white card with a silver engraving of the Pudding Hall crest.

Below was printing in a beautiful seraph font in black ink.

Dear Christa,
You are cordially invited to Pudding Hall on
24th December to celebrate your birthday with
cocktails and dinner and entertainment.
Dress: Formal
Time: 7pm

There was not a single mention of it being Christmas Eve or Christmas the next day. It was simply about her birthday. She looked at the boys and then hugged them both.

'I can't wait, thank you,' she said, hearing her voice break with her emotion. She stood up and waved at Marc who waved back.

'Thank you,' she mouthed and he nodded and gave her a look that made her want to run and kiss him.

Rain started to fall and she looked up at the sky.

'Scoot – into the car, both of you,' she said as the rain began to fall sideways with more force than she had seen in a while.

The boys raced to the car and they waved as Marc drove away with a toot of the horn.

A formal dinner? She didn't have a thing to wear.

Everything formal was back in London and she didn't want to wear anything she had ever worn with Simon.

She wanted to be the new Christa, one that Simon knew nothing of.

She turned over the card to find more writing.

Stay for Christmas. Please.
M x

God, what was he doing to her, she thought, as she closed the front door. She took a deep breath and put the card back into the envelope and put it in her room before she went back into the kitchen.

Petey was putting the leftover fudge into a box.

'I'll take this down to the van for the staff. Nice for them to have a treat, don't you think?'

'That's very kind of you, Peter,' said Peggy. 'A generous heart is a good heart, I always say.'

Christa sat down. 'That was the boys. They asked me to dinner tomorrow night,' she said.

'How lovely,' said Peggy.

Christa looked at her and at Petey, who was now folding the top of the box.

'Did you know about this?'

Peggy shrugged. 'Not at all, they didn't ask me to cook,' she said. 'Which was just as well. I'm a terrible cook.'

Christa started to laugh. 'I thought you loved your shepherd's pie.'

'Loathe it. I don't even eat it, but it's easy,' Peggy admitted.

Christa sat in thought for a moment.

'I think I'm going to go back to my maiden name,' she said. 'I don't want to be a Playfoot anymore.'

'I don't blame you,' said Peggy. 'I bet he was playing foot with all sorts of people.'

Petey laughed. 'What's your maiden name then, love? I did a lot of reading on surnames when Annie and I did research on the family tree. My surname is Chandler, which was the name for a candlemaker back in medieval times.'

'I suppose Peter Fudge isn't really an appealing moniker,' said Peggy. 'My surname is Smith,' she added, 'which is my married name, but my maiden name was Ramsbottom. That was hell when I was at school.'

Christa rubbed Peggy's arm. 'Children can be so mean.' Peter stood up from the table and left the room and returned with a thick book.

'What's your maiden name then? I have a book of names that might have yours in it?' Petey put down the well-leafed book and Christa looked at front.

'*The Big British Book of Surnames*, updated 1999,' she read aloud.

Petey picked up the book and held it in his hand.

'Go on then, what's your name?' he asked.

'Hartley,' she said. 'I have no idea what it means. Something to do with hearts I guess?'

Petey flicked through the book and then looked at her. 'H.A.R.T?' he spelled out.

She nodded. 'L.E.Y.,' she finished.

Petey looked up from the book. 'That's a popular name around Yorkshire,' he said. 'Your family come from here?'

'I don't know,' she admitted. 'Dad didn't talk about family much – only his grandmother from time to time – but then again, I didn't ask. Self-absorbed teenager I guess.'

Petey looked at the page, running his finger down the list and then stopped.

'Hartley. Stag clearing,' he read aloud.

'A what?' she asked.

'In Anglo-Saxon times, "hart" meant a male deer, a stag, and "lea" meant a clearing of wood. It would have meant your family lived where the deer stood in the clearings.'

Christa put her hands over her face. 'Ever since I have been here I keep seeing this stag near Pudding Hall. I've seen him three times and once in the dell,' she said to Peggy. 'He was so close I could see the velvet on his antlers. And then Marc gave me a Christmas decoration of a deer family. Don't you think that's weird?' she asked.

Petey shook his head. 'No, I think you have an affinity with them and now you know why. I know Pudding Hall was once home to large deer clearing and hunters used to come before Mr Ferrier bought it. I don't think he hunts though?' he asked Peggy.

She shook her head. 'No, never, there isn't even a gun in the house.'

'I love knowing the meaning of my name, Petey. Thank you for telling me.' Christa stood up. 'And now I have to go and find something formal to wear to my dinner,' she said, feeling excited at the thought of wearing something other than jeans and jumpers.

Peggy grabbed her bag and patted Petey on the shoulder. 'I'm off to run some errands.'

'Do you want a lift anywhere?' asked Christa but Peggy declined and soon Christa was on her way to find a dress worthy of the new Christa Hartley.

35

Christa drove her car towards Pudding Hall, turning off at the driveway. It was already dark and she put her driving lights on high as she navigated the driveway. She really didn't want to hit a fox, or a deer for that matter.

In the distance she saw the lights of beautiful Pudding Hall, welcoming her, and emotion welled up inside her. She thought her time at Pudding Hall was gone but now she was having her birthday dinner there and Christmas as well. *Don't cry*, she told herself. Not only had she bought a dress but she'd also had her short hair washed and dried so it was a shiny, beautiful cap and her makeup had been done by a girl whose had more piercings in her face than Christa had ever seen but she made Christa look like a beautiful version of herself, with smoky eye makeup and flawless skin.

And when Christa had shown her the dress, which was carefully hung in a dress bag, the girl had exclaimed she had a perfect shade of plum lipstick to go with it.

Christa stopped her car on the driveway and took some deep breaths and tipped her head back to stop the tears from falling.

When she finally trusted herself not to ruin her face, she

looked out of the window and she saw the red stag in the centre of the driveway staring at her straight on.

Please don't run at my car. The stag lowered his head for a long moment and then lifted it again and slowly walked across the drive and into the darkness.

But what did the deer mean? she wondered. She wasn't a superstitious person but she knew it meant something. She wondered if her dad knew what their name meant. It probably didn't mean much when you were a lorry driver in London but she knew there was significance even though she couldn't work it out.

She drove slowly in the dark, not just for safety but also to savour the drive to the house. She wanted to make a mental snapshot of the lead-up to this moment.

She didn't know what would happen – maybe she and Marc were just a flirtation and it was only desire but it felt so good to be wanted again and she had never felt more beautiful.

Her phone rang and she pressed the hands-free device.

'Baby girl, happy birthday,' cried Selene's voice. 'I'm sorry I haven't spoken to you for the past week, but my God my life has been crazy since you recommended me to Avian. I signed the contract today and then they had me filming promos right away. I'm in the middle of every shot with the other judges because I'm the woman. A black Frenchwoman no less. I am going to change the world one plate at a time. I'm sick of writing reviews for already well-known places. I'm excited to find raw talent!'

'You were always going to be a star,' Christa said, meaning it. She had recommended Selene to Marc who had told Avian. There was no one better who was camera-ready and who was both smart and funny.

Selene sounded genuinely excited as she told her about the day, and how one of the guest chefs from France had asked her opinion on his next career move. Giving advice was Selene's favourite thing to do, so when combined with restaurant and food industry conversation, Selene shone like no one else.

'What are you doing for your birthday?' Selene asked.

'Dinner at Pudding Hall,' she said. 'Nothing special.'

'Oh? How are things with the fancy billionaire?' she asked.

'Complicated and involved but I can't tell you now, as I'm arriving at the house. I do need to debrief though. Can I call you on Boxing Day?'

'I don't know why you still have this Boxing Day. We don't have it in France – silly holiday,' Selene complained.

'That's because French people don't eat their own weight in goose and pudding and drink too much on Christmas and then get indigestion and need to spend the following day moaning about how awful they feel.'

Selene laughed. 'I will be at my parents' but will fly back to London that night. Call me. Happy birthday again, my friend.'

'I will. Bye,' said Christa and she finally parked the car at the house and smoothed out her dress.

It was pink. Of course, it was pink. When she had been with Simon her evening wear was always black and quiet. Minimal and streamlined.

This was nothing like that.

Fuchsia pink silk that fell below the knee, with a fitted top and a flared skirt.

The V-shaped neckline showed off her creamy skin in both the front and back, and the gathered shoulder strap detail was delicate and flattering. A thin black velvet ribbon was tied around the waist and she had black velvet pumps that were surprisingly comfortable.

There was so much fabric in the skirt that Christa had to resist the urge to do a spin in the dress as she walked towards the house.

Something cold fell on her back and she put her hand out and saw snow.

'Oh come on,' she said aloud, looking at the sky. She really was living the fairy tale. Before she got to the front door, she stood in the snow and looked up at the sky and twirled around, letting the pink skirt spin out around her.

'What a moment,' she heard and stopped twirling and looked up to see Marc standing in a dinner suit on the steps of the house.

Christa smiled. 'I just felt so pretty, and it's snowing,' she said. He looked incredible, as though the dinner suit was cut just for him. It probably was, she reminded herself, hoping her pink dress was enough.

'You look incredible,' he said and he came down to take her hand and they walked to the front door together.

'Happy birthday, Christa,' he said turning to her.

'Thank you, Marc,' she said and he kissed her on the cheek and opened the door.

The Christmas tree was dressed in all her glory and beneath the tree were piles of presents in all colours.

Marc led the way to the formal sitting room, a room Christa hadn't seen but to walk past. She didn't think anyone had used it during her time at Pudding Hall but now when he opened the door she wondered why it wasn't used every day.

The fire was burning in the grate and the room was filled with pink flowers.

Candles and soft lighting warmed the room and Marc took her to sit in a large armchair with an archway of balloons in different shades of pink over the top, and a sign above reading, *Christa, the Birthday Queen.*

Christa felt the tears fall as Marc helped her sit and she bit her lip to try and stop them falling.

'Happy birthday,' she heard and then the door burst open and in came her favourite people.

The twins in little dinner suits, which was too cute, she thought, and Adam and Paul looking so handsome and glamorous.

'Oh wow, you're wearing a velvet dinner jacket,' she said, touching Pauls' arm as she went to hug him.

'And you have on velvet shoes. Do they come in men's sizes?' he asked as she squeezed him tight. Paul had been a true friend to her during her time at Pudding Hall.

Adam kissed her cheek and looked her in the eye. 'Happy birthday, Christa. You are one in a million, and I mean that.'

She hugged him. 'Thank you, Adam.'

And then walked in Peggy and Petey. Peggy in a sparkling

top and a long black skirt and Petey looking like a happy penguin in his dinner suit.

'Oh my God,' she cried. They were like surrogate parents and now she knew how much they meant to her.

'You knew!' she accused them.

'Of course I knew, Christa, I know everything that happens in this house,' Peggy said firmly and Christa laughed.

Waitstaff in white shirts and black trousers came in then with trays of drinks.

'This is a Love Potion,' said Marc to Christa as he handed her a gold-rimmed martini glass, with what looked to be a steaming liquid but then she realised it was dry ice.

'Goodness,' she said as she took the glass from him. 'What's in it?'

The waiter answered, 'Pomegranate juice, strawberry vodka, and Chambord.'

There was a gold arrow with strawberries cut into heart shapes speared on it, sitting in the drink, and Christa thought she could have died in this moment and been happy but decided against it since she knew there was more to come.

Everyone had their drinks, and Marc raised his glass to Christa, the birthday queen of hearts he said, and then everyone raised their glasses and said, 'To Christa,' and she cried.

She couldn't help it but no one seemed to mind.

More staff came into the room with canapés and drinks and somewhere Christa could hear music playing.

'Where is the music coming from?' she asked Marc and he showed her out the door, where there was a small swing jazz band playing on the landing of the stairs.

'Are you kidding me? It's Christmas Eve. Where did you get all of this from? The staff, the food, which is excellent by the way. Did you try those blinis?'

Back in the sitting room, Seth and Ethan both wanted to sit by Christa.

'When can Christa open her presents?' asked Seth.

'Now,' said Marc and Seth and Ethan ran to the table and came back holding two large boxes.

'Two presents?' she said and looked up at Marc. 'This is a lot.'

He looked unconcerned at her worry and took a sip from his cocktail.

'Too bad, we're only just beginning. So, get ready for the best birthday you've ever had in your life.'

Love Potion #9 Cocktail

Ingredients

 1 cup pomegranate juice
 80ml/2¾fl oz strawberry vodka
 80ml/2¾fl oz Chambord Black Raspberry Liqueur
 2 small chunks dry ice (optional)
 2 strawberries cut into hearts for garnish (optional)

Method

1. In a cocktail shaker, combine the pomegranate juice, vodka, and Chambord. Shake to combine.
2. Place one chunk of dry ice into the bottom of each glass.

3. Pour the martini over a very small piece of dry ice.
4. Garnish with skewered strawberry hearts if desired. Pretty cute :)
5. Wait 5–10 minutes for the dry ice to dissolve (and enjoy the fun show!) before drinking.

36

Marc worried it was too much for Christa but if he could have tied up the world in a pink ribbon then he would have.

The evening had gone perfectly, with presents given. The boys had given her a Lego set of a bakery to make together.

'I can't wait,' said Christa, clearly meaning it, and Marc saw how happy they were to be around her.

Avian had left without much fuss. At times Marc wondered if they even realised they could have a close relationship with their mother but he knew it was her job to create the connection, not the boys, and he hoped it would happen one day.

Paul had given her a silk pillowcase and sleep mask and Adam had given her a gift box of Jo Malone perfumes.

Peggy, ever practical, gave her a book of traditional Yorkshire recipes that Christa had been very enthusiastic about.

'There's more to us than just Yorkshire puddings,' announced Peggy to the room.

'No doubt,' agreed Paul and she smiled at him.

'He's the cultured one,' Marc heard her whisper to Petey.

Petey gave her her own fudge that he had named after

her. 'Christa Pudding,' he said and she laughed, and opened the bag and took a nibble.

'Brandy. Lemon.' She paused. 'Glacé cherries. Nutmeg. Molasses?'

She looked at Petey who nudged Marc. 'She's got a fine set of taste buds on her that one.'

And Marc.

He handed her a small box and she opened it carefully.

'Oh, Marc, it's beautiful,' she whispered, and she took the delicate chain from the box and held it up to admire the charm.

'It's a pudding,' said Marc feeling silly now she was holding it.

'I know,' she said holding it to the light.

'It's tourmaline and the holly is emeralds and rubies, and the custard or icing, I don't know what you call it, they're diamonds,' he said hurriedly but she was already trying to put it on, not listening to him as he tried to convince her of the credentials of the jewels.

'I love it so much,' she said as he took over and fixed the clasp around her neck.

'It feels so nice against my skin,' she said and she turned to him to show him. 'Look how cute it is,' she said looking down at the charm.

'You can change it,' he said. 'If it's too childish.'

'Are you kidding?' She laughed at him. 'I love pink and Lego and pudding and you,' she said and then caught herself and he smiled at her.

'Sorry, too much,' she said and pretended to rewind her words. 'Probably the Love Potion playing tricks on me.' But he saw her blush and the way she touched the charm and he kissed her cheek before leaning in close to her ear.

'I love you too, Christa, so much.'

She grabbed his hand and he resisted the urge to carry her upstairs to bed because they still had dinner to go.

There wasn't a single low point of the night. Christa sat at the head of the table, and they ate their way through a delicious dinner of bruschetta, salmon and lemon risotto, salad, fresh bread and beautiful wine. It was light and fresh and everything he knew Christa loved.

And then the pièce de résistance was brought in.

Marc opened the door and Peggy carefully carried in a large cake covered in pink iced roses and with tapered candles glowing and flickering as Marc started singing 'Happy Birthday' and everyone joined in. Christa cried happily as she blew out the candles.

'Make a wish,' yelled Ethan.

Marc saw her glance at him and smile as she then cut the cake. Peggy served it and they drank tea and laughed and the boys performed magic tricks they had been teaching themselves from the internet. Finally Marc said it was time for the last part of the night.

'Come on, everyone,' he said, standing up and opening the door to the foyer.

The waitstaff were lined up holding coats and everyone slipped into them.

'This is exciting,' said Peggy.

'You do know it's snowing,' said Christa as she zipped up the coat.

'We won't be out for long,' he said as he was helping the boys into their coats.

The party stood on the front steps and looked out into the dark night. There was a light dusting of snow on the steps and Marc wondered why he had thought even for a minute he would sell Pudding Hall.

The sound came first and then the sky glowed as the first firework exploded and the party clapped and cheered. The boys yelled as the Catherine wheels and rockets flew through the night sky. The sky glittered with fiery rain and then burst into peony-shaped flowers of pink and red and orange and blue until the last one fired into the sky and the night fell silent again.

'Happy birthday, Christa,' he said to her and she turned to him.

He wasn't sure when everyone had left them alone on the steps, but all he knew was her lips were on his and he had never felt happier than in that moment.

'You are so beautiful for going to all this effort for me,' she said when she finally pulled away and Marc held her cold face in his hands.

'That's the thing, it's no effort. I would do this every day if I could but I know you would hate it.'

Christa kissed him and again and shivered.

'Inside. It's freezing. And I have to put those kids to bed.'

Peggy and Petey said their goodbyes and held Christa close.

'We are coming back for lunch tomorrow. Marc invited us,' Peggy said.

'Who is doing the cooking?' asked Christa.

'He has someone apparently, a chef whom he paid huge money to so you don't have to cook, he said to me.'

Christa waved them goodbye and closed the front door.

Adam and Paul had gone to bed and the waitstaff had cleaned up.

She kicked off her shoes and sat on the long sofa in front of the dying fire in the sitting room, watching the coals glow.

It was such a beautiful birthday, she thought. Not because of the excess and largesse but because everyone made themselves available. They didn't say there would be more presents tomorrow or not to eat too much because there was Christmas lunch the next day. They all made sure she was celebrated and that was enough. She could happily never have a birthday again, as this night would be enough to see her through till she died.

'You okay?' she heard Marc ask as he closed the door behind him.

She turned and smiled. 'I'm more than okay, I'm content,' she said.

Marc came and sat next to her. 'I never knew what contentment was until the first night you were here,' he said.

'How? You yelled at me twice.'

'Let's not talk about what an idiot I was,' he said, as his thumb rubbed the back of her hand.

'It was this feeling when we were sitting around the table and laughing, your incredible food was being served, and I thought, "This is as good as it gets". But now I know there is something better. When you have someone to share it with you.'

Christa rested her head on his shoulder and the clock on the mantel struck midnight.

'Merry Christmas,' she said to him and turned to him and kissed him.

'Merry Christmas, Christa,' he said and kissed her in

return. Suddenly, he stood up. 'Wait here, I want to give you your present now.'

'Really? You can't wait till tomorrow morning?' she asked, laughing at his eagerness.

He disappeared and then returned with something behind his back.

'I didn't wrap it,' he said as he sat next to her and handed her a plain white envelope.

She turned it over and opened it and then pulled out a sheaf of papers stapled together.

She started to read but couldn't make head nor tail of it and so looked at him. 'I don't understand. This is the pub? The one that sold?'

Marc nodded. 'I bought it for you for Christmas, so you can create the place you wanted. I know it seems excessive but I spoke to Zane and he said that St William's Charity can work alongside you and it's totally doable.'

Christa turned over the page and kept reading. Marc had bought her the pub?

'Why?' she looked at him, still confused.

'Are you angry? Do you think I've gone too far?'

She shook her head. 'It's your money; you can do what you like with it. No, I wanted to know why you did this for me?'

Marc sat back and thought for a moment.

'You know I say I help people but all I do is give people money. I don't know what it's doing, or even if it's helping anyone at all. I mean, I funded trees once because I liked gin. It's not that I don't get there is need but I have avoided seeing the need close up because of what I saw as a kid.'

Christa listened intently as he spoke. He stared at the fire.

'I was ashamed and when I see poverty, I freak out. It reminds me I could lose everything and end up back trying to work out how to feed my family. But you showed me what help is and why it matters. You showed up and I realised I need to also.'

She laid the papers on her lap and turned to him.

'So that's why?'

But Marc shook his head.

'No.' He thought for a moment and finally looked at her. 'I did it because I believe in you. Because you're remarkable and you make me want to do better and put more good into the world. Because you make me want to be a better father and ex-husband and because you can help people in a way that is generous and kind; something I need to do more of.'

She put the papers on the table. 'These are wrong,' she stated.

'Why?' He picked them up and leafed through them.

'I'm not Christa Playfoot anymore. I'm going back to my maiden name.'

'Good idea, what is it?'

'Hartley,' she said and looked at him. 'It meant deer clearing in Anglo-Saxon times.'

'That's nice, deer,' he said and she smacked his leg. 'Terrible pun.'

He laughed and took her hand.

'Would you change your name again if you remarried?'

'Probably not,' she said. 'I didn't want to the first time but Simon insisted, said it would be best for business. That was a lie.'

'Just so you know, I wouldn't expect you to change your name.'

She laughed. 'Are we getting married?'

'Most likely,' he said and he sounded so sure that Christa didn't doubt him for a minute, nor did she panic. She didn't know when she'd come to the realisation but she knew Marc and his boys were her future.

'You bought me the pub for Christmas,' she said incredulous. 'You're going to be really disappointed when you open my present tomorrow.'

'Oh? What is it?' His fingers were tracing patterns on her leg now, pulling the pink silk of the skirt up to show some of her thigh. She felt goose bumps on her skin and she shivered a little.

'A woollen scarf and some fudge,' she said. She took a moment and then pushed her leg against his hand.

'But I can let you unwrap me upstairs if you like,' she teased and saw Marc blush. 'I might be able to deck your halls as they say.'

Marc jumped up and pulled her up, put his hands around her waist and pulled her to him, close. 'Oh you're very punny,' he said and without another word he led her upstairs.

37

Early Christmas morning, Christa woke in Marc's arms. The sky was dark still, though she could hear birds singing outside, and she moved in closer to him. He stirred then kissed her and pulled her to him.

'Good morning,' he said and before she could answer they were tangled up together again.

Later, they woke again to the sounds of the twins yelling.

'Santa's been,' said Ethan.

'Dad is Santa, you big baby,' yelled Seth and Christa looked at Marc and made a sad face.

'When did you stop believing in Santa?' he asked her.

'I don't think I ever did to be honest,' she admitted.

'Me neither, otherwise Santa was an arsehole who totally forgot about us and that would be too hard to take as a kid.'

Christa kissed him. 'We should go and see the kids,' she said, but Marc pulled her close.

'One more kiss,' he said and she kissed him and then jumped from bed and pulled on his robe that was on the chair.

She went to the window and pulled back the curtains and squealed.

'Oh it's snowed; like proper snowed. God it's so beautiful.

Come and see,' she said and Marc pulled on sweat pants and a top and stood behind her and wrapped her arms around her.

'Okay, that's pretty awesome,' he said and he kissed her head.

'Do the boys know yet?' she asked and then she heard the boys yell.

'Dad, Dad, it's snowed.'

'Better get going,' he said.

'Wait, I'll go to my room and come from there,' she said picking up her bag.

'Why?' Marc frowned.

'Because they don't know I'm in here with you,' she said. 'We can't force us upon them. They need time to adjust.'

Marc snorted. 'Put on some clothes. I want to show you something downstairs.'

Christa showered quickly, dressed in the nice pants and a pretty lace-pattern woollen jumper and boots. She put on a slick of pink lipstick and walked into the hallway where Marc was waiting.

'You look amazing,' he said. 'Black suits you, so does pink.'

She touched his face. 'I could wear a potato sack and you would say that it was made for me.'

He took her by the hand and led her down the stairs.

'The boys are dressed and outside in the snow,' he said. 'They're making a snowman.'

'Oh that's so cute,' she said. 'Let's go and help them.'

'Yes, but before we join them, I want to show you something.'

They walked past the tree and down the hallway and into

the kitchen and there on the table stood the gingerbread house.

It was a very wonky version of Pudding Hall, complete with garden at the back, on green icing and with paths and the maze, made from cardboard.

'There's Bill and Meredith,' she said. 'And some deer,' she added. 'The monkeys are in the trees.' She laughed.

'Look in the maze,' Marc said and she moved closer to look over the top. There in middle were two cardboard figures facing each other, propped upright with sticky tape. A woman with short black hair and an apron on, holding a wooden spoon. And a man with sandy hair and a computer in his hand.

'That's us,' Marc said.

'Am I about to whack you with my spoon?' she joked.

'I don't know that I'm not boring you to death, talking you through my next deal,' he said. 'I don't always take my laptop to the maze but clearly I did this day.'

Marc gently lifted the figures from the maze.

'Oh don't break them,' said Christa, looking out in case the boys where coming.

'Look,' said Marc and he showed her the faces of the figures. There were words written on Marc's face in tiny writing, coming from his mouth.

'I love you.'

She bit her lip. 'Oh my God, that's so cute. We clearly did a terrible job at hiding our feelings.'

She held the little Christa in her hands. She had 'Are you hungry?' written on her face and she burst into laughter and tears.

'This is perfect, truly.'

Marc put the figures back into the maze and pulled her to him.

'I love you,' he said.

'Are you hungry?' she asked.

'Always.'

Two Years Later

'I'm going to call you train tracks from now on,' Christa gently teased one of the young students in her class.

'Why?' the older boy looked belligerently at her.

'Because you haven't cut all the way through the leeks.' Christa picked up some leek that was still joined.

'You have to cut all the way through,' she said to the group of teens.

They came every Wednesday and she taught them how to cook basic meals. Today was potato and leek soup. A staple that was cheap and easy and nutritious.

'You should now have your onion, potato and leek chopped,' she said. 'And one clove of garlic crushed and at the ready.'

The kitchen was quiet after the lunch rush, which is when the teens came in and cooked. Some had been in trouble with the courts, some had been recommended by social workers and others by Zane and the team at St William's.

Hartley House, as the pub had been renamed, had become a place to meet, get help, give help, connect and learn.

While it wasn't an easy process to create Hartley House, with the paperwork and permits and convincing the council, eventually Zane and Christa got it over the line and then more hard work began.

Paul had helped design a place that was both warm and comforting, but not over the top, under Christa's guidance.

'I don't want people to feel they're in McDonald's but I also don't want them to feel intimidated as though they're at a wannabe Cliveden,' she had said.

And Paul had delivered something lovely and welcoming. The old wooden panelling had been painted a soft blue and with white walls, papered in a faux pressed metal, it gave the old pub a sense of style without being piss-elegant.

Paul had loved that phrase when Christa said it to him.

'Piss-elegant. I know a few celebrities who adhere to that style. Namely one ex-president's wife who has a penchant for white and gold. Only the Pope is allowed to wear white and gold, although he teams it with red shoes, which is a lot, you know, even for the head of the Church.'

The kitchen was completely fitted out with the largest space for the lunch preparation and then a smaller kitchen with ovens for the cooking classes. It was Selene who came and consulted on the kitchen design after working on the smash hit *Blind Baking*.

Selene was the star of the show and her French candour, mixed with her natural warmth and kindness, shone through in every episode.

Avian had suggested they do an episode at Hartley House and show it to the rest of the world. They would be arriving to shoot next week and the twins would be coming with her to stay at Pudding Hall for the summer.

Christa saw Marc come through the back door and speak to some of the staff, and he waved with his free hand.

She waved back.

She walked the class through the rest of the instructions for the soup.

'Now you can take a break but set a timer. I don't want the stink of burned potato and leek soup lingering in here for days on end.'

Christa undid her apron and left the kitchen, saying hello to a few of the social workers who were talking to clients and the dentist who had just finished packing up after some check-ups.

'Hi.' She beamed at Marc and she leaned over and kissed him and then kissed the soft downy head in the crook of his arm.

'How is she?'

'Terrible. All she does is sleep, eat and poop,' he said and he passed Christa their daughter.

Juniper Beatrice was born on a warm summer evening with little to no trouble, while Marc cried and Christa swore like a kitchen hand. Juniper delivered herself and promptly suckled at Christa's breast and sighed as though she had been waiting for her moment.

Christa rocked her now and touched her little cheeks. 'She looks like Seth at times and then Ethan at other times,' she said, completely smitten.

'They're identical twins,' he reminded her.

'But they're so different,' she said looking up. 'Ethan's hair sticks up at the back and Seth's at the front. When Seth frowns he squints but when Ethan frowns he almost sneers. Not to mention the freckle – that was the first way I could tell them apart.'

'The freckle?' Marc asked.

'Yes, the one on Seth's cheekbone. Ethan doesn't have one.'

Marc groaned and then slammed his hand on the arm of the chair but Juniper didn't stir.

'Are you telling me for twelve years I've struggled telling them apart and all I had to do was notice the freckle on a cheek.'

Christa shrugged. 'This is why you're a terrible parent,' she teased.

'I know I am,' he said. 'Lucky I have you to show me the way to salvation.'

But in truth, both Marc and Avian had stepped up as parents. They shared custody comfortably and easily and the boys were going to finish high school in America but were hoping to attend university in England in the years to come. And they were back and forth all the time, both adoring their baby sister.

Juniper woke and stared at her mother and then smiled a gummy smile but Christa could see a hint of a tooth.

'She has a bottom tooth coming through,' she said to Marc.

'No wonder she's been grumpy,' he said, leaning over and rubbing his finger over her gum and nodding.

Christa sat her up on her lap and Juniper grabbed the Christmas pudding on her mother's necklace and tried to suck it and scrape her tooth on the jewels.

'No pudding for you, missy,' said Christa and she tucked the necklace away from the little hands.

'I have to finish this soup class and then we can go,' she said, standing up and rocking Juniper so she laughed, delighted with her mother's tricks.

'Yes, Peggy said she had made something for Junie, and Petey wanted to show me the agreement for the sale of the business.'

Petey had sold the fudge business to a small confectionary brand and he and Peggy were planning on travelling to Scotland to celebrate soon.

Now that they were living together, Christa had teased them about a wedding but Peggy had refused.

'I've been married once – that was enough for me.'

'Not for me, it seems,' Christa had joked.

She and Marc had married at Pudding Hall early in the summer after they met, a small event with only Peggy, Petey, Adam, Paul, Selene, Bill and the twins in attendance.

They had a lunch in the garden and then they napped and lolled about the house, and it was perfect for everyone. Christa wore a blush pink sundress with pink roses in her hair and Marc wore jeans and a white shirt and in every photo they were laughing and kissing and holding the boys close.

Christa saw Zane waving at her from the office.

'Okay, let me finish up here,' she said and handed Juniper back to Marc, who started to blow raspberries on her protruding baby tummy.

'What's up?' she asked Zane.

'I have the council mothers' group in the phone. They want to know if they can discuss a cooking for babies series?'

Christa clapped her hands. 'Oh yes please, I've been thinking about this.'

She walked back to the kitchen where her teens were starting to blend their soups.

'How does it taste?' she asked and the young cooks nodded and some said it tasted great.

'Now you all have your large containers. This will keep it warm until you get home, and then you can serve it to your family for dinner. Won't your parents be happy they don't have to cook for a change?'

The kids laughed and some looked embarrassed.

'I have bags of rolls for you all, left over from lunch, and some butter portions. For dessert there's chocolate brownies. Healthy ones,' she said as the young cooks moaned, used to Christa's continual discussions about nutrition and the importance of supporting their mental and physical health. 'They have zucchini in them, but don't tell your younger brothers and sisters or they won't eat them – but I know you're all not immature like that.'

She saw a few looks exchanged but she knew the brownies would all be gone in every house. They were so good to eat and so easy to make.

'Next week we're making shepherd's pie,' she said and she heard some groans.

'But not your usual shepherd's pie,' she said. 'This is a shepherd's pie devised by a Michelin-hatted chef.'

One of the teen boys frowned. 'You wear a car tyre as a hat?'

Christa laughed. Served her right for showing off, she thought. Those things didn't matter to these kids and nor should they; it was all smoke and mirrors, as Simon had proven.

After losing his role to Selene, and losing Avian, he had a new restaurant – bankrolled by his parents again – but this time, with no Christa, the reviews weren't as complimentary as he was used to. It was all over the tabloids that Simon had gone to a reviewer's house and had relieved himself in the man's shoes by his back door.

Except the man had caught him on camera and the footage was released to the papers.

'The second time a camera undid him,' Marc had said to Christa as she was reading the story on her iPad while she fed Juniper.

'I don't understand where he would get the idea to do that to someone's shoes,' she had said to Marc. The twins had laughed hysterically at this but she paid them no attention. Poo jokes were still very popular with them both but for some reason this story, in particular, seemed to amuse them for days on end.

As the teens were leaving with the soup and extra goods, Christa called out, 'Jackson?'

The young man walked away from the group to join her.

'You know, I need some help around here, and I think you show real promise in the kitchen,' she said to him.

It was true, Jackson had a natural way with the knife and seemed to understand food at a higher level than the others. But she also knew he needed a job. His mum was undergoing cancer treatment, Zane had told her, and his dad had been laid off. His home was loving but money was tight.

She gave him an extra container of soup and more bread. 'For the freezer,' she said.

Jackson looked like he was about to cry as he took the soup. 'Thank you, miss,' he said and she smiled at him. 'You have the makings of a chef, Jackson – I can see it. So have a chat to your dad and you can work here a few afternoons a week and can do more in the holidays if you like?'

Jackson nodded.

'You can be my commis cook,' she said.

'What's that?' he asked, looking worried.

'That's the most important role in the kitchen,' she said with a smile. 'The new cook.'

Acknowledgements

Thanks to Hannah Todd, my editor and task mistress who keeps me on track. To Tara Wynne, my agent and protector. To David, my husband and super sidekick and cup of tea maker extraordinaire. To Kelly Walker, my friend, and accountability wrangler.

Thank you for all your special gifts you share with me.

About the Author

KATE FORSTER in lives in Melbourne, Australia with her husband, two children and dogs and can be found nursing a laptop, surrounded by magazines and talking on the phone, usually all at once. She is an avid follower of fashion, fame and all things pop culture and is also an excellent dinner party guest who always brings gossip and champagne.

Hello from Aria

We hope you enjoyed this book! If you did, let us know – we'd love to hear from you.

We are Aria, a dynamic fiction imprint from award-winning publishers Head of Zeus. At heart, we're committed to publishing fantastic commercial fiction – from romance to sagas to historical fiction. Visit us online and discover a community of like-minded fiction fans!

You can find us at:
www.ariafiction.com

 @ariafiction

 @Aria_Fiction

 @ariafiction